COZY
CAMPING

A Lexie Starr Mystery
Book Six

Jeanne Glidewell

Cover and Book design by eBook Prep
www.ebookprep.com

First Edition, July 2014
ISBN: 978-1-61417-636-7

ePublishing Works!
www.epublishingworks.com

DEDICATION

I'd like to dedicate Cozy Camping to RVers everywhere. Writing this novel brought back many fond memories of the twelve years my husband, Bob, and I owned and operated a large campground in Cheyenne, Wyoming. We found 99.9 percent of our customers to be the nicest, friendliest, and most fun-loving people you could ever want to meet. The tiny fraction of our customers who didn't fit into this category were just freaks of nature who had probably spent too many hours on the road that day. Marc and Jane, the current owners of A.B. Camping, Inc., have added their special touch to the RV Park and made it an even better place to stay. They are now making fond memories of their own.

I'd also like to dedicate this novel to my beautiful niece, Kylie Rae (Goodman) Moore, who stepped in to run the office of A.B. Camping for me one summer when I became gravely ill. She took over a week before Cheyenne Frontier Days, when the job always became very intense, and handled it with exceptional grace and professionalism for an eighteen-year-old. I like to pretend Kylie inherited her amazing creativity from me. She didn't, but I still like to pretend she did.

ACKNOWLEDGMENTS

I would like to thank my dear editors, Judy Beatty, of Madison, Alabama, and Alice Duncan, of Roswell, New Mexico, who help keep me from butchering the English language with words I make up when I feel the situation calls for it and punctuation that has no rhyme or reason to it.

I'd also like to thank Nina and Brian Paules, of eBook Prep and ePublishing Works, for all the long hours and hard work they put in to make my books available to readers. They save me a lot of frustration and anxiety from trying to do it on my own.

CHAPTER 1

"Have you lost your mind?"

"Not at all, Lexie. The clean air and scenery in Wyoming is incredible. And camping there will be a lot of fun. You know how much you enjoy new adventures," Stone Van Patten, my husband of one year, replied.

"Adventures, yes! Sleeping on the ground with spiders and other creepy crawlers is definitely not my idea of a fun adventure. And I cringe at the idea of a snake slithering in next to me to curl up in the bottom of my sleeping bag! Sitting next to poison ivy while eating gritty hotdogs turned into burnt leather over a blazing fire, does not sound all that appealing to me either."

At age fifty-one, I had no desire to hone my survival skills in the deep, dark woods, where danger might lurk around every corner. With the snap of every limb, I'd fear I was about to be mauled by a bear or a mountain lion. I'd run out of pepper spray before we reached our camping site, just reacting to phantom assailants. I had my own little pink-handled gun now, too, but randomly firing bullets at figments of my imagination might make my fellow campers uneasy.

Stone would probably insist I catch my own supper in a rippling stream, too, and he should have learned from his first attempt to teach me to fish that was a recipe for disaster. He would spend his entire vacation untangling my fishing line and digging hooks out of somebody's flesh, most likely his own.

Stone and I own and operate a bed and breakfast lodging facility in Rockdale, Missouri, called the Alexandria Inn. Alexandria is my given name although everyone calls me Lexie. We'd both lost our first spouses years ago, and then met and fell in love when I was in Schenectady, New York, investigating a murder case that involved the welfare of my only child, twenty-nine-year-old Wendy.

Now we were celebrating our first anniversary, and Stone thought we needed to get away for a couple of weeks to rest and relax and enjoy ourselves. Ever since he told me he was planning a secret vacation to celebrate the end of our newlywed status, I'd been hoping he had booked a Caribbean cruise during which we could ingest entirely too many calories at a midnight chocolate bar and stuff ourselves like throw pillows at the endless buffets. The onboard entertainment and nightly shows would no doubt be fascinating, and the ports of call would offer endless possibilities.

I could visualize myself snorkeling at the second largest barrier reef in the world in Belize, and riding a zip line through the forest in Roatan, Honduras. I hoped to swim with the dolphins in Cancun as well. For some odd reason, being eaten alive by sharks or plummeting to earth from a high cable did not scare me as much as the thought of a boll weevil finding its way into my sleeping bag. A walking stick, no matter how harmless Stone assures me it is, can creep me out like nobody's business. To me the camouflaged critters harbor evil intentions and mean to harm unsuspecting people in some fashion or another.

You see, I really do enjoy new adventures, but roughing it in a tent and having to squat behind bushes to relieve myself were not my cup of tea. My idea of roughing it is when room service is late. I was mentally preparing my rebuttal when Stone's next words made me stop in my tracks.

"Not tent-camping, honey. I've rented three class-C motorhomes, and reserved sites at an RV park in Cheyenne, Wyoming, during the largest outdoor rodeo in the world, called Cheyenne Frontier Days. I've even purchased tickets to a couple of nightly concerts, including a concert featuring one of your favorite country music artists."

"Oh, well, that's different then. I can picture us driving down the interstate while I fix lunch at the same time," I said, my spirits instantly lifted.

"Yes, and these rigs have all the comforts of home, just in slightly smaller proportions. And not only that, I won't have to pull over at every single rest stop between here and Cheyenne, since you always have a cup of coffee in your hand. You can use the john in the RV at seventy miles an hour," he said with a laugh.

"It's not just me who needs to visit the rest stops on a regular basis. You tend to need to stop frequently too," I said, a little insulted by Stone's comment.

"I can't help that I have an enlarged prostate, my dear. Besides, I was only teasing you. Getting out and walking around intermittently helps prevent blood clots from forming in our legs. We probably need to do that even when traveling in a motorhome. The exercise will be good for us. Adequate circulation becomes more of an issue at our ages."

"Isn't getting older a barrel of fun? I can remember the days when we never gave issues like those a second thought," I said. "Now, just forgetting where I laid my keys makes me panic. I'm sure a rapid-onset case of Alzheimer's is kicking in. It does run in both of our families, you know."

As Stone was responding, it suddenly occurred to me that I had led us far away from the initial topic of conversation, and also that we must not be going on the trip alone. "Why did you rent three motorhomes, by the way?"

"I've talked Wendy and Andy and Wyatt and Veronica into joining us on our adventure. I knew you'd be delighted to have them all along on the trip. They were sworn to secrecy, because I wanted to surprise you for our first anniversary."

Wendy was living with Stone's nephew, Andy, who, like his Uncle Stone, had also relocated from South Carolina. I was certain it was only a matter of time before they tied the knot and began producing some grandchildren for me. So far, the closest they'd come to giving me grandkids to spoil, was adopting two baby alpacas, which they'd named after a '70s sitcom. I could just see us inviting Mork and Mindy to sit in on our next family portrait.

Wyatt was a dear friend of ours whom we'd met when a guest was murdered in our inn on its opening night. Detective Wyatt Johnston had served on the Rockport police force for sixteen years, and he dropped by nearly every morning to devour enough pastries to provide any normal person with his entire daily recommended caloric intake. His girlfriend, Veronica, was the only daughter of the murder victim from that inaugural evening at the Alexandria Inn. She had moved back home to Rockdale from Salt Lake City after inheriting her father's historic Italianate mansion here. Like us, she had turned it into a bed and breakfast, which she called Little Italy Inn.

I knew Detective Johnston thought very highly of Veronica, but I wasn't totally convinced she'd be that delightful to travel with. Although I hadn't had a lot of interaction with her, she came off, to me anyway, as being a little self-absorbed, and not awfully personable. But I adored Wyatt, and would make an effort to get to know his girlfriend better on Stone's proposed trip to Wyoming. If nothing else, I was curious to find out what it was about her that Wyatt found so irresistible.

I was afraid that all the lotions and potions Veronica couldn't live without would more than fill the small bathroom in a motorhome, and probably the storage space under the bed, as well. High-maintenance was an understatement when it came to Wyatt's girlfriend. And the young lady couldn't ever manage to get anywhere on time, which drove me crazy. We couldn't join her and Wyatt on a run to Dairy Queen for ice cream without waiting an hour for her to get ready. How incredible does one have to look to drive up to a window and have a chocolate sundae passed out to her by a sixteen-year-old pimply-faced boy on summer vacation?

"How nice to have company on our trip," I told Stone. "Traveling with two younger couples will only enhance our vacation and keep us entertained and amused, I'm sure. Besides, I've been wanting to get better acquainted with Veronica. And now that I know I won't have to share my bedding with a rattlesnake and my meals with a swarm of ants, I'm getting excited. After all the murder cases I've unwittingly gotten myself involved in during the last couple of years, I could use a vacation."

"Unwittingly?" Stone asked. "I'd describe it more as

continuously throwing yourself in front of moving trains."

"Well, whatever," I replied. Then I quickly changed the subject back to our upcoming trip before Stone began reprimanding me for my habit of needing to be rescued while investigating murder cases I wasn't supposed to be involved with in the first place.

"I got the idea from Stanley and Emily Harrington—you know—that couple who stayed in our inn last fall and own the campground in Cheyenne.[1] By the time I called for reservations they were already completely booked for Frontier Days, but they managed to work us in with the first three cancellations they had. Emily said our sites are not side-by-side, but they're in the same section. Stanley and Emily also helped me procure some tickets to already sold-out concerts. I think the fact that you took them on the historical home tour of Rockdale and fixed them a huge bowl of cheesy potatoes to take to their family reunion while they stayed with us, scored us enough brownie points that they felt obliged to accommodate us as best they could."

"Gee, I guess I was sucking up without even knowing it would benefit me. It will be nice to see the Harringtons again. I really liked them. I'd guess they are about Wyatt and Veronica's ages, late thirties or early forties," I said. "So tell me about the motorhomes you've rented."

"They are Coachman Concords and thirty feet long with two slide-outs that make them even roomier. I'd say they're similar to the one Sheila and her husband bought last year."

"Theirs is very nice," I replied. Sheila was my best

---

[1] *The Spirit of the Season (A Lexie Starr Mystery, Holiday Novella)*

friend and I knew she and Randy enjoyed traveling in their RV.

"I could have rented a larger motorhome that slept six, but I thought everyone would be more comfortable with their own unit."

"I agree. That way it won't feel crowded and we won't have to deal with six adults sharing one small bathroom," I said.

With a guffaw, Stone said, "Don't think I didn't take that into consideration. With three women on board, each of us men would have been allotted about two minutes of restroom time per day."

"You're probably right. Wendy and I aren't particularly high-maintenance, but I'll bet anything Veronica spends more than an hour every morning just putting her face on."

"Putting her face on? Is it removable?" Stone asked.

"Applying her makeup, silly. Just out of curiosity, do you know how to hook up to the electricity, water, and sewer connections at the camping site?" I asked.

Stone gave me a so-so hand gesture, and said, "They gave me a briefing and short demonstration, so I don't think I'll have much trouble. But Stanley assured me he shows novice RVers how to connect their cords and hoses all the time. I'll show Andy and Wyatt the basics so they can handle hooking up their own rigs, because I doubt you ladies have any desire to mess with water and sewer hoses."

"A truer statement has never been uttered. I'd actually rather share my sleeping bag with a snake while sleeping in a bear's den, than deal with anything sewer related."

A week later, the six of us stood out in front of the inn admiring three identical motorhomes, lined up like an Army convoy in the circular driveway. Stone

pulled Andy and Wyatt aside to show them the basics
of setting up one of the Coachman Concords once we
were at our sites at Cozy Camping RV Park in
Cheyenne, Wyoming.

Puffing his chest out like General Custer leading his
troops into battle, he turned to Veronica, Wendy, and
me and said, "You gals can start loading up the rigs
with our clothes, food and all, while I explain the
intricate details of setting up a motorhome to Andy
and Wyatt. You three don't need to be concerned with
all this technical jargon."

As the three of us turned to walk away, I heard
Stone say, "Now first you want to take that
thingybobber in the storage compartment, and hook it
up to this doohickey over here."

"Come on, ladies," I said. "This so-called 'technical
jargon' is way over our heads. We just need to
concern ourselves with all the heavy lifting, loading,
and other strenuous work involved with getting ready
to head out for the week. Is it just me, or do you two
get the feeling we are being played like banjos in a
hillbilly hoedown?"

Several hours later, we exited off I-80 West and
pulled into a cafe in Kearney, Nebraska. The men
decided it was a good opportunity to stretch their legs
and get a bite to eat. We all enjoyed a hand-battered
tenderloin sandwich and steak fries, except Veronica,
who ate roughly a third of her dressing-free garden
salad. I suppose it took great diligence and self-
restraint to maintain a size zero body.

I admired Veronica's figure only to a point, because
I considered her severe slimness to be more skeletal
than the modelesque look I'm sure Veronica was
shooting for. If someone who already wore a size zero
dress lost weight, convinced they were still too fat,

what size dress would they shop for then? I've never seen a negative-zero sized dress hanging on a rack anywhere, but I'm sure they'd make better use of their time at that point by shopping for a burial plot. A body could only sustain itself without adequate nourishment for so long, after all. And that's just what I reminded myself of every time I reached for my favorite treat, a dark chocolate candy bar, which for the benefit of my health, I was always able to suffer through.

To be honest, I could stand to lose ten pounds or so, but I wasn't obsessed with it since Stone had assured me he'd love me no matter how much I weighed. Anyhow, he could stand to lose even more than ten pounds. Misery may love company, but chubbiness absolutely adores it. Even though I was truly fond of his Teddy-bear quality, standing next to Stone, with his slightly protruding paunch, I felt I looked rather trim. But standing between Veronica and my daughter, Wendy, I'm pretty sure I looked like the cream part of a double-stuffed Oreo.

My daughter, Wendy, was several inches shorter than Veronica and managed to sustain a slender, yet not quite anorexic, physique, while frequently eating like a grizzly bear that's just come out of hibernation after a long cold winter. Having the metabolism of a hummingbird certainly wasn't a trait Wendy inherited from me. I could lick a celery stick and gain two pounds.

After finishing our lunch, we all decided to utilize the restaurant's restrooms before continuing on our journey. While we waited in line to use one of the two available stalls, I asked Wendy and Veronica if they had packed their swimsuits. I'd read that the campground had just recently added an in-ground pool on the premises. Wendy assured me she'd brought her suit along, and Veronica informed me that she didn't know how to swim and was terrified of water.

"We could buy you a suit at a Wal-Mart in Cheyenne. Any town with over twenty residents has at least one Wal-Mart. Then I could teach you to float, dog paddle, and tread water, at the very least. And once you've mastered the basics, we could move on to some of the standard swim strokes. I'm sure you'd be relieved not to have to be so afraid of water. Besides, not knowing how to swim could potentially be dangerous, I'd think."

"Oh, no, thanks for the offer, but I'm afraid I'd sink like the *Titanic*," Veronica replied. "Besides, I wouldn't want to mess up my hair and makeup. It's an arduous task to maintain this kind of natural beauty. It may be a bit difficult for you to appreciate, but I feel it's crucial to always look presentable when I leave the house."

Ouch, I thought. *That barb stung.* Why hadn't I thought of that? No one should be caught camping while not appearing as if they were attending a black-tie ball at the White House. Who knew it took so many gels, lotions, potions, and gobble-de-gook to maintain such a "natural" beauty? And what had Veronica meant by her last statement? No, regardless of how "crucial" it was, I didn't make it a habit to apply tons of mascara, eyeliner, and foundation, every time I left the inn. And I didn't feel the need to touch up my lipstick every five minutes as Veronica seemed to do—if I even found it necessary to wear lipstick in the first place. Today, like nearly every other day in my life, lip gloss to moisten my lips was sufficient to serve my purpose.

But, even without makeup, I didn't feel like I looked completely hideous. I had short curly hair that I occasionally turned into a work of art—using that term very loosely. And I stood just a few inches over five feet, a good six or seven inches short of Veronica's stature. And, yes, I really did need to make a better effort to lose those extra pounds. Yet, with all that going against me, I still managed to face the public without feeling like I should be on display at a freak show. I had enough self-esteem to get by, albeit nothing like the level of pride in herself that Veronica appeared to possess.

Perhaps Stone should have given more thought to the idea of inviting Wyatt and Veronica along on this trip. I loved Wyatt to pieces, and in general, I got along fine with his girlfriend as well. But Veronica seemed more concerned about her looks than in having any excitement or joy in her life. I hoped having her along wouldn't put a damper on our vacation. But for now I just nodded and walked into the now-empty restroom stall.

The men were standing next to the motorhomes waiting for us to return. For some reason, Veronica had found it necessary to spend five or six minutes at the washbasin, reapplying foundation, as well as dabbing a little powder on her nose and forehead. Had she not figured out there was a bathroom and several mirrors in her motorhome? I guess it was just a "crucial, arduous task" that needed to be taken care of before presenting herself to the three men waiting impatiently for us in the parking lot.

I don't mean to sound disparaging of Wyatt's girlfriend. They made a wonderful couple, both tall and incredibly good-looking, and they seemed to have a lot of interests in common. For instance, Veronica liked to cook, and Wyatt liked to eat. It amazed me that someone who enjoyed cooking as much as she did could manage to ingest so little of the end product.

And they both enjoyed watching movies, although his tastes tended to be a bit bloodier and more edge-of-your-seat thrilling than hers. But for Veronica's sake, Wyatt suffered through an occasional chick flick, too.

I reminded myself I just needed to concentrate on Stone and me enjoying ourselves, and let Veronica and Wyatt do their own thing throughout our vacation. After all, we were celebrating our anniversary, and I planned to have a restful, laid-back vacation so we could unwind a bit from the pressures and responsibilities of owning and operating a lodging establishment. But you know what they say about best-laid plans…

CHAPTER 2

Friday was a pleasant, fairly uneventful day on the road. Although the scenery in western Nebraska never changes all that much, we did spot a variety of wildlife, including deer, antelope, wild turkey, a coyote, and a road-killed bobcat.

When I spotted a rare albino raccoon in a tree not far off the shoulder, I made Stone turn around and go back, with the other two motorhomes in tow, so I could snap some photos of it. I thought it'd be a cool thing to post on my Facebook page. As it turned out, the albino raccoon was a highly disappointing Wal-Mart shopping bag hung up on a branch and flapping in the breeze. After a few sarcastic remarks about my optometrist, Stone pulled back onto the interstate and we all continued our journey west.

As you can imagine, Stone did not slow down or even flinch when I told him I was sure I'd seen a moose behind a row of trees next to a cornfield. He did find time, however, to make yet another chiding comment. "That's amazing! A moose right here along I-80 in the flat plains of Nebraska. What are the odds?"

"Um, zero?" I asked, slightly embarrassed.

"Pretty much," he replied. "I think you were referring to that oil well pumping in the field back there…not that it bore any resemblance to a moose."

The most interesting event of the day was when we spotted a barred owl sitting alone in the grassy median. Fortunately, I wasn't the only one who saw it or we would have whizzed right by and left it in its precarious location. Knowing the location of this barred owl was not normal, particularly in the bright sunny afternoon, Stone had pulled over, and the other two couples followed suit. I could just imagine them saying to one another, "Reckon she's spotted a giraffe up ahead?"

When Stone got out and approached the owl, he noticed it was alive but unable to fly. When it struggled to get away, Stone backed off, not wanting it to cause further injury to itself. Apparently, it had been struck by a vehicle and sustained damage to one of its wings.

I snapped a few photos of the odd-looking creature and pleaded with Stone to seek help for the poor thing. I just couldn't stand to leave an injured, helpless owl to fend for itself when it was in such a hopeless situation. Stone agreed with me, as did the other four in our party.

We were just a couple miles east of Sidney, Nebraska, where there was a large Cabela's sporting goods store located right next to the interstate. We decided to stop there to find help for the owl. With the assistance of a member of their staff, Stone was able to contact the Nebraska Fish and Game Association, who assured him they'd rescue the barred owl and transfer it to a wildlife rehabilitation center for medical assistance.

Stone gave the game warden the owl's location,

including what mile marker it was closest to, and then the three men decided to browse through the store, since we were there already anyway. I believe Stone's justification was the necessity of moving around to prevent blood clots in our legs, as he'd mentioned a concern about earlier. I was wondering if he'd be as worried about the potential health hazard had we stopped at a Vera Bradley store to find assistance for the stranded owl. I doubt he'd have had the patience to wander around the store for forty-five minutes while we three ladies admired the newest brightly patterned purses and clutches.

Veronica retreated to the restroom located at the front entrance of the sporting goods store, presumably to refresh her makeup, while Wendy and I looked around in the store's clothing department. I found several shirts I liked and Wendy found a jacket she couldn't live without. I don't know about the other two couples, but that damned owl cost Stone and me almost six hundred dollars.

We filled the entire storage compartment up with Stone's purchases, such as fishing equipment, a new pair of binoculars, some hunting paraphernalia, and a lot of camping equipment I didn't think was particularly necessary to have in an RV park. A propane lantern? Really? Couldn't we just flick on the light switch inside the motorhome? It even had exterior lights if we needed light while sitting in our lawn chairs under the awning at night. When it came to sporting goods, Stone was a salesman's new best friend.

When we finally reached the campground at eight-thirty Friday evening, the Cozy Camping RV Park was a total zoo. We had heard Cheyenne Frontier Days was a popular annual event, but we had no idea of its true magnitude until we pulled into the campground's driveway.

Our three rigs sat behind several others still waiting to pull up to the sidewalk leading to the office so their drivers could go in and register for the sites they had reserved. There was a "Full" sign at the entrance gate, so people without reservations wouldn't waste their time waiting in vain.

There were people everywhere I looked, and recreational vehicles of all sizes and shapes seemed to occupy every square inch of the park. I could sense a frenzied titillation in the air, similar to the droning buzz of a fluorescent light bulb. I could feel a sensation, like static electricity, that caused the hairs on my arms to stand straight up, and was instantly awash with excitement for the week ahead. As if looking into an imaginary crystal ball, I had a premonition that our anniversary vacation would turn out to be even more memorable than Stone had anticipated.

As we pulled up closer to the office, I saw an area full of tents, and for a split second, I had visions of water leaking through the roof while folks tried to sleep during a thunderstorm, with all types of creatures slithering in to get out of the rain. I actually saw a young lady sitting next to a fire pit waving a charred hamburger patty back and forth as if it were a Polaroid photo. I wondered if she'd dropped it on the ground and was trying to displace ants and dirt from her supper.

Across from the tent area was a family struggling to set up what Stone told me was a pop-up camper. The young couple was arguing and doing a lot of pointing, eye rolling, and head shaking, while four young children ran amok in the vicinity. One little boy was picking up rocks and throwing them at the travel trailer parked next to them. It looked more like a chore than a vacation to me, and the notion of six people occupying that canvas-topped camper made me shiver.

Thank you, Lord, for the good sense you gave Stone to rent motorhomes and not pop up campers or tents, I thought. I also greatly appreciated the fact he'd rented a separate motorhome for each couple. We were just too old to have *that* much fun.

When we pulled up to the second spot in line, Stone asked if I could handle going in to register for our site. From his tone, he clearly thought it would test my capabilities.

"Yes, I'm pretty sure I can handle that," I said, laughing as I exited the rig with my Mastercard and our confirmation slip in hand. When I walked into the office, a tanned, well-toned woman, most likely in her mid-to-upper thirties, was at the counter complaining about her site. I waved at Emily Harrington, who cheerfully returned my greeting before turning her attention back to her loud and obnoxious customer.

The unhappy customer's hair was bleached so blond it was nearly white, making her look older than she probably intended. The fact that she had no frown lines, crow's feet, or any other visible sign of movement on her forehead made me think she might have gone overboard with Botox as well.

"When I called to make a reservation for my husband and me, I specifically asked for a site next to the pool, under a shade tree, with a concrete patio and grill. We have no tree, no grill, and are at least ten sites down from the pool, so I am not happy at all!" The woman spoke to Emily in an assertive and intimidating fashion that I found unnerving.

A young and, no doubt, naturally blond-haired gal waiting on another customer looked up and glared at the discontented woman as if she'd just seen her whack a puppy on the head with a stick. I'm sure she was thankful to be helping an exuberant jolly old man in a cowboy hat instead of the broad who was hammering Emily with her grievances.

I was uncomfortable even being near the cranky woman, and felt sorry for Emily, who stood behind the counter. Soon, however, I realized she was not fazed one iota by the customer's rude behavior. She responded calmly and matter-of-factly.

"I assume you'd like to be next to the shower house and laundromat too?" Emily asked.

"Well, of course I would!" The irate woman replied, obviously not picking up on the scoffing tone in Emily's voice. "That's what I requested when I made reservations over the phone."

"Then perhaps you should have called for a reservation more than a week ago. My husband and I own this campground, and I remember taking your call myself, because it was nearly midnight and you woke us both up. I told you then that I had only one site available, and that was only due to a last minute cancellation. You were lucky to get a site at all, as we fill up very quickly for Frontier Days."

"Listen, lady, I am not here for some silly rodeo. I'm here for a book signing at Barnes and Noble tomorrow morning. Two other authors involved in the event had no problem securing nice sites, and I am way more successful than either of them," she said. I could sense the muscular woman's sense of self-importance was hefty. Based on my first impression of this customer, I knew she wasn't someone I'd want to befriend. I also knew I didn't want to tick her off in a dark alley either.

"And the other authors' names?" Emily asked.

"Norma Grace and Sarah Krumm—two wanna-be

best-selling authors."

"Oh, yes, I remember their names. Very congenial ladies, I might add. They called months ago to reserve sites—in plenty of time to secure premier ones—something you would have been wise to do, too."

"I'm a very busy woman, and I didn't have the time to spend on trivial little details like that. The point is that I did get a site, and it is not at all what I requested."

Emily glanced up and looked straight into the customer's eyes, as she replied. "Obviously, it's not such a 'trivial detail' now that you're here and are finding out you should have taken a few moments of your precious time to reserve a site when your friends had the foresight to do so. And I'm sure every customer in the park would like a deluxe site like the one you requested, which I told you at the time was impossible. The vast majority of them are just happy to have been able to get a site with full hookups in a high quality, well-appointed Good Sam park. There are hundreds of RVs parked out in overflow lots and fields with no hookups at all, that were unable to secure a site in a real campground such as this one."

"Perhaps you don't know who I am," the customer said haughtily, while placing her hands on her hips in an attempt to show her superiority.

"Perhaps I don't care who you are," Emily said, without flinching or even raising her voice. "You could be Mother Teresa and your husband the Pope, and you would have still been assigned the same site."

"Humph! I don't appreciate your smart aleck comments, lady. I happen to be Fanny Mae Finch, the renowned author. I'm practically a household name," the surly woman replied.

"Not in my household! Sorry, never heard of you." Emily spoke as I echoed the same words in my mind.

Perfect retort, I thought. I wanted to applaud, and say, "Campground owner one, pompous ass zero."

"Well, you must be illiterate, then. My new novel is currently on the *New York Times* Best Seller list," the egotistical woman stated, with obvious pride in her self-proclaimed awesomeness.

"How nice for you, Ms. Finch. Do you want the site or not? You're holding up the line. There are plenty of people who would love to have your site if you'd like to take your business elsewhere."

"I do not appreciate your attitude at all. Have you not heard the mantra of most professional business owners, that the customer is always right?"

"Well, Ms. Finch, you are *about* to be right! Right out the exit gate of this campground, that is!"

"You know, I could write an article about how rude and unprofessional the staff is in this so-called RV Park. *Cozy* Camping? Really? What fantasy world are you living in, lady? Even the man on the golf cart outside had the gall to tell me I needed to pull up because I was blocking the driveway. As you just suggested, I sincerely do have half a mind to take my business elsewhere."

"Please do, because I have more than half a mind to give you a refund and send you on your way so you can enjoy looking for a site in a town that's been booked up for months. The closest RV Park where you have a prayer of finding an open site in is probably forty-five minutes south of here in Fort Collins, Colorado. Otherwise, you can rent a dry-camping site in an overflow field up the street. That way you can also write a book about how much you enjoyed parking in a field full of rutted, dusty roads, anthills, and prairie dog mounds, with no electric, water or sewer hookups and no shower house to use. You might even be gifted with an antelope's calling card at the bottom of your doorsteps some morning. And don't look around for a laundromat, a café and coffee shop, or a bus to transport you downtown or to the rodeo grounds, either. We offer those amenities, but for use by our paying guests only. Guests not staying in our park are not allowed on the premises to take advantage of any of our facilities. Hey, maybe that book will hit the best-seller's list too!"

I had to admire this businesswoman's composure. Wendy and Veronica were now standing behind me and had only heard the last response by Emily. Having not heard the entire conversation, they were probably thinking she didn't have the social graces necessary to deal with the public. I would fill them in on the entire exchange later. I'd become very fond of both of the Harringtons when they'd been guests at our inn just before Christmas. Emily was a kind woman, but like me, she was not the type to take undeserved crap from anybody.

I watched Fanny brush an imaginary object off the sleeve of her jacket as if it were spittle that had shot out of Emily's mouth. The white fur coat she wore, even though it was in the lower seventies, was obviously an attempt to flaunt her success and appear classy. A t-shirt and shorts would be more comfortable and appropriate for the situation. In my opinion, the novelist didn't have an ounce of class in her entire body.

Fanny Mae Finch must have been weighing her options and found her other choices to be unappealing, because she snatched her receipt and a park map off the counter and stomped out of the office.

"Bravo," I said, as I approached the counter. "You could not have handled that self-absorbed witch any better than you just did, my friend. Obviously you've dealt with customers like her before."

"Not too often, fortunately," Emily replied with a smile. "But when this place fills to overflowing during Frontier Days, occasionally some of the nastiest creatures come out of the woodwork. I particularly dislike those with no room to complain because they failed to make a reservation in advance and I'm forced to turn them away. But the vast majority of them are as polite and understanding as they could possibly be."

"Thank God for small favors," I said, as I handed Emily my reservation slip.

"It's so nice to see you again, Lexie. I spoke to Stone a few weeks ago, and I'm so happy we were able to accommodate you all. After he told me of his desire to surprise you for your anniversary, I was praying for cancellations. When a woman called to cancel four sites her family had reserved due to an unexpected death in their family, I tried very hard not to sound pleased with her family's misfortune."

"Emily! That's just awful!" I chuckled, as I signed my credit card slip and told her I didn't want to hold up the line. Ms. Fanny Finch already had people backed out the door because of her long-winded tirade.

"I'm just pulling your leg about the last-minute cancellation. Actually, the entire group decided to bypass the festivities this year to be present for the imminent birth of a new family member. So it was a joyous reason, not a death, and I was happy for them. But I was happier still that I could call Stone and tell him we could accommodate your three rigs. Oh, by the way, Lexie," Emily said, as Wendy, Veronica and I turned to leave. "I apologize in advance, but unfortunately her royal highness is parked right next to one of your three sites. I made the mistake of giving her the fourth site that opened up due to the last-minute cancellation."

"No worries," I responded. "Even though I may not be able to display the patience you did, I'm sure I can hold my own with the esteemed Ms. Finch. I'm afraid I would have sent her packing the second after she walked in and slammed her reservation form down on the counter in front of me."

As we walked back to the rigs, two men in golf carts prepared to lead us to our assigned sites. I told the one parked in front of our motorhome to put us right next to the last camper he had parked, which would have been the Finches. I didn't want to saddle either of the younger couples with an unpleasant neighbor.

As we pulled into our site, I spotted Fanny Finch yelling and gesturing wildly at a man I assumed was her husband as they stood outside their Fifth Wheel. The slightly overweight man had his back to us as he attached his cord to the electrical pedestal. We couldn't see his face but it was apparent he was ignoring his traveling companion as if she were nothing more than a fruit fly buzzing around a rotting cantaloupe on the picnic table. I was sure he'd learned to tune her out many moons ago—to maintain his sanity, if nothing else.

It was at that moment I had a fleeting feeling of uneasiness. That niggling premonition in the back of my mind when we pulled into the campground had come back in full force, and I feared I hadn't seen or heard the last of the disagreeable author. To my chagrin, in most cases, I had found that my premonitions were almost always spot on.

CHAPTER 3

As I had expected, Stanley Harrington had to be called upon to give the men a refresher course in connecting all the utilities to the motorhomes. Somewhere between the thingybobber and the doohickey was a whatchamacallit that Stone didn't know what to do with. Stanley explained that it was a regulator, designed to keep the water pressure at an optimal level.

It was a Friday night in late July, and the opening night of the rodeo festivities. We didn't have tickets to the concert that evening, so the six of us sat in lawn chairs on the patio next to our site. The campground was a beehive of activity, and it was fun just watching the other campers coming and going. We saw a bus pull up in front of the office and a swarm of excited people rush to board it for a ride to the fairgrounds where Toby Keith would be entertaining the crowd in concert that evening.

At an elevation of over six thousand feet, it was remarkably cool for a mid-summer evening. I was wearing my Kansas Jayhawks sweatshirt, and relishing the fact that all my friends back home in

Kansas and Missouri were probably sweating like an ice-cold glass of lemonade on a hot Midwestern night.

For a late supper, the six of us had purchased barbecued pork sandwiches and fries from the little restaurant on the premises. I had remembered Emily and Stanley talking about it being a new addition to their campground one evening as we gathered in the parlor of the Alexandria Inn for an after-supper cup of coffee.

The food was delicious and we devoured it as we visited and relaxed in our lawn chairs. I had my ever-present cup of coffee in my hand as I listened to a lively debate between Andy and Wyatt about which political party was most apt to put us in a deep depression and ruin our country the fastest. In the end, it was a six-of-one and half-a-dozen of the other consensus. We all agreed, no matter which party was in power, our country was destined to go down the toilet faster than we could holler, "Impeach him!"

To veer the conversation toward a less depressing subject, I said, "I wonder if our owl was rescued and how it's doing tonight."

"I'm betting he's being well taken care of," Stone replied. "The gentleman on the phone assured me that if the owl's injuries were limited to a broken wing, or something of that nature, it would be rehabilitated and allowed to recover at the wildlife center. It would then be set free once it was completely healed. If the owl's injuries were too severe for it to ever be able to return to the wild, then the bird would make its permanent home at the center, where children often take field trips to learn more about wildlife indigenous to their area."

"That would be kind of like being condemned to the Shady Acres Nursing Home for birds of prey," I said. "I sure hope the owl can be set free eventually so it can live out its life in its natural environment."

"I'm sure they do all they can to make their habitat as close to what they're accustomed to as possible," Wyatt said. "Occasionally, while we're on patrol, we find an injured animal and transport it to a rehab center outside of St. Joseph. Just a couple of weeks ago, I took a red fox there that had gotten tangled up in a metal snare and was attempting to gnaw off its leg to get free."

"Oh, my goodness! How disturbing. Those traps should be illegal," Wendy said, taking the words right out of my mouth, and probably the others in our group.

Veronica turned to Wyatt and asked, "Isn't that the one you went to check on at the rehab center last week?"

"Yes, I was worried about the little critter and wanted to see how he was faring. I'm happy to say the vet told me that other than that injured leg, it looked pretty healthy. He felt confident he'd be able to return to the wild after he'd had some time to heal."

"What wonderful news," I said. I wasn't surprised at all that Wyatt would make a special trip to check on the animal's welfare. He was a kind, compassionate man with a heart of gold. "Sounds like a great rehab facility."

"It is, Lexie, as most of them tend to be. The center I took the injured fox to is a protected wildlife sanctuary that appears to be a really well-kept—"

Before the detective could finish his comment, a piercing scream filled the air and startled us all. I spilled coffee all over my sweatshirt when I jumped in reaction to the sound, which was immediately followed by the sound of something hitting the inside wall of the Jayco Fifth Wheel just a matter of feet from where we were sitting. We heard the shattering of glass and a male voice shouting out a very graphic obscenity. There was a loud commotion inside of the RV where very descriptive name-calling was being exchanged and a scuffle appeared to be taking place.

Since I knew Fanny Finch was in the site next to us, it was apparent she was in a lively tussle with her husband and it was his voice we'd heard cussing in anger. Detective Johnston was often called out to investigate domestic disputes, and had told me they were often the most dangerous calls to respond to. I looked at him and raised my eyebrows in question. I felt we needed to do something to prevent the quarrel from escalating, but didn't know what the best course of action would be.

"Wyatt, what should we do?" I asked, always willing to butt in to other people's business, particularly when their business appeared to me to be in dire need of butting into.

"By *we*, I assume you mean me. I can't just push my way into their RV and arrest anyone, Lexie. I am out of my jurisdiction, obviously, and am nothing more than a regular citizen here. However, if it sounds like their squabble is getting to the point someone could get seriously injured, I'll call 9-1-1 and go knock on the door to try to intervene until the officers arrive."

Just then, we heard the door of the Fifth Wheel open and immediately slam shut. We watched silently as Fanny Finch, carrying a bathing suit and beach towel, headed up the road toward the pool area. She walked quite briskly and it was clear she was livid. When Fanny got to the gate leading into the pool area, she slipped inside it and disappeared from our sight.

Wendy broke the stunned silence by asking, "Do you reckon she's going to go for a swim while she waits for her husband to calm down?"

"Probably," Wyatt replied. "That is usually the best

course of action. It gives both parties a chance to cool down until they can discuss whatever provoked the argument in a civil manner."

Witnessing the spirited spat effectively squelched the light-hearted camaraderie we'd been engaging in. Everyone stood and folded up their lawn chairs, wished each other a good night, and retired to their own motorhome. I couldn't help wondering what had started the Finch's dispute. I couldn't understand how anyone could get along with someone as full of herself as Fanny Finch. I didn't care if she'd written *Gone With the Wind.* As far as I was concerned, she was still no better than any other person in the campground. If she were Margaret Mitchell, the actual author of that famous classic, I might have been tempted to modify my statement a touch — but she wasn't!

I just prayed that being parked next to Fanny Finch and her husband didn't take the joy out of our vacation in some unforeseeable way. But I'd also prayed I'd be celebrating our anniversary on a Caribbean cruise, and here I was in a Wyoming campground instead and enjoying almost every minute of it. Sometimes there was a good reason for not having your prayers answered the way you want them answered. Could this vacation turn out to be one of those times? I wondered.

After a good night's sleep, I fixed French toast for breakfast and then called Wendy to see if she wanted to go for a swim with me. She did, and she met me at the pool gate about five minutes later looking very attractive in a two-piece blue and white bikini that had less material than the last hot pad I'd purchased.

In comparison, I felt like a ninety-year-old lady in my matronly one-piece suit with the hip-camouflaging skirt and high-cut front that completely covered any hint of cleavage—not that I had an over-abundance of cleavage to cover. In Kohl's dimly lit dressing room, I thought the yellow with black trim swimming suit had looked decent enough on me. But in the presence of my daughter and other swimmers in the unforgiving light of day, it looked frumpy and outdated. If I gained ten more pounds, I'd probably resemble a school bus and require a back-up alarm stitched into the suit.

I was reluctant to unwrap the beach towel from around my body and put my swimsuit-clad body on display. I was relieved when Wendy remarked on how cute the suit was, and how nice it looked on me, as I slowly revealed myself. I complimented her on her suit, as well.

There were four other women and one man in the pool. The man's flabby abdomen lapped over the rim of a red, white, and blue Speedo that was twenty years too young and forty pounds too small for him. I was afraid the waistband would snap like a banjo string strung too tightly past its limit. It was the most unpatriotic display of our flag's colors I'd ever seen.

The chubby man stepped onto the diving board and executed a painful-looking belly flop. He then glanced around to see if the other swimmers had watched and admired what I'm sure he thought was an Olympic-quality swan dive. He might even be delusional enough to think he looked like Greg Louganis in his skimpy swim trunks. The two middle-aged women standing in the shallow end doing water aerobics looked at each other, rolled their eyes, and quickly went back to the routine they were performing. The third woman, a very attractive redhead, had on a bone-dry bikini, and her long red hair was blowing slightly in the breeze. She had no beach towel with her and I was pretty sure she'd only come to rest and relax with the book she was reading, not to partake in any swimming. As I walked past her, she glanced up, nodded at me, and returned to the book she held out in front of her to shade the sun from her eyes. She almost appeared to be hiding behind the book whose cover bore the image of a handsome, dark-haired man strumming a guitar.

The last of the four women was donning a black swimming cap and paying no attention to the man, who crossed her path on his way to the ladder as she swam toward the deep end with a well-executed butterfly stroke. She looked like she was involved in an intensive training routine to compete in some form of swim meet.

Wendy jumped right in, but I stuck a toe in to test the temperature of the water, which was as chilly as I had expected it to be, with the cool Wyoming evenings. Inch by inch I worked my way down the steps into the pool, wondering if Wendy's method of entering the water would have been preferable to prolonging the agony of taking so long to submerge. Granted, it was a heated pool, but anything more than five degrees cooler than what you'd find in the average hot tub was too cold for me. I was a cold-blooded person—sometimes in more ways than one, I'm ashamed to admit.

When the woman doing laps swam toward me looked up, I was surprised to see it was Fanny Finch. She stopped swimming long enough to stand up in the pool and shout at the man who had just leapt off the diving board a second time, looking like a bloated bullfrog jumping into a pond.

"Please quit embarrassing yourself, Avery! I swear, if I didn't need you to be my driver, I'd leave your hideous hide at home." The man dried himself off and

strode purposely toward the gate. He left the pool area
without a word to Fanny. I wondered if Avery, who
I'd felt certain I'd recognized as her traveling
companion, really was just her driver, or had the
misfortune to be her husband as well.

I didn't have to wonder long, though. The two
women in the shallow end had stopped exercising and
were standing with their mouths open in obvious
disbelief. Wendy, who was warming up with some
water aerobics near them, glared at the verbally
abusive author. Fanny turned to the three of them, and
asked, "Would any of you like a worthless,
overweight husband who looks like the American flag
was painted on his fat bum? I happen to have one I'm
willing to let go—cheap."

Wendy continued to frown at Fanny, and the other
two women, mouths still agape, shook their heads
woodenly and didn't speak. The redhead in the chaise
lounge appeared oblivious to the entire exchange even
though I'd noticed Fanny turn her way as she spoke,
as if the comment was made specifically on the
stunning sunbather's behalf.

I turned away as nonchalantly as I could and began
to swim toward the deep end of the pool. Within
seconds, Fanny passed me as if I were parked at a red
light. She was doing the American crawl, but I was
the one who looked like I was crawling. As fit as
Fanny was, it shouldn't have surprised me that she
swam like Esther Williams, albeit in a snooty writer's
body.

I was winded after swimming two laps, and it
shocked me how quickly I had run out of gas. As I
dragged my weary body up the ladder, I made a vow
to try to get myself into better shape. Working on my
endurance by swimming laps while staying at the
campground would be a good way to start on my new

resolution. I decided that I'd try to get in as much pool time as I could before we headed home.

When Wendy and I left the pool about fifteen minutes later, the two women exercising in the shallow end had already departed and Fanny was in the middle of what seemed like her hundredth lap. The sunbather was hastily packing her book, bottle of water, and sunglasses into a beach bag, as if preparing to head back to her campsite. It seemed almost as if she didn't want to be left alone with Fanny Finch in the pool area. Having witnessed Fanny's rude and mean-spirited remarks to her husband, I couldn't blame the red-headed beauty. I wouldn't trust the venomous author either.

I was anxious to get back to the motorhome and tell Stone what we'd witnessed. Wendy and I parted ways with plans to meet at her motorhome after we'd had a chance to put on dry clothes. The men were going to the rodeo after lunch, and we gals were left to amuse ourselves until they returned. We'd been invited to go along with the guys, but had unanimously agreed that watching the daily rodeo's highlights on the Cheyenne TV station each evening was all the bull-riding and calf-roping we needed to see. As far as I was concerned, if you'd seen one guy fly off a bucking horse, you'd seen them all. Besides, I had a tendency to cheer for the animals, and that didn't always sit well with the folks in the stands around me.

After we all gathered outside Wendy and Andy's rig, Wyatt winked at Wendy before turning toward Veronica, and saying, "I've got good news and bad news for you, sweetheart. A little birdie told me that Vex Vaughn is your favorite country singer and I was able to snag six tickets to his concert on Thursday night."

Veronica squealed and turned into Wyatt's embrace

in pure bliss. "You are the best, honey! I am super excited to go see him perform! Did you get good seats?"

"Well, that's the bad news, I'm afraid. The only tickets I could find are in the standing-room-only section." Wyatt sounded apologetic with his response.

"Awesome!" Veronica said, with a fist pump as an exclamation point. "That's even better. I want to get as close to the stage as I can, just in case he throws a guitar pick or something into the crowd."

I muttered under my breath as Stone groaned loudly and dramatically. I'm sure he was as excited as I was to stand in a frenzied crowd of Vex Vaughn's adoring fans for two or more hours, no doubt being doused in beer by screaming young women as our toes were being stomped on by their leather boots. At five-foot-two, I wouldn't be able to see anything over the sea of cowboy hats anyway.

His mood unaffected by our discontent, Wyatt was grinning from ear to ear, delighted that he could bring such happiness to his girlfriend. I didn't want to rain on this young couple's parade, so I would be a good sport and suffer through the concert silently, with a forced smile on my face and a feigned lilt to my voice.

I turned my attention back to Wyatt, to whom Veronica clung as if he were a porcelain throne on prom night. The detective looked at Wendy and me, and said, "It was Emily who secured the tickets for us, from a customer who had six tickets to sell. Could you gals pick them up at the office? Andy, Stone, and I want to catch the next shuttle bus to the fairgrounds so we can walk around a while before the rodeo begins at one."

"Are you going to try to win Veronica a teddy bear by knocking over three bottles with a baseball?" I asked Wyatt in a teasing manner.

"I doubt it," Veronica said with a chuckle. "More likely he wants to chow down on hot dogs and funnel cakes."

Everyone laughed, knowing Veronica had no doubt hit the nail on the head. The man was a bottomless pit when it came to food. "Well, I did have my mind set on snacking on a foot-long chili dog with shredded cheese, onions, and jalapeños on top," Wyatt said.

"Just promise us you won't ride the Scrambler afterward," Stone said to his buddy. "I don't want to be anywhere around when you start spraying everyone with that conglomeration you call a snack."

"I promise you I won't go anywhere near any ride that spins in circles. I'm at that age now that I can barely tolerate a Ferris wheel without tossing my cookies."

I volunteered to go pick up the tickets so I could express my appreciation to Emily for going out of her way to accommodate us. While Wendy and I were swimming, Veronica had been baking oatmeal raisin cookies for the group, and they were absolutely delicious. After gobbling down two cookies, I'd told the young lady she'd missed her calling as a bakery chef and that I'd like for her to give me some cooking lessons some day when she wasn't tied up with work at her own inn. But for now, with nothing else pressing, the two younger gals decided to accompany me.

The young blond woman I'd seen working the desk the day before was alone in the office ringing up a teenage boy's potato chips, Coke, and postcards. She smiled at the young man and wished him a fun day at the rodeo before turning her attention to us. I told her our names and in return, she introduced herself as

Kylie Rue and said she'd only been working at the campground for a few weeks.

"You must be a quick learner, Kylie," I said. "You appear to be very professional for a gal who looks like she should still be in high school."

"I'm not *that* young, I'm afraid," she said with a smile. "I'll be twenty-nine on my next birthday, which is the day after Christmas. That kind of sucks in a way, but I certainly clean up in gifts in late December."

"I'll bet you do. We're the same age, girlfriend. Except I'll be thirty in mid-August, so I'm still an elder to you, since my birthday is just about three weeks away," Wendy said to Kylie.

"Time seems to pass quicker and quicker the older I get. I'll be thirty before I know it," the office helper said.

Kylie had a youthful and bubbly disposition, and it amused me the way she talked about her age. I put my hand on top of hers, and said, "Don't rush it, sweetie. Your birthday is still five months away. When you're my age, you'll be saying you just turned fifty-one until the day before your fifty-second birthday. Are you from around here? I detect a faint touch of a southern accent in your voice."

"Yes, you're right, Ms. Starr," she replied. "I just moved out here from Longwood, Florida, but I'm originally from Tennessee. I was fortunate to land this job so quickly."

"Really?" I asked. "What did you do in Florida?"

"I went to cosmetology school and got a job at The Hair Affair Salon, but after several years of dealing with disgruntled old women...um, no offense, Ms. Starr, I'd had enough and decided to move out here. I wanted a change and to experience new places, starting with Wyoming. I hadn't anticipated being so homesick, though. I'm adopted, but I couldn't love my mom and dad any more than I would if they were my biological parents. I miss them even more than I thought I would, but I'm hoping I'll get over that eventually. And, Ms. Starr, I apologize again for the disgruntled old women comment. That was a little insensitive of me."

"Please call me Lexie, dear. And I wasn't offended about your comment until you told me not to be." Including me in the category of disgruntled old women really was kind of discouraging. I didn't feel terribly old, and I certainly didn't see myself as disgruntled. "Trust me, Kylie, I may seem ancient to youngsters like yourself, but I'm at least a decade younger than dirt, and as *gruntled* as they come."

I could see her mulling over the question of whether "gruntled" was a real word, or not, when I continued. "Why were the old ladies so disgruntled?"

"They blamed me when I couldn't make them look like Halle Berry or Jennifer Lopez. They'd show me a photo and say, 'I'd like to get the *Rachel* hairstyle,' and then totally blow a gasket when they didn't look exactly like Jennifer Aniston when I was finished. Jeez Louise, I might barely make a hundred bucks on a good day. I'm not sure I could even make Jennifer Aniston look like Jennifer Aniston."

"I'm sure you're more talented than you give yourself credit for," Wendy said. "But your job must have been challenging at times. That's why I like working with cadavers. They never complain, and I haven't ever witnessed one blowing a gasket. And I'm smart enough to leave the hair styling to the funeral home to take care of, because if you don't make a dead person look like they did when alive, or even better in some cases, there can be some very unhappy family members."

After chuckling over Wendy's remark, Kylie pointed at my daughter's feet and said, "I absolutely love your boots. If I ever win the lottery, the first thing I'm going to buy is a pair just like them. Well, maybe the second thing, after I buy the biggest, plushest mansion in the country, complete with a huge, elaborate swimming pool, and a fleet of customized Rolls Royces in the eight-car garage."

"It better be a big lottery payout or you might not have enough left over for a pair of boots like mine," Wendy said, chuckling at Kylie's remarks.

Just as Wendy finished her sentence, the queen of gasket-blowing walked in the door. Ignoring Wendy, Veronica, and me as if we were grease stains on the linoleum floor, she marched straight up to Kylie and demanded to see the owner. Kylie's jubilant mood vanished like dollar bills in a strip joint.

"I'm afraid she doesn't start working in the office until noon. She's up late every evening doing paperwork after she locks up the office, which stays open until ten, and often later than that during this annual event," Kylie answered with as much politeness as she could summon. "Can I help you?"

"No, you can't. I have an issue to discuss with her that is way above your pay grade."

Remaining calm and collected—almost stoic—Kylie told Fanny Finch to come back later if she needed to talk directly to Emily Harrington. I think I would have been compelled to slap the scowl right off the author's face. The woman must have been born disgruntled. She was like the tiger that couldn't change its stripes—a fitting description of Fanny. I was impressed with Kylie's poise, something I'd have been hard-pressed to emulate.

Even though Fanny had said she'd speak only to Emily, she launched right into a laundry list of complaints. Between griping about the unevenness of her site and the park's lack of a payphone, she managed to work in the fact that she was the author of the best selling novel *Fame and Shame*, a biography detailing the disgraceful truths about Vex Vaughn's past behaviors and actions.

I didn't have a clue who Vex Vaughn was earlier when Wyatt announced he had acquired tickets for us to attend the performer's concert that evening. This wasn't surprising, since my tastes leaned toward old-timers like Merle Haggard and Johnny Cash. I'd still be listening to my old Elvis tapes if my car had an eight-track player in it, something the three gals I was with would look at as if they were viewing something from the Jurassic period.

When I glanced at Veronica, whom I now knew was a fan of Vaughn's, she had an angry, hateful expression on her face, and fists tightly clinched. When she took a step forward, I thrust myself between her and Fanny as I heard Kylie respond, "I'm sure you are profiting handsomely on the book, despite how it might affect other people's lives."

Fanny replied with venom. "The scumbag should have thought about that when he was taking illegal drugs, getting young women pregnant before dumping them, and racking up one DUI after another. Not only that, but he was arrested for assault and battery several times, and charged with resisting arrest twice. Oh, but I don't want to give away everything in the book. You'll have to purchase a copy at my book-signing this afternoon if you want to know all the juicy details."

"No, thanks!" Kylie replied. I could tell that she, like Veronica, was a fan of the subject of Fanny's unsanctioned biography. I wasn't sure why they seemed so fond of him if Fanny's description of him was accurate. I listened as Kylie practically spat out her next comments. "I have no desire to read a disrespectful book like that! And one more thing, Ms. Finch. When was the last time you've seen a payphone? They're practically obsolete now that nearly everyone from nine to ninety owns a cell phone."

Yes, I thought, *this young gal would definitely consider an eight-track player comparable to a Tyrannosaurus Rex.* I hadn't really even taken notice of the disappearance of pay phones until I thought about Kylie's remark. The fact I'd recently crossed over to the downhill side of fifty was becoming more and more apparent. Odd as it might seem, I couldn't remember ever being happier or more content in my life.

As Fanny turned and stomped out of the office, she let out a loud huff, and said, "I'll come back later when somebody with a little authority is in the office."

It's probably fortunate she left when she did. I was afraid Kylie, with her younger, fit, and athletic body, was on the verge of punching the author's lights out. And, even though Veronica was an ultra-delicate size-zero woman, she was livid. In her furious state I would have placed money on her if she'd goaded the older, but much stronger, Fanny Finch, into a hair-pulling, bitch-slapping catfight—particularly if Kylie jumped in to assist her in the impromptu smack-down. The two women working as a tag team would make mincemeat of the mouthy broad.

"I'm sorry if I sounded rude to Ms. Finch, but there's just something about her that rubs me the wrong way. I guess I lost my patience, which is rare for me. I usually don't let much of anything get under my skin," Kylie said, apologetically. "Now I feel really badly that I spoke to her the way I did."

"Well, don't feel bad for one second, my dear. She was the rude one, not you," I assured the affable young gal. "I'm fairly certain Fanny rubs everybody the wrong way. I lost my patience with her two seconds after I laid eyes on her. What took *you* so long?"

Everybody laughed, and Kylie appeared visibly relieved. I could tell she felt bad about losing her cool, and it was obvious it went against her nature to do so. It was also obvious that Veronica still wanted a piece of Fanny Finch. I found myself praying she never got the opportunity to carry out her wishes, because I was certain it wouldn't be a pretty sight.

CHAPTER 4

Sitting around a table at the small campground café, I asked Wendy and Veronica if there was anything special they wanted to do while the men spent the afternoon at the rodeo. The response I got from Veronica took me completely by surprise.

"I would like to go to Fanny Finch's book signing at Barnes and Noble."

"Are you serious?" Wendy and I asked in unison.

"Yes, I am. As much as I dislike the author of *Fame and Shame*, I'm dying of curiosity about the dirt she's spilling in her tell-all book about Vex Vaughn. I suppose it's people like me who are to blame for her book being a *New York Times* best-seller."

"I guess I have to agree with Kylie," Wendy said. "Aren't you concerned about how a book like hers could adversely affect the singer's life, and his family's, too?"

"How much could it affect him? He's rich and famous and probably could care less about what Fanny's written in her book. Celebrities like Vex Vaughn are usually happy to get any kind of exposure they can, good or bad. I would be surprised if this book didn't actually help boost his record sales, maybe even substantially. The bad boy reputation goes over big with his female fans. I know I find it pretty sexy, myself. Not as sexy as Wyatt, mind you."

"Well, I don't doubt you're probably right, but are you sure you want to support Fanny Finch's writing career by buying a book from her? Isn't that windbag egotistical enough already?" I asked Veronica. "I can already imagine the arrogant expression she'll be sporting when you hand over money for her book after the scene in the office this morning. Are you sure you're not just interested in getting within slapping range of her?"

"Of course not!" She replied with an ornery grin that said otherwise.

Despite Wendy's and my efforts to dissuade her, Veronica was dead set in her desire to make the trip to Barnes and Noble. She agreed to buy the book directly from the store instead of standing in line to have her purchase signed by the author. She thought it most likely Fanny Finch would never even notice we were there. I was not at all thrilled to be going to the bookstore with Veronica, but Wendy and I agreed it wouldn't be very hospitable of us to make her go alone.

While I was digging money out of my fanny pack to pay for our lunch, Emily walked in to speak to the lady standing behind the cash register. We spoke briefly with Emily after she ended her conversation with the clerk. When Veronica told her we were going to the book-signing event, she looked at me as if I had deserted her camp and joined the enemy's. After Wendy and Veronica walked outside and left me to settle the bill, I felt obliged to explain my decision to go to Barnes and Noble with Veronica. "Trust me, Emily, this was not my idea. I'd never do it if I didn't

feel responsible for Veronica, because Stone invited
her to accompany us on our vacation. I can't stand the
sight of Fanny Finch, and I'm going to do everything I
can to make sure she doesn't see me at the book-
signing."

"Oh, don't worry about it. My issues with her are
yesterday's news. Now I'm dealing with a customer
who won't pick up after his German shepherd and
three Rottweilers. Stanley threatened to throw the man
and his wife out of the park if he catches him letting
his dogs poop on someone else's site again without
picking it up afterward. It's always been an issue, but
has eased up quite a bit now that Stanley has added a
fenced and gated dog run."

"Wow, that is the most rude and disrespectful thing
a person could do in a beautiful place like this—or
anywhere else, for that matter," I told her. "People
like that shouldn't be allowed to own pets. Why would
anyone even want to travel in the confined space of an
RV with four large dogs?"

"You've got me! But it seems like the vast majority
of our customers travel with pets, mostly dogs.
However, many of them have smaller breeds like
terriers and poodles. We did have one older couple
staying here who traveled with seven greyhounds in
their twenty-four foot motorhome. They told us they
had adopted them when the dogs got too old to
compete in racing at their local dog track. I guess I
can understand the Warners not wanting to see the
dogs put down when their former owners could no
longer profit off them. Dogs like that deserve a family
to love them after being used in that way."

"I agree whole-heartedly, but I'd have to think twice
before dragging them around the country in a small
motorhome," I replied.

"You and me both! By the way, Lexie, how are you

gals going to get to the bookstore? It's on the north end of town and too far to walk from the fairgrounds if you took the shuttle bus there," Emily said.

"I don't know," I replied. "We haven't even considered the transportation aspect of our plans. Do you know the number of a local taxi service?"

"Yeah, right. This ain't New York City, my friend, but I'd be happy to loan you my car whenever you need it." Emily dug her keys out of her pocket, and said, "Take it. I certainly won't need it today. I couldn't get away from this campground right now if I wanted to. Just park it in the carport when you get back. You'll feel right at home in it. It's small and yellow, just like your little VW bug you let us take to go to the casino in St. Joseph while we were staying at your inn."

I thanked Emily and decided to look for a book of Sudoku puzzles to give her as a token of my appreciation. I'd seen her working on one a couple of times while she and Stanley were our guests the previous fall. Suddenly, I felt a spark of anticipation, anxious to see what the afternoon would bring.

Using the GPS feature in Emily's car, we had no trouble driving straight to the Barnes and Noble on Dell Range Boulevard, not far up the road from Frontier Mall where we thought we might do a little shopping later on. When we walked into the bookstore, we saw a crowd of people gathered around a table in the most prominent location in the building. In the midst of the mob, I heard the squeaky laugh of Fanny Finch a time or two. I didn't want to get anywhere near her table, but I could visualize the author busily signing books for her adoring fans with the air of the Queen of England addressing the commoners.

"Go get your book, sweetie, and let's get out of here," I said to Veronica.

While Veronica wandered around the store looking for a copy of *Fame and Shame* on a shelf in the biography section, and Wendy went over to the snack bar area to buy all three of us a bottle of water, I felt obliged to walk over to where another table was set up with two dejected-looking ladies sitting behind it. No one was in line to make a purchase, but I thought it would be a pleasant diversion to chat with them about the books they'd written. As I approached, I noticed several tall stacks of unsold books on the table in front of them almost shielded them from view. I knew from overhearing Fanny's conversation with Emily that these ladies were the "wanna-be best selling authors" known as Norma Grace and Sarah Krumm.

Both Norma and Sarah looked bored and disgusted, and Norma was tapping her ballpoint pen against the edge of the table in an attempt to relieve her boredom. I felt bad that Fanny Finch was monopolizing the crowd, even though I realized her book was quite relevant in Cheyenne this week, with Vex Vaughn headlining the concert at the rodeo arena on Monday evening.

After purchasing a bundle of Sudoku puzzle books that I found on a clearance table, I stopped to dispose my gum in the trashcan. By the time I reached their shared table, which was almost hidden behind a row of bookshelves, and a long way from Fanny's table, they were searching for something inside a box of books and having an animated conversation. I heard Sarah say, "I can't believe Fanny got them to put us over here by the restrooms so we wouldn't be within sight of all the people who want to purchase her book. Can you, Norma? Not only is she hogging the attention, as usual, she's managed to get us put back in this secluded area where hardly anyone will even notice we're here."

"I'm sure that was her intention," Norma replied. "It's not like she doesn't do that at every book signing event we go to. Sometimes I feel like pushing her in front of an oncoming bus. I really despise that conceited blowhard!"

"Me, too! I don't know why we even go to these book signing events with her."

With that last exchange between the two ladies, I found myself wanting to do a little more eavesdropping in order to better hear Norma's response. I like to think it was more of an "inquisitive mind" kind of thing rather than it being the inherent "nosy Nelly" trait I was saddled with. I squatted down in front of Norma's table to mess with the shoestring on my left tennis shoe, as if it had come undone and needed to be retied. I didn't think I would be noticed by the two authors, who were still involved in their lively discussion.

"I know why, Sarah," Norma said, as she pulled a cell phone out of the box. "We have the same agent as Fanny does, and if Nina didn't let us go to book-signing events with Fanny, we wouldn't get to go to any at all. As much as it pains me to admit it, you and I are nowhere near to being in the same league as Fanny when it comes to book sales and writing careers. Of course, that's due to the 'accident' she orchestrated at that one book-signing event a few months ago. Still, we're lucky Nina agreed to represent us, and we don't want to make any waves and risk being dropped as her clients."

"Yeah, you're right," Sarah replied. "I don't know about you, but it took an act of God for me to get an agent, not to mention mailing out hundreds of query letters. My self-esteem was practically bleeding from so many rejections before I got a positive response from Nina."

"I know the feeling. I could have wall-papered my living room with the rejection letters I collected before Nina accepted me as a client. I was just a query letter away from the self-inflicted death of my writing career. The few agents who took the time to reply to my queries invariably sent a form letter that basically said, '*No way, Jose! Don't quit your day job, lady!*' I feel extremely fortunate to have Nina as my agent. And the fact that she was able to sell my book to a notable publisher was even more amazing. You and I both know, it's not the kind of book that would appeal to the masses like *Fame and Shame* obviously does."

"Same here," Sarah agreed, with a long-suffering sigh before standing up and looking down at me as I finished retying my shoe. "Can I help you, ma'am?"

"Oh, no, thank you," I replied, caught off guard. "I'm fine. I was just trying to get a knot out of this shoestring and retie it before asking you two about your books."

When both of their faces lit up with delight, I knew immediately I was going to have to buy a copy of each book, whether they interested me or not. And, as it turned out, it was the latter. Norma Grace's book about her life as a so-called "Coupon Queen" and Sarah Krumm's tome on the principles of multi-generational households and their effect on society did nothing to pique my interest.

I had clipped coupons in the past only to forget to dig them out of my fanny pack and hand them to the checkout cashier when actually buying a product I didn't really need in the first place. And living in a multi-generational household wouldn't appeal to me for very long. I'd give it a month at best before I started circling classified ads in the *Rockdale Gazette* and presenting the list of available apartments to Wendy. And she's the only close relative I had left, except for Stone, who already shared a home with me. I loved my daughter more than life itself, but there was such a thing as too much togetherness.

However, I was pretty adept at feigning interest in things I had no interest in. I perfected this talent after having been married for a year to a man who could talk about the pros and cons of different kinds of bait and tackle for hours on end. Stone, on the other hand, could not resist yawning and sighing when I babbled on about a deal I'd found on faux leather shoes and how I thought I should return to the store to buy one in every color they offered. In fact, he'd once fallen asleep as I was telling him about my desire to search the Internet for a good chicken Florentine recipe. I was just explaining the importance of using the perfect seasoning combination of garlic, basil, and thyme, when Stone's head fell back on the couch and he began to rattle the blinds with his snoring.

I exchanged introductions with the two ladies, while Norma was signing her book, which she guaranteed would save me a lot of money on groceries and household products. I asked Sarah about the crowd around the third author's table, as though I'd never heard of the book or its author.

"Oh, that's Fanny Finch, signing copies of her book about the country and western singer, Vex Vaughn. Personally, I find the sensational facts she attributes to 'a reliable source' to be questionable and unethical, but apparently, there are a lot of people who like that kind of thing. Personally, I think she used a liberal dose of creative license in the process of debasing the singer."

"But it appears a lot of people enjoy seeing a famous person humbled, or in this case, demeaned," I replied in agreement. "Not me, however. If the singer wanted to air all his dirty laundry in public, he'd write his own autobiography about his life. I find it rather distasteful, myself."

"Exactly!" She responded, as she handed me back my change for her book, which she'd already signed. "Just between us, she treats Norma and me as if she's Cinderella and we're her ugly stepsisters. In her opinion, we are so far beneath her that it's an injustice that we're even allowed to participate in book-signing events with her. I'm pretty sure she's appalled we're even allowed to breathe the same air she does."

"You should ignore her high and mighty attitude. You've both earned your own degree of success, and you deserve respect for it," I said, with as much conviction as I could muster.

Wendy had joined me at Norma and Sarah's table and handed me a water bottle. After glancing at the titles of the two books in my hands, she looked at me quizzically. Before she could humiliate me by asking what on earth had prompted me to buy the books, I said, "I know you're dying to read these books too, honey, but you'll just have to wait until I've read them first."

"Oh, darn!" She said, not bothering to pretend she had any interest in reading the two books.

"Where's Veronica?" I cut in quickly, before Wendy began inquiring about why I had any desire to read a book on either topic.

Wendy pointed toward the crowd across the room, and said, "The only copies of Fanny's book that are available are at her table, so Veronica's standing in line to buy one and have it signed."

I heard Sarah gasp, and I was too embarrassed to explain the situation, so I thanked them for signing my books and walked away with Wendy in tow. We each sipped our water while we sat on a couch in a reading nook of the bookstore. We chatted about everything from the recent recall of a popular brand of baby strollers, to how to treat an alpaca with stomach ulcers caused by an overproduction of gastric acids. We even discussed possible names for my imaginary grandchildren as we waited over an hour for Veronica to join us. I was chewing over Wendy's name choice for a son, should she have one. I wasn't sure I could ever get used to referring to my grandson as *Major,* no matter how popular Wendy insisted the name was. I didn't want to feel as if I should salute my grandson every time our paths crossed. I was trying to visualize telling an ER physician that "Major" had a crayon stuck up his nose when Veronica walked toward us with the coveted book about her favorite singer clutched tightly in her arms.

That inherent nosy-Nelly trait reared its ugly head again as I looked at the likeness of an incredibly handsome man wearing a black cowboy hat and holding a well-worn guitar on the cover of *Fame and Shame.* I wasn't surprised to see it was the same book the pretty redhead had been reading at the pool earlier that morning. It was apparently being snatched up by many readers.

I was ashamed of myself for suddenly wondering what kind of "sensational facts" were laid bare on the pages of the best-selling book. But I vowed never to read it—not even to satisfy my curiosity.

I can't remember the last time I laughed as hard as I did when Stone, Wyatt, and Andy got off the shuttle bus dressed like actors in a John Wayne western. From their brand new ten-gallon hats and pointy-toed boots, to the oversized silver belt buckles on their braided leather belts, they looked like they'd just pilfered stuff from Ty Murray's closet.

The most amusing part was that I could tell they all thought they looked pretty hot in their new cowboy regalia. At least Andy actually owned a cattle ranch, and the expensive purchases he made might come in handy for him. Stone's new get-up, however, would collect dust and moths in the basement for the rest of its life after we returned to Rockdale, Missouri. I didn't point this out, however. I had a multitude of "must have" shoes doing the exact same thing in my closet.

"I see you all spent a lot of time, not to mention money, in a Western Wear shop this afternoon," I said, with a smile. "And you can't imagine how smart you all look in your new costumes."

"Costumes? These are not costumes, Lexie Marie!" Stone said adamantly. "This is Western apparel, which is very stylish and suitable for the occasion. We stopped by the Wrangler Western Wear store downtown after we had delicious prime rib sandwiches for lunch at the Albany Inn next door to it. We put on our new gear before we went to the rodeo, which, by the way, was awesome. In my next life I want to be a rodeo clown."

I wanted to tell him he was already halfway there in that get-up. But as silly and out of character as Stone looked, I could tell the men had thoroughly enjoyed their afternoon together and I was happy for them. Wendy, Veronica, and I had also had a pleasant afternoon shopping at Frontier Mall and visiting the Capitol building, the Union Pacific "Big Boy" locomotive steam engine, which was on display in Holiday Park, and the historic downtown area. I remembered seeing the exact western wear store that had drawn the three men into its web.

I had been surprised when we stopped at a gift shop and Veronica bought a number of souvenir-type trinkets to hand out at Rockdale Meadows, a nursing home back home, where she told us she visited every Thursday to play cards with some of the residents. She spent time with many of the residents that seldom had visitors and who always welcomed someone to converse with. There was definitely more to this young lady than met the eye, I was discovering. She was certainly caring and thoughtful.

We'd also stopped for tourism information at the visitor's center along I-25, which was conveniently located close to the Cozy Camping RV Park. We picked out a few cards from the rack advertising tourist sites we thought we might want to take in while we were in Cheyenne. If time allowed, we all agreed we should consider taking a day trip to Rocky Mountain National Park, not far south of town in Estes Park, Colorado.

That evening, we accepted Emily's invitation to take Stanley's extended cab pickup truck, which was much roomier than her economy car, to Poor Richard's Steakhouse for supper. We indulged in wonderful cuisine and entertaining camaraderie as we discussed the events of the day. I, in fact, *over*-indulged on the "wonderful cuisine" and I could feel my jeans getting snugger and snugger with every bite of my Buffalo sirloin steak and loaded baked potato, not to mention the full plate of food I'd selected at the delectable soup and salad bar. In lieu of passing on dessert, I promised myself I'd get up early the next morning and swim a couple dozen laps at the pool before breakfast. Then I'd spend a relaxing day with my husband and friends at the campground. It sounded like a perfect day to me. Too bad it didn't work out that way.

CHAPTER 5

Wendy agreed to join me for an early Sunday morning swim, but when we arrived at the swimming pool, the gate was locked. The "Open" sign was lit up on the office door so we walked over to ask when the pool would be available to use.

Kylie greeted us warmly when we walked into the office, friendly and gregarious, as was her nature. "Good morning, ladies! What are you two up to this early on a Sunday morning?"

"Good morning, Kylie!" Wendy and I said in stereo. I told the young woman we were hoping to get a few laps in before breakfast and were wondering when the pool would be open.

"Oh, I'm sorry," she replied. "I had customers lined up outside the door when I opened the office about a half hour ago and haven't had a chance to go unlock the gate. There's a lull in the action right now, but it's not apt to last long. Come along and I'll unlock it for you before the next wave of customers arrive. We usually open the office and pool at eight, but during these annual festivities we open at six because the RV Park is already busy at the crack of dawn during

Frontier Days."

Kylie related a funny anecdote about a customer she'd checked in the day before as we walked over to the pool area. "I asked her how many people were in their party because the rate is for two adults only. We charge an extra two dollars for each additional adult, as is a common practice for campgrounds, according to Emily. But we never charge for kids under twelve, because the Harringtons don't want it to be too expensive for young families with lots of children. The customer told me there were two adults and a child in her party. So I asked her how old the child was to see if I needed to charge for him or not. I couldn't help laughing when she kind of hung her head in embarrassment, and replied, 'He's thirty-nine.'"

"What? Thirty-nine?" I asked Kylie in astonishment. "That's a little old to be considered a child, isn't it?"

"That's what I said to the customer," Kylie said. "And she responded, 'Well, he's *my* child!' So I let the thirty-nine year old *kid* stay free because I didn't want to get involved in a confrontation with the customer. But, jeez, I mean, thirty-nine? Really? Some people will do anything to save a buck, won't they?"

We were still laughing at her story as Kylie turned the key in the lock on the pool area gate. As she swung open the gate and turned to hurry back to wait on a gentleman walking up the sidewalk to the office door, she said, "Have a nice swim, ladies, and enjoy your day."

We thanked her and I followed Wendy onto the concrete patio that surrounded the pool. I almost swallowed my tongue when Wendy looked into the pool and cried out in alarm, "Oh, my God!"

I rushed to the side of the pool and looked down into the water. Just as it was registering in my mind what had startled my daughter, Kylie appeared at my side to see what had caused Wendy's outburst. It had been loud enough to potentially wake half the people in the campground. When it dawned on her what she was seeing, she echoed Wendy's exclamation, and her face paled. She put her right hand over her mouth. I saw her stagger a bit and I grabbed her by the shoulders to steady her, in fear she might pass out on the pavement.

"Is that what I think it is?" Kylie stammered. "Is that a body on the bottom of the pool?"

"Yes, I'm afraid it is," I replied. "And not just any body. I recognize the suit she's wearing. That's Fanny Finch!"

"Oh, dear Lord," Kylie said, her face drained of color. I could tell from her reaction that she'd never seen a dead body before. Unfortunately, I'd seen a few too many in the past couple of years. But, even so, it was a jolt to my senses every time it occurred.

"I'll call 9-1-1 while you run and get the Harringtons, Kylie. And Wendy, perhaps you should go inform her husband that there's a problem, and let Stone know what's going on, too. I wouldn't go into detail with Mr. Finch if I were you," I instructed.

I was getting accustomed to situations like this, having been involved in the investigation of a number of deaths in the last couple of years. Because of those past experiences, I was able to maintain control of my emotions and react with a sense of calmness in the face of a crisis like this one, after the initial shock had worn off. But Wendy, who makes a living as an assistant to the county coroner, deals with deaths and cadavers on a daily basis. She immediately pulled her cell phone out of her pocket and said to me, "I'm probably better equipped to speak to the 9-1-1 operator and emergency technicians, so why don't you go get Stone and Mr. Finch while I take care of this matter."

It wasn't a question. It was an order. I knew she was right, but I couldn't help resenting the fact my daughter didn't seem to think I was competent to speak with the emergency personnel. But I also knew she'd get some degree of perverse pleasure in detailing the specifics of the dead body to whatever poor sucker answered the call. I still couldn't stomach her morbid fascination with cadavers, which had resulted from her occupation in the coroner's lab. Besides, now was not the time to quibble over minor injustices, so I merely nodded and followed Kylie out through the gate.

Mr. Finch was sitting in a lawn chair on the small—and not adequate in Fanny's opinion—concrete patio. He was drinking a cup of coffee and chuckling at two squirrels chasing each other around a large cottonwood tree. I hated to have to disturb his peaceful morning by bringing him bad news.

"Mr. Finch?" My voice quivered but the gentleman seemed unaware of my trepidation.

"Good morning, sweetheart. It's actually Mr. Bumberdinger, but please call me Avery. Finch is Fanny's—or actually Claudia's—pen name. She gets almost physically ill if someone refers to her as Claudia Bumberdinger...not that I think being referred to as Fanny is much better. You may not believe this, but she can be a real hard bugger at times." Avery smiled as he spoke, and, naturally, I smiled back at him. But I was thinking I'd also prefer to be called Fanny Finch rather than Claudia Bumberdinger if my name was going to be plastered across the cover of a book I'd written.

Avery Bumberdinger seemed like a very soft-spoken, laid-back guy. It was hard to visualize him as the same man I'd heard viciously squabbling with his wife two short nights ago. He wasn't half-bad looking, either, when he was fully dressed and not doing belly flops off the diving board in a too-tight Speedo.

I smiled at the kind man now as he took another sip from his coffee cup and I introduced myself. I wasn't sure how to best break the horrid news to him. Out of an ingrained sense of politeness, I let him know I was happy to make his acquaintance. "My name is Lexie Starr and it's a pleasure to meet you, Avery."

"And you, as well, Ms. Starr. What can I do for you this fine morning, pretty lady?"

"Um, well, um, you see..." I stuttered, trying to get my nerve up. I finally took a deep breath, and said, "I'm afraid there's been an accident at the pool involving your wife and your presence is needed there immediately."

I spoke with as much discretion as I could, considering the gravity of the situation. I assumed he could tell by my frayed nerves and haunted expression that the situation was dire, but I didn't want to be the one to tell him his spouse had expired.

Avery shook his head like a man at the tattered end of his rope. He let out an expressive sigh and set his almost full coffee cup down on the patio. I looked at it with longing. I wanted to ask him if I could finish it off for him if he was just going to let it go to waste. I was very much in need of a strong dose of caffeine.

Good thing I hadn't just taken a big gulp of coffee, because I almost choked on my own saliva when Avery asked, "What has Fanny done now? Held someone under water for daring to disagree with her? I'd like to hold *her* under water for a minute or two myself, and probably would if I thought I could get away with it. I'm just kidding with you, of course. Seriously though, Ms. Starr, what is the problem with my wife now? Is she being a bugger again?"

"I'd rather let the Harringtons explain it to you," I said. I didn't have it in me to tell someone about the death of his loved one, even if Avery Bumberdinger had just jokingly stated he wouldn't be above killing his spouse if given half a chance.

"Oh, all right. I don't know what's gotten into that woman, but she's become nearly impossible to get along with recently. She's been gnawing on my last nerve all week. We'd been getting along fabulously until her silly book soared to the top of the *New York Time's* best best-sellers list. Her success has gone to her head and now she's almost impossible to get along with."

I knew that would no longer be a problem that would plague Avery, but I limited my reply to telling him he really should hurry to the pool area. He shook his head again and stood up. He pulled a black comb out of his back pocket to smooth down his hair, which was wavy, the exact color of his comb, and very sparsely accented by gray streaks. Finally, after assuring every hair was in place and the door to his fifth wheel was locked, he began to walk nonchalantly up the gravel road toward the pool.

My next order of business was to get Stone. When I walked into the motorhome, he said, "I thought you and Wendy were going for a swim. You've only been away for ten or fifteen minutes."

After briefly studying my face, he asked, "Honey, what's wrong? Are you okay? Sit down, and let me pour you a cup—"

"No, not now—"

"Okay, now I'm worried. What's going on? I've never known you to not welcome a cup of coffee. Did I hear Avery say something about drowning his wife?"

"Not exactly, dear. It was more of a new item on his bucket list, I think. But you're half-right, because Fanny did drown, Stone! Wendy and I found her at the bottom of the pool. She wasn't breathing! She's dead! I can't believe it, Stone! I just can't believe she's dead!" My voice rose another octave with every word I spoke. I knew I was beginning to hyperventilate and sound as if I was on the verge of hysteria, which I was. The seriousness of the situation was just beginning to hit me. There might be a killer staying in our friend's RV Park, I realized, and his RV might just be parked right next to our site.

"Settle down, honey," Stone said, as he wrapped his arms around me. "You're in shock and I don't want to have to slap you."

He smiled to let me know he was only kidding, but his comment helped to calm me down. I explained to him as quickly as I could what had transpired. Then, together, we rushed back to the scene, where numerous emergency vehicles were beginning to arrive. We'd heard the sirens approaching as we had been briskly walking up the road.

Wendy was introducing herself to an EMT who was stepping out of an ambulance, while Emily and Stanley were speaking to Avery. I thought Stone really might need to slap Fanny's husband, because his expression never wavered as he listened to the campground owners explain the situation to him. His face looked like it had been carved into the side of a mountain, so I knew he was in such a state of disbelief that the finality of his wife's death had not yet sunk in.

As squad cars and a fire engine pulled into the campground, people began emerging from their RVs and tents, following the source of the activity. Despite the fact that it was just past seven o'clock in the morning, a crowd formed quickly. Two divers in neoprene wetsuits were entering the men's shower. They had obviously retrieved the body from the bottom of the pool and were changing back into their regular outfits.

As the news spread about what the commotion was regarding, I could hear the blending sound of many conversations occurring simultaneously. The grapevine was operating at full force. I saw Fanny's fellow authors, Norma Grace and Sarah Krumm, standing off to the side. Neither of the ladies, still wearing their pajamas and bathrobes, looked particularly astounded by the horrific turn of events, nor upset about the death of Fanny Finch. In fact, they wore identical contented, almost-evil, expressions.

They appeared to be happy about the shocking tragedy and relieved to be seeing the last of someone they despised. If I had to adequately describe their demeanor, I'd say they looked like two women watching a fireman rescuing their pet kitten from a high, flimsy branch up in a tree; pleasure, mixed with relief. I mentally vowed that I would never treat others so badly that they might some day be looking down at my dead body with that same expression on their face.

I saw Kylie, who'd been rendered speechless, wipe a tear off her cheek before returning to the office—most likely in the event a customer needed attention. I think it was safe to say there were no customers in the office, due to the mob that surrounded the pool area. At that moment, discovering what had a huge crowd abuzz was more intriguing than the idea of purchasing a bag of ice or Wyoming keychain.

The police officers on the scene were trying, without much success, to push the crowd back from where the body bag had been laid out next to the once-energetic body of Fanny Finch. They realized that observing something of this nature could be very traumatic to the curious onlookers, so they were trying to shield the body from the crowd's view as much as possible.

After the coroner zipped up the bag in which Fanny's body had been placed, several men worked together to hoist the bag up and load it into the back of the medical examiner's van to be transported to the morgue. I glanced over at Avery to gauge his reaction. His stony expression was that of someone watching men load a large burlap bag of turnips they'd just purchased at a farmer's market into the bed of a truck.

I wondered if somebody really did hold Fanny's head under water until she drowned; perhaps even Avery, who might have been attempting to cast suspicion away from himself. I couldn't imagine anyone who wouldn't be at least tempted to do such a terrible thing to the self-centered and unpleasant woman, given the opportunity. I mentioned the possibility to Stone.

He rolled his eyes in response, and said, "Oh, good grief. I hope this isn't going to turn into another unfettered determination to prove the woman was murdered and her death wasn't an accidental drowning. After all the harrowing events surrounding Ducky's death[2] last fall, I should think you'd steer as far away as possible from getting involved in the matter."

"Well, of course, Stone. I'm merely intrigued by the situation because I've seen Fanny Finch swim. She was the embodiment of what the offspring of Michael Phelps and Esther Williams would be."

"Seriously?" Stone asked, with a chuckle. "I can't quite visualize Michael Phelps, who's in his twenties,

---

[2] *Just Ducky (A Lexie Starr Mystery, Book 5)*

hooking up with Esther Williams, who's got to be nearing ninety if she's even still alive."

"Okay, smart-aleck. Esther Williams passed recently, and I know she and Michael would be an unlikely pair. My point is that I can't imagine her drowning accidentally. She appeared to be the picture of health, and was definitely an impressive swimmer. She was like a dolphin on speed in the water."

Stone rolled his eyes again and walked over to greet Andy, Veronica, and Wyatt, knowing they'd be interested in what was going on. They'd been among the throng of people ascending on the scene from their RV sites.

The next thing I knew, Wendy was standing in front of me, having finished her conversation with the coroner. I had not been surprised to see her speaking with him. With my daughter's passion for all things cadaver-related, and her unseemly desire to immerse herself in every discussion involving the cause of someone's death, I would have been more astonished if she hadn't spoken to him.

"You know, Mom, I'm finding it hard to believe she drowned accidentally. When you two were swimming laps yesterday, Fanny swam by you like you were a warning buoy floating on the surface of the water. It was like watching greased lightning flash past a dying slug."

"Well, I think your analogy might be a gross exaggeration," I said, rather miffed by the comparison. "I wasn't trying to break any speed records, just warming up."

"No offense intended, Mom. She'd have passed me as if I were in a coma had I had been swimming a lap myself. I'm just saying the woman was an advanced swimmer."

"Yes, I agree, and I do get your point, Wendy. She

was too accomplished a swimmer to drown accidentally, barring a sudden health impediment that rendered her unable to function, of course. I was just saying the exact same thing to Stone."

"Eli, the coroner, said her liver temperature was eighty-four degrees, which indicates she's been dead for around nine hours, which would make her drowning somewhere about ten last night. The pool is heated because of the cool evenings here, but the temperature of the water still factors into the formula to determine the time of death. So she could have died even later than that; maybe around eleven."

Wendy loved to flaunt her knowledge of the science of mortality, even to someone like me, who was likely to turn a deaf ear as soon as she began spouting words like rigor mortis, lividity and dissection. I often wondered where I'd gone wrong raising my only child to make her turn into someone so fascinated by what caused some unfortunate person to bite the dust. But out of an inborn curiosity I wasn't proud of, I reluctantly paid attention to what Wendy was saying.

"As you just mentioned, I'd guess her drowning was probably precipitated by a heart attack, aneurysm, stroke, or seizure. I'm sure that an autopsy will determine what caused her to lose consciousness and drown." As an assistant to the county coroner back home in Missouri, Wendy sounded confident of her assessment. I had to agree it was the only reasonable explanation for Fanny's untimely death. Or, at least it was until I spotted a shiny silver object under the hedge row just inside the fence surrounding the pool patio. It was barely discernible, but something told me it would turn out to be an important factor in Fanny's demise.

CHAPTER 6

The shiny object turned out to be a hair dryer hooked to a long orange extension cord rolled up and used to hide the hair dryer in the dense foliage. If not for the sun glinting off a tiny exposed area of the silver plastic, I wouldn't have noticed it, even though it would have been just a matter of time before one of the detectives discovered it. The unplugged and spooled-up extension cord appeared to have been plugged into an electrical outlet behind the pool's pump. It was now being photographed from every imaginable angle by a team of homicide detectives who'd been called in when I brought the hair dryer to the attention of the closest police officer.

Wendy tapped me on the shoulder, and I turned to face her. "Now I'm certain the official cause of death will be listed as asystole of the heart."

"Layman's terms, please."

"Basically, it's ventricular fibrillation, or cardiac arrest. Detective Colmer told me the hair dryer is fried and nonfunctional. It's probable that someone attached that hair dryer to the electrical cord, turned it on, and tossed it into the pool near Fanny, causing her to die of electrocution."

Wendy was obviously proud of her ability to explain the chain of events leading to Fanny's death to her slightly queasy mother. The smugness she exhibited was almost disturbing. It was a trait she'd inherited from her father, Chester Starr. Chester, my first husband, had died from an embolism many years ago when Wendy was only seven years old. But I can still remember Wendy's exact expression on Chester's face after he'd correctly guessed something as trivial as the outdoor temperature.

Wendy left me and walked over to where the rest of our little group was discussing the new discovery, presumably to impress them with her expertise in the field of necropsy. I saw Emily giving information to a homicide detective. Rather than follow my daughter and listen to her repeat her reasoning, I decided to go over and wait for the campground owner to finish up with the detective. I was anxious to get Emily's take on what had happened in her RV Park.

After relating what little she knew about the events that unfolded the previous evening, she moved away from the detective and turned to me with a look of total exasperation.

"I was afraid something like this would happen when we put the swimming pool in last year, because a pool is such a liability," Emily told me. "Our insurance went up substantially, as you can imagine. Now I assume we'll be embroiled in a major lawsuit. Not to mention that a murder occurring here on the premises is not exactly going to encourage other campers to stay here in the future. I'm wondering if an RV park could lose it's Good Sam status when customers start getting whacked on the premises. That distinction is very important to the success of the campground."

I could relate to the fact that Emily's main concern was how it might potentially harm their business. I'd been in her shoes before, worried a murder at the Alexandria Inn on its opening night would adversely affect the success of our new bed and breakfast establishment.[3] I assured her that it hadn't hurt our business and I doubted it would hurt Cozy Camping RV Park either.

After listening to my opinion, Emily asked, "But why did this have to happen during Frontier Days, the busiest ten days of the season?"

"Just fate, I guess. You know what they say about the Lord working in mysterious ways. It could have happened on any day, and could have just as easily been one of us whose number was up last night."

"Yes, but I can't see either one of us having a line of people waiting to have first crack at bumping us off. Oh, well if it had to happen, I couldn't have picked a better customer for it to happen to," the park owner said.

"Emily!" I gasped.

"Oh, I'm sorry. I didn't realize I'd said that out loud," she said with a sly smile. "But, truthfully, I wouldn't wish something like this on anybody, not even my worst enemy."

"You have enemies?"

"You know what I mean, Lexie. In all the years of owning and operating this campground, I've found that every customer brings me pleasure."

"Oh, how wonderful for you," I said, wondering how a pain-in-the-tush like Fanny Finch could bring anyone pleasure, least of all Emily. I had watched the deceased browbeat her just a couple of days ago. "You can't tell me it's true that every single one of

---

[3] *The Extinguished Guest (A Lexie Starr Mystery, Book 2)*

them actually brings you pleasure!"

"Yes, it really is true. Some bring me pleasure by coming here and others by leaving. And, in this case, even by leaving zipped up in a body bag."

"I can't believe you said that, Emily!" I exclaimed. I might have thought the exact same thing, but I'd have never verbalized it for fear of looking extremely cold-hearted. I expected Emily to tell me she was only pulling my leg again, the way she had when I checked us in at the office on Friday evening.

"Did I mention she brought me pleasure?" Emily said instead, with a wink. "Seriously, I'm very upset about Fanny's death, but I'm not particularly surprised she'd tick someone off to the point they'd want to kill her. Who do you think might have done it? Her poor hen-pecked husband? Or maybe even one of the authors who participated in the book signing event with her? None of those three seems to be capable of such a horrific act, but you never know, I guess. How often do you see the next-door neighbor of a serial killer being interviewed on TV saying they'd have never guessed their kind, quiet, and thoughtful neighbor capable of cutting the eyes out of their numerous victims and serving them up like Brussels sprouts with a steak and salad for supper?"

"Egads, could you be any more gruesome, my friend? But I admit you're absolutely right, Emily. I don't believe I've ever seen one of those neighbors being interviewed say something like, 'Yeah, my neighbor's a psychotic nut job, and I've always wondered how many people he'd strangled, disembodied, and stored in his freezer.'"

Emily chuckled and replied, "And you called me gruesome? Is that not the pot calling the kettle black? But I suppose a serial killer would shy away from carving up a number of people living on his own street. After a while, the authorities might get a clue and start looking into the whereabouts and alibis of the other residents living near the victims. I'd assume the serial killer would make a big effort to appear normal and neighborly around the people they see day in and day out. But in this circumstance, the perp may have just been pushed over the edge by one too many mean-spirited insults by the victim. I imagine it was a spur-of-the-moment type of execution."

"That makes sense. I've found in past experiences with murder cases I've been involved with that the perpetrator often turns out to be the person you'd least expect. In this case it doesn't necessarily have to be somebody staying in the campground, you know. I've noticed that people come and go from here at will, even at night when the security guards are manning the gate."

"That's true. We can't lock the entrance and exit gates and restrict our customers from using them whenever they please. But your comment made me wonder if the guards noticed anything unusual last night. We only hire Mike and Jack to man the gates and patrol the campground during Frontier Days. Their job is to make sure no one's being rowdy and disturbing other campers, and to assist late arrivals with reservations needing help in locating their assigned sites."

"I'd love to speak to the guards, but Stone wouldn't be happy if I got involved in this investigation in any way, even remotely. I'm sure Wendy wouldn't be thrilled about it either. They seem to be birds of a feather when it comes to me helping the authorities investigate murder cases without their approval."

"Could that be because you've almost gotten yourself killed numerous times by butting into homicide investigations you had no business butting into?"

"Oh, I get it. You talked with Stone while you were staying at the Alexandria Inn, didn't you? And it seems as if he's recruited you into his and Wendy's camp," I said in mock dismay. "I really have no particular reason to care who killed Fanny other than pure curiosity, so I would never put myself in any potentially dangerous situation just to discover who did it. I have more sense than that."

"Hmm, that's not the impression I got from speaking to your husband." I knew Emily was just messing with me, but I was still annoyed by yet another person inferring I was crazy to put my neck on the line by getting involved in police business—a little too frequently, I'll admit. The list of people who outright accused me of being foolish was getting longer all the time.

Personally, I thought I'd been quite successful in my attempts to aid detectives in murder cases I'd been involved with. If I were thirty years younger, I'd seriously consider enrolling in the police academy and doing all I could to get a position in the homicide division of any nearby police department. I seemed to have a knack at tracking down killers and bringing them to justice.

But Stone and I were on this trip with family and friends, celebrating our one-year anniversary, and I really had no desire or intention of doing anything to interfere with our vacation.

The six of us hadn't made any plans for the day, and given the events of the morning, we decided to just hang around the campground for the remainder of the afternoon. RVers were clustered in groups, discussing the demise of the famous author, who'd only recently become well known because of the unsolicited biography she'd penned.

Listening to the grapevine chatter, I could see it was clear the campground was buzzing with theories and possible motives for her death. I particularly liked the one that had the subject of her *New York Times* best-seller, Vex Vaughn, sneaking into the park's fenced-in pool area and exacting revenge on the woman who had publicly degraded and demeaned him by airing his dirty laundry in her tell-all biography.

When I repeated this theory to the group, after I'd heard a customer relating it to a small group of people standing outside the women's shower house, Wendy replied, "I'd say it's actually as feasible as any other possibility. I know I'd be tempted to take out anyone who targeted me the way Fanny did him."

"Wendy!" I was taken aback by her statement. This was a young woman who used to sob and grieve for days over the loss of a goldfish in the twenty-gallon aquarium I'd given her for her tenth birthday. I'd had to tell her I'd had the beloved pet buried at a special cemetery so it could go up to fish heaven, and then unceremoniously flush the fish down the toilet when she wasn't looking. Occasionally, it was just easier to replace the goldfish at the pet store. Since the solid orange-colored ones all looked alike, she was never the wiser. I made sure I never bought one with distinguishing features for just that reason. As a single mother, after the death of Wendy's father, it was all I could do to stay one step ahead of her.

"Well, wouldn't you want to retaliate in some way, Mom?" Wendy asked.

"Of course I would! And if I couldn't squash my desire for retribution, I'd spill red wine on her expensive white fur jacket, sneak laxatives into her food, or something of that nature. I certainly would never throw an electrical device into a pool to fry her brains, for God's sake!"

"It doesn't seem to me you'd get much satisfaction out of those lame excuses for revenge unless the despicable woman pooped herself to death." Everyone laughed at Wendy's comment, as did I, but it made me wonder what the chances were that the country singer really was involved in the author's death.

By five-thirty we were all restless and bored, so we decided to take the shuttle bus down to the fairgrounds to walk around and eat carnival cuisine for supper. A big doughy pretzel liberally sprinkled with salt sounded very appealing to me, as did a funnel cake smothered in powder sugar. It was a matter of which level—my sodium or my blood sugar—needed a boost at the time I placed my order. If possible, I would chase either one down with a large cherry shaved-ice snow cone.

It was standing room only on the bus, which was full of people with tickets to the evening's concert featuring a band with several new hits currently at the top of the charts. The opening act for the band was the recipient of a CMA award for new entertainer of the year. With the much-anticipated concert that evening, there was gaiety and excitement on the shuttle bus. No one seemed to notice they were squeezed together like Veronica's breasts in the push-up bra she wore under a spaghetti-strapped tank top. I couldn't fathom how she could even catch her breath in the too-tight top, but I'm fairly sure breathing was not at the top of her priority list that evening.

I personally didn't mind the lack of space as much as I minded the combined smells of liberally applied perfume on nearly every female, and the body odor radiating from a young man in a sweat-stained Aerosmith t-shirt. And the stench being expelled frequently from the man in front of me, who apparently forgot to lace his chili with *Beano* earlier in the day, almost gagged me.

I was relieved to exit the crowded bus, and happy to have the unpleasant odors replaced by the mouth-watering aroma of the carnival food I was more than ready to sample. Everyone else was hungry too, so the first order of business was to eat.

While ingesting a week's worth of saturated fat, I could feel my cholesterol and triglyceride levels elevating with each bite and experienced a moment of regret. But it didn't take long to convince myself that unlimited calories were allowed, if not obligatory, while on vacation. I had the other fifty-one weeks of the year to worry about the excess baggage I was carrying around in my shorts, as well as the results of my next lab work ordered by my physician. If I really felt motivated, I could use the fifty-one weeks to do something proactive to resolve those issues.

But for now, I was thoroughly enjoying a greasy funnel cake with what seemed like a pound of powdered sugar piled on top of it, and seriously considering getting a corndog from the stand where Stone was standing, waiting on the foot-long chili-cheese dog he'd ordered. Apparently, he was adhering to the same "calories are inconsequential on vacation" principle that I was.

An hour later, our group had split into three pairs. Stone and Andy were looking for silver and turquoise bolo ties to complement their new cowboy wardrobes. Wyatt and Veronica were walking hand-in-hand from booth to booth and partaking in public displays of affection. Wendy was leading me to the Ferris wheel, determined to get me to ride on the carnival's most prominent ride. The ride was festively lit up with bright colorful lights and accompanied by the aptly named song, *Ferris Wheel*, being sung by country and western singer, Jason Jones. I could already feel the funnel cake looking for an exit route out of my stomach.

But, despite the fact that, like Wyatt, spinning in circles had a habit of making me toss my cookies, I still couldn't resist riding Ferris wheels once in a while. Besides, I didn't want to disappoint my daughter. Ferris wheels normally spun so slowly that I wasn't affected by their movement. Anyhow, now that I was married, Wendy was involved in an exclusive relationship, and we were living in different towns, we rarely had an opportunity to spend time together. I hoped to make the most of this vacation time.

As we were getting close to the front of the line, Wendy whispered in my ear that Norma Grace and Sarah Krumm had just joined the end of the line, which placed them about a zillion riders behind us. "Hey, Mom," she said. "I have an idea. Why don't we go back to the end of the line behind the two authors and see if we can learn anything new about Fanny's death. They surely know a lot more about it than we do."

Naturally, I loved the idea. Nosiness was my middle name, and I frequently found that idle gossip was very informative, eye opening, and much more interesting than cold hard facts that could be validated. But having my normally reluctant-to-get-involved daughter suggest such a thing kind of threw me for a loop.

"Are you serious?" I asked.

"Yes, even though I know it's the kind of thing I lecture you about and beg you not to do. There's just something about this case that intrigues me. That's probably because I was the first one to discover Fanny's dead body."

"Well, okay then, but are you planning to tell Stone what we did later on and get me relegated back into the dog house?"

"Heck no, Mom! It was my idea, and it'd be I who ended up on Stone's bad side, not you. Besides, I have no intention of 'interrogating' them, as you have a habit of doing."

To nip her lecture in the bud, I clutched her by the elbow and led her back to the end of the long line. We greeted Norma and Sarah as if totally surprised to see them.

"You two were the next to board the ride," Sarah said. "Why in the world did you give up your place in line? It will be at least another half-hour before you get that far up in line again."

Wendy was not as quick on her toes as I when it came to making up crap at the spur of the moment, so I quickly replied with what was only a slight exaggeration of the truth. "I am scared spitless of carnival rides, so I needed a little more time to build up enough courage to go on this contraption with Wendy."

"You're scared spitless of a Ferris wheel?" Norma asked. "Then am I to assume you wouldn't get within twenty feet of a roller coaster?"

"Yes," I said, with as much uneasiness as I could muster. "Even fifty feet is too close for me. I know it's silly, but it's just one of those irrational phobias that everybody seems to have at least one of."

Norma nodded, and replied, "My primary phobia is fear of flying. But that's kind of on a whole different level, I think."

"Why's that?" I rebutted. "If you fell from the top of this Ferris wheel, I'd bet you'd be just as dead as if you fell from the sky in an airplane 30,000 feet up in the sir. In fact, it'd probably be a slower, more agonizing death, because you would surely die instantly if you crashed in a plane. Having plenty of time to anticipate your impending death while falling from such a height in an airplane does not sound too appealing, but at least your life would be snuffed out like a candle when you eventually hit the ground. A fall from the Ferris wheel might result in a long drawn out passing. It might even render you a vegetable, or a quadriplegic, which to me would be a fate worse than being instantly vaporized in an airplane exploding on impact with the ground."

"Okay, point taken," Norma said with a laugh. "Now I'm not so sure I want to ride this thing, either."

"Speaking of which," I said, knowing I didn't have much time left to segue into a discussion about their fellow author's untimely death because the line seemed to be moving much faster than it had been earlier. "Aren't you two shocked by what happened to Fanny Finch late last night?"

The two ladies agreed the death of their *friend* was unbelievable and they were devastated by the loss of such a dear colleague. I could see them literally biting their tongues as they tried to portray a close relationship to the deceased. When questioned, they reiterated the same information we'd already heard or known about, and we were inching toward the front of the line again. "Oh, I almost forgot, Sarah. I had some questions relating to your book about multi-generational households that I wanted to ask you. But, oh dear, we are almost to the front of the line already. Would you mind terribly accompanying me on the ride, while Wendy rides in a basket with Norma? As a young lady on a strict budget, I think Wendy could learn a thing or two from her, as well."

Wendy glanced at me with an expression that spoke volumes, but thankfully, she fell right into step with my deceptive ploy. "Yes, that's right, Sarah. I was just telling Mom I hoped I'd get an opportunity to discuss some saving strategies with you."

They both looked as if they'd been awarded the Pulitzer Prize for their cleverness, and quickly agreed to switch partners to try and help us out as much as they could. I could almost see tiny wisps of smoke escaping Wendy's ears as her mind whirred, trying to think of sensible questions to ask the coupon-clipping expert. She was the type who didn't care if something cost ten dollars or ten thousand. If Wendy wanted the item badly enough, she was willing to pay whatever it cost to purchase it. I could picture her clipping coupons out of circulars about as easily as I could picture me, with my God-awful, eardrum-splitting singing voice, joining the Mormon Tabernacle Choir.

A short time later, Norma asked if anyone wanted a snow cone to eat while we waited. There was a stand just across from the Ferris wheel. I told her I didn't think we should lose our place in line again.

"Tell you what," she said. "Sarah and I will go get them while you two hold our place in line. Okay? We'll have to eat them fast, though, because we can't take food or drinks on the ride."

They were back within two or three minutes carrying four purplish-blue snow cones. Wendy and I thanked them and began to eat the frozen treats. I couldn't quite make out the flavor, but it was a strange combination of a sickening sweet initial taste, followed by a bitter aftertaste. Not wanting to appear rude or unappreciative, I ate it quickly, as did the other three ladies, who all seemed to genuinely enjoy their snow cones. Most likely, my problem was that I was cold in my light windbreaker, and I'd have preferred a warm beverage to ward off the chill of the cool Wyoming evening.

When we approached the front of the line, all four of us tossed our paper cones into a trashcan next to the ride operator. Once we were seated, strapped into our seat and the Ferris wheel began to turn, Sarah said, "So tell me about your family's living situation."

"Well, you see, my daughter moved out and just as I was adjusting to living alone, my mother came to live with me, and I'm wondering what kind of issues this new living arrangement might entail."

I don't like to out-and-out lie to anyone, but I've been known to stretch the truth on occasion, sometimes to the extreme when I feel the situation warranted a white lie. My mother did reside in the Alexandria Inn with Stone and me, albeit it was in a small vase that had its own honored location on the fireplace mantel.

"Well, first of all, although it might take a little time to get accustomed to having your mother live with you, I can assure you it can ultimately work out to be very rewarding for both of you," Sarah began.

"Okay, terrific! That's really all I needed to know," I replied, before she could start explaining the many ways we could benefit by living together. After all, I'd adjusted to have my mother's ashes in an urn on the mantel a long time ago. "So, let's get back to Fanny's vicious murder. Who do you believe could have been the perpetrator?"

Sarah seemed thrown off balance by my sudden change of subject. I'm sure she'd been mentally preparing a list to recite to me regarding issues I might expect in my new living arrangement. But she recovered quickly and replied, "I really don't know, but I have to wonder if her husband had something to do with it. Even though they haven't been married long, I've rarely heard a civil exchange between the two of them during the last few months of attending book signings with her."

"Um, yes, that does sound suspicious," I agreed. "Any other ideas?"

Sarah looked around in all directions—I suppose to ascertain no one had crawled into our basket with us while we revolved around in space. She then leaned in toward me to whisper in my ear. "Just between you, me, and the lamp post, I also have to wonder if Norma might be capable of a cold-blooded murder like that. Truthfully, she had no use for the woman. There was no love lost between Fanny and Norma, I assure you. Incidentally, just before the tragic murder, Norma said that she'd like to push Fanny in front of an oncoming bus."

"No kidding?" I asked as if I hadn't heard the woman say that very thing while eavesdropping the previous day. I had considered it a figure of speech used to vent frustration with her fellow author. I think I may have even threatened to push Stone in front of a speeding train one day when he had hidden a candy bar from me as a joke. I was just kidding of course, but I'd been craving chocolate at the time, so it was totally understandable.

"Why, as a matter of fact, it was just before you joined us at our table to purchase copies of our books! You might have even overheard her make that comment."

"Now that I think about it, I did hear her say such a thing. But I didn't take her remark seriously. It's the kind of thing anyone might say about another person they were annoyed with. I never for a second thought she might actually do something like that. Do you seriously believe she might be responsible for Fanny's death?" I asked.

"I think it's possible, given the hatred and bitterness she felt toward her. For what it's worth, Norma can be a bit unpredictable, even mentally unstable at times. She spent three months in a pysch ward a couple of years ago after trying to stab the guy she was dating at the time."

"Wow, that's a lot to digest," I said. I really didn't know what to make of Sarah's comments but could hardly wait to repeat them to Wendy.

"And, remember, Lexie, this goes no farther than the two of us—and the lamp post of course. I wouldn't want my suspicions to get back to Norma, you understand. If she could kill once, she could surely do it again to someone who had implicated her in a murder that might get her put away for life."

"Absolutely, Sarah. My lips are sealed," I promised, even though I felt as if she was just being melodramatic.

"And another thing," Sarah continued. "Norma heard Fanny referring to us as 'aspiring authors,' and she has not gotten over it yet. She was offended by Fanny's inference that we weren't bona fide authors when we've both published books that we hadn't had to resort to self-publishing to get printed. Fanny even expressed surprise that either of our books got published in the first place."

I didn't want to tell her that I couldn't quite believe it either, or that their "aspiring authors" status had been upgraded to "wanna-be best-selling authors" in Fanny's opinion. So instead of being frank I replied, "How rude! She sounds like she was a real piece of work."

"Precisely!" Sarah retorted with such vehemence that I had to wipe spittle off my cheek. "And I want you to know that I don't believe in gossiping, but I consider this more a case of information-sharing."

"Yes, of course, especially since everything you told me is based on first-hand knowledge on your part and not just assumptions and conjecture."

"Exactly! And remember, mum's the word. Oh, by the way, Lexie. I have to commend you, because you are remarkably calm for someone with a phobia like yours. I'm proud of you for facing down your fear so admirably."

I had completely forgotten about my earlier remarks about being scared spitless to ride the rather sedate carnival ride, so I thanked her and said, "You can't imagine how hard it is for me to hide my anxiety and not be overcome by my rather irrational fear."

Just then there was a loud, eerie squealing sound as the Ferris wheel gears began to grind, which caused the baskets to jerk spastically to and fro. The basket Sarah and I were in ground to a halt at the very highest point of the ride. I turned around to look at Wendy and Norma, who were still slowly swinging in the basket behind us. Wendy shrugged, and turned her palms face up in a gesture of uncertainty.

I shouted loud enough to be heard by Norma and everyone else within six baskets of us, "Now do you see why I don't like these damned carnival rides?"

What followed the sudden stalling of the carnival ride were the longest two-and-a-half hours of my life. Every ten or fifteen minutes the Ferris wheel would roar to life, make ungodly crunching and squealing noises, advance two feet in its rotation, and come to a screeching halt again. I had figured out that at the rate we were going, it would take about ten to eleven hours for us to get low enough to the ground to be able to disembark our basket, as the people who were fortunate enough to be at the bottom of the ride had done after the Ferris wheel had stopped operating.

I wasn't totally surprised about the untimely breakdown. I had seen young men, who didn't look like they had the wherewithal to put a "some assembly required" bookcase together, assembling elaborate carnival rides in the past. When assembling a bookcase, a person might dispose of any leftover nuts, bolts, or other leftover hardware, without any adverse consequences. Granted, a poorly assembled bookcase might crumble to the floor when overburdened with hundreds of pounds' worth of books, but it wouldn't be likely to take any human lives with it when it fell. On the other hand, left-over parts cast aside by carnies with an eighth-grade education, trying to put together a more highly complicated carnival ride, could prove catastrophic. I shuddered, just imagining the potential outcome of such a situation.

The operators of the Ferris wheel were aware that people stuck on the ride were getting anxious, frustrated, and increasingly incensed. One young lady several baskets ahead of us was freaking out, crying and screaming to be let off the ride immediately. There was only one way off the ride at that moment, and the operators below were obviously reluctant to point that out to her. The result of exiting the ride in that fashion would certainly be unpleasant, if not lethal, for the hysterical woman.

Frequently, a man on a loudspeaker announced that mechanics were working on the problem and it would just be a few more minutes before the problem was corrected. *Liar, liar, pants on fire....*

Sarah Krumm did not seem disappointed or frustrated in the least about the situation. It gave her more time to explain every possible thing, no matter how remote, that could come into play in a multi-generational household. Did I know that approximately fifteen percent of elderly adults in the United States were living with their children? *No, I didn't.* Did I really care how many elderly adults were living with their parents? *No, I didn't.*

Had it ever occurred to me that my "live-in" mother could potentially want a new love interest to move into my house too sometime in the future? *No, I didn't.* Had it ever occurred to Sarah that if a person could truly die of boredom, they'd be taking me off this ride on a stretcher, and putting me in a body bag the way they had Fanny Finch? Sarah seemed to think I was as enthralled with our conversation as she was.

I wanted to tell her that I wasn't particularly worried about my mother moving her new beau into my house. For one thing, she'd always been totally devoted to my father, even after his death in the 1990s. More importantly, there wasn't enough room for another urn on the fireplace mantel.

Just about the time I began to think my eardrums might start bleeding from Sarah's incessant talking, the Ferris wheel fired up again and managed to keep running long enough for the four of us to vacate our baskets. Stone, Andy, Veronica, and Wyatt were sitting on a bench, waiting patiently for us to be rescued from our plight. When they had no success looking for us, they'd noticed the Ferris wheel had malfunctioned, and looked up to see us in baskets at the top of the ride. The men appeared to be content to sit on a bench and gorge on junk food while they waited. Veronica just looked bored out of her skull, to which I could completely relate to.

Stone and Andy had on rather gaudy western shirts and carried plastic bags holding the shirts they'd worn to the fairgrounds. They'd also donned the shiny silver and turquoise bolo ties they had hoped to score. I half expected them to break out in a rendition of the old country song, *Streets of Bakersfield*, because their "costumes" would have made Buck Owens proud.

I had to admit, however, that Stone looked

handsome, or at least as handsome as he could look while shoveling spoonfuls of sloppy food in his mouth and wearing a liberal amount of it on his chin. He'd be lucky if his new shirt survived the gorge-fest, because getting mustard, ketchup and chili sauce out of clothing was not one of my fortes. I'd ruined more shirts with splattered grease spots than I care to admit before Wendy gifted me with a monogrammed apron the previous Christmas. I wondered if Stone would be offended if I gifted him with a monogrammed bib for Christmas.

I had to smile as I watched Stone eating the messy conglomeration in the plastic bowl he was holding. His silver hair and light blue eyes were accented by the silver studs on the pockets and wingtips of the collar of his blue-and-tan, and now chili-stained, plaid shirt. I thought for the umpteenth time in the last year that I couldn't have landed a better or more compatible husband than Stone Van Patten. The fact that he was easy on the eyes was merely an added bonus as far as I was concerned. He could have been the homeliest man on the planet and I wouldn't have loved him any less, or agreed to marry him any quicker than I had.

Veronica was filing her fingernails as all three men were working their way through large containers full of Fritos buried under heaped-up servings of chili and cheese. I watched as Stone pulled a roll of Rolaids out of his pocket, tossed two in his mouth and soon after, spooned up another large bite of the Frito pie, complete with jalapeño rings on top. I could have sworn he'd brought a new roll of Rolaids to the fairgrounds, but it was nearly empty. My husband seemed to have an odd green tint to his face, which I feared was a preview of coming attractions.

As we walked back to the shuttle bus loading area, I

almost swallowed my own Rolaid when Wendy whispered to me, "Wait until I tell you what Norma told me about Sarah. She thinks there's a good chance she's the person responsible for Fanny's death, and I think she might possibly be right."

"I have a lot to tell you, also," I said. "Sarah was wagging her accusatory finger in Norma's direction, while Norma was apparently pointing hers at Sarah. I'd gotten the impression the two ladies were close, but with friends like that, who needs enemies?"

"Well, Mom, there's an old saying that one should keep their friends close, and their enemies closer. Maybe the appearance of closeness between the two gals is based on more than a true friendship. And, as much as I hate to admit it, I'm finding that the circumstances regarding Fanny Finch's murder are getting more intriguing all the time."

Music to my ears, I thought. It was nice having my daughter, who I rarely got to see anymore, interested in the murder case as much as I was, even though our involvement was only on the peripheral of the investigation. The outcome of the case would have no direct bearing on either one of us. It was the fact there seemed to be a growing list of people who might have wanted to kill the author that piqued my interest, and apparently Wendy's also.

There was a nagging voice in my head telling me to step aside and let the Cheyenne homicide detectives track down and exact justice on the killer without any interference from Wendy and me. Unfortunately there was a louder voice in there drowning it out, asking, "*What harm can be done by snooping around a bit, just in case we accidentally stumble on to something the detectives have overlooked*?"

It was not a question I wanted to ask out loud though, in fear that Wendy would present me with a lengthy and detailed list of examples of harm I'd encountered in similar situations in the past.

CHAPTER 7

There were only three other campers accompanying us on the shuttle bus back to the Cozy Camping RV Park. Because of the incident responsible for my two-and-a-half hours of mind-numbing boredom, it was late, and the fairground was nearly empty of people by the time we boarded the last scheduled bus ride of the day.

As expected, Stone had a well-deserved bellyache, and I was preparing for the unpleasant potential of a Frito pie being unpleasantly hurled all over the occupants of the vehicle. I handed him a sack that had held a handcrafted leather dream-catcher I'd purchased in the Indian Village vendors' area to hang from my rear-view mirror. The sack was small but would do as a barf bag if necessary.

Fortunately, Stone was able to keep the food down until we got back to our motorhome, at which time he rushed into the tiny bathroom to expel pretty much everything he'd eaten at the carnival—enough to have fed a small Ethiopian village. I was so proud of him. He had obviously put a lot of effort and expense into this nausea episode, and the results were proving he'd been very successful.

My now puny husband went straight to bed with a plastic trashcan on the floor next to him in case of an encore. It was cool outside, as was typical of Cheyenne evenings, but I was comfortable in my ratty old Kansas City Chiefs sweatshirt. So while Stone sought solace from his nausea by falling asleep, I sat in a cheap plastic chair on our patio. I was ruminating over who might have wanted Fanny Finch dead badly enough to commit the crime, when a voice behind me caused me to nearly jump out of my skin.

"Oh, Mom, I'm so sorry I startled you," she said. "Andy went straight to bed because he could feel the foot-long chili dog he ate staging a comeback. Those men are like little kids when it comes to stuffing themselves with junk food at a carnival. At least they were wise enough to avoid two of my childhood favorites, the Scrambler and the Octopus, both of which frequently precede a hurling episode."

"Been there, done that."

"Me too, but I was nine," Wendy said with a chuckle. "You up for a short chat? I want to tell you what Norma told me today about Sarah, and hear what Sarah said about Norma."

"Good, I'm glad you're still up, because I wanted to discuss it with you, too. Stone is sick to his stomach, and I'm beginning to feel a bit queasy myself."

Speaking as quietly as possible so we wouldn't disturb any of our fellow campers, I told Wendy what Sarah had said about suspecting Norma of Fanny's murder. Wendy shook her head in wonderment as I related Sarah's sentiments about her cohort.

"Wow," Wendy said, after I had finished my story. "You are not going to believe why Norma told me she suspects Sarah of being involved in Fanny's death."

"I'll believe anything at this point. So go on. I can't

wait to hear it!"

"She's adamant that Sarah should be considered a prime suspect in the murder."

"Why? What makes her think Sarah could have killed the woman? I was under the impression that Norma and Sarah were close friends, weren't you?"

"Apparently not as close as they might lead others to believe," Wendy replied. "Norma told me that what originally started Sarah's bitterness toward Fanny was an incidence of sabotage perpetrated by Fanny against Sarah."

"Go on!"

"Well, according to Norma, the incidence occurred the very first time the three authors' mutual agent, Nina-something, set them up for a group book-signing at a popular New York bookstore. Fanny's book had just been released and the initial sales were underwhelming. All three authors were promoting their debut book releases. So Sarah, who had been a client of Nina's the longest, was assigned the table in the most prominent location in the store. According to Norma, the prime location is almost always assigned to the most noteworthy author, and at that time, Sarah had probably sold eighteen copies of her book to Fanny's dozen."

"I'm guessing that didn't set well with Ms. Finch."

"It appears it didn't set well with her at all. While Avery Bumberdinger was bringing in boxes of all three of the author's books, Fanny 'accidentally' spilled an entire thermos of hot chocolate into the case containing copies of Sarah's tome. Norma used air quotes around the word 'accidentally' so I knew both Norma and Sarah thought it was intentional. All but a couple of the books were rendered useless and considered by Sarah Krumm to be casualties of Fanny's spite and connivingness."

"Is connivingness a word?" I asked. My experience as a librarian was coming out in me.

"Well, if it ain't, it oughta be!"

I cringed when my college-educated daughter used two more words that weren't recognized by Funk and Wagnalls as Standard English to answer my question, but wanted her to get on with her story. "Oh, my! I bet Sarah was furious. I'd have been a bit ticked off myself, if I were in her shoes."

"Me too," Wendy agreed. "So you know what happened next?"

"Sarah pummeled Fanny with a sodden copy of her boring book?" I guessed.

"No; although that course of action was probably considered. The bookstore owner turned the coveted table near the entrance of the store over to Fanny since Sarah now had a grand total of two books she could sell and sign."

"And because of that nasty but crafty incident, Sarah was incensed enough to commit murder? I don't buy it," I said.

"Let me finish. There's more to the story."

"Okay, please continue."

"The first person through the door of the bookstore that morning was the producer of a daytime talk show whose studio was right across the street in Times Square. Because of a major traffic jam, he'd had two last minute cancellations by individuals scheduled to appear on that day's show. The producer was desperate for a replacement and had but minutes to find one. Because she was stationed right next to the front door, he approached Fanny and asked her if she'd appear on the talk show in a few minutes. Even though he'd never even heard of Fanny Finch or her book, he thought the show's host could interview her and, with his talent for making even the most tedious conversation seem spellbinding, the interview could make the host almost a shoe-in for an Emmy. Naturally, she jumped at the opportunity."

"Well, of course," I said with a nod. "Who wouldn't have?"

"Then, to make the interview of an unrecognized author even more scintillating, the host managed to make *Fame and Shame* sound as if it contained a slew of unfathomably sensational and mind-blowing revelations about the popular country and western artist. The talk show host convinced a multitude of viewers that it was the must-read book of the century because, as it turned out, the tell-all book really did contain a lot of unimaginable details of Vex Vaughn's life, and sales took off like a gazelle being pursued by a cheetah," Wendy said.

"Jeez, what a stroke of luck for Fanny. I'll bet that Sarah thought it would have been her fate instead of Fanny's had Fanny not destroyed her books and claimed her assigned table at the entrance?" I said in the form of a question.

"Yes, she did. Norma told me that she, herself, was realistic enough to know that her book about coupon-clipping would only appeal to a limited audience, but Sarah was naïve enough to believe her book about multi-generational households was worthy of the same level of success as *Fame and Shame*. Norma told me Sarah was still under the impression that anyone who had a published book to her credit was destined to make a killing off their 'masterpiece'. Norma said she personally didn't expect to break even, with what it had cost her to write and promote her own book, but it was a labor of love for her more than an attempt to make a profit," Wendy explained.

As a response, I simply simulated the sound of snoring. Wendy ignored me and continued.

"According to Norma, when Sarah approached Fanny with this theory of Fanny 'stealing her thunder,' so to speak, Fanny told Sarah that she'd be legally able to marry her pet Shih Tzu before her 'silly' book ever became a best seller. Sarah was so livid, Norma said, that if looks could kill, Fanny would have been dead several months ago."

"Legally marry her Shih Tzu? Well, you've got to give Fanny credit, she did have a way with words—an important skill for a writer, you know."

"Yeah, right, Mom," Wendy said, with a dramatic display of eye-rolling. "So, to put it in a nutshell, Sarah feels that Fanny stole her prosperity and fame. It was something Sarah could not let go of. She's been allowing it to suck the joy and happiness right out of her life. Norma thinks Sarah might have been looking to settle the score."

"That's really a shame," I said. "It seems to me that the person who wants revenge almost always suffers worse than the person they want vengeance against, who often don't even realize, or care, that they're the subject of that other person's wrath. It ends up hurting the hater worse than the hated."

"Yeah, that's for sure! Oh, before I forget, since Wyatt bought us tickets to the Vex Vaughn concert tomorrow, I wish there was some way we could get to meet him."

"I thought it was Veronica who idolized him, not you," I said. "I wasn't aware you even liked country music. I thought you liked artists like Pink and Bruno Mars."

"I do. But I also like George Strait, Pitbull, Bob Marley and Mumford and Sons. I like all musical genres. And I really don't care about meeting Vex Vaughn, or any other artist, for that matter. I'd just like to see what Vaughn has to say about the death of his nemesis, who was determined to undermine him. But, frankly I don't think there's any way we could get within a hundred feet of him," Wendy said.

Her comment floored me because nosiness was normally my bad trait, not hers. Was this the same daughter who had gotten up on her "don't be such a fool" soapbox and railed at me time and time again about getting involved in murder investigations? Was my reckless and impulsive nature rubbing off on her? For her sake, I hoped not. But at the moment I was happy to see I had lured her over to the dark side.

Wendy yawned and told me she was getting sleepy, so after she headed back to her own rig, I went inside and joined my husband in bed. I stayed as far away from him as the queen-sized bed would allow.

I felt another wave of discomfort and, for a second wondered if I'd been poisoned with something intentionally added to my nasty-tasting snow cone. I'd been poisoned before and had that same light-headed and confused feeling now that I'd had then. But I couldn't see how either Norma or Sarah could have a clue that I suspected either of them of murder, or about my penchant for taking it upon myself to find people responsible for committing a deadly crime.

Then a bout of nausea hit me like a prizefighter. I leaned over Stone and grabbed the bathroom trash container just in time. It occurred to me then that perhaps a liberally salted pretzel, powdered sugar-coated funnel cake, corn dog dipped in spicy mustard, rancid blue snow cone, and half of Wendy's nachos and cheese, had made for a dangerous combination. My empathy for my husband instantly went up a notch.

As I lay in bed waiting for the nausea to abate, I thought about how the way I felt now was reminiscent of the way I'd felt when I'd been poisoned before. It crossed my mind that Norma, Sarah, or both, had ample opportunity to slip something into my snow cone between purchasing it and handing it to me to eat. It would explain the bitter aftertaste of the frozen concoction. But what had I said or done at that point to raise a red flag? How could they know I wanted to elicit damning information from them and turn it over to the cops?

Had they spoken to Emily, who was aware of previous incidents when I'd done that, and been apprised by her of my ingrained inquisitiveness, as I like to call it? Or, as Wendy, Stone, Detective Johnston, and the Rockdale, Missouri, Chief of Police are apt to call it, my bad habit of intrusive meddling.

I convinced myself I was over-reacting to a well-earned case of *carnivalitis*. It seemed to be contagious amongst our little party of vacationers.

Although discovering Fanny Finch's killer did not have any personal bearing on me, as previous cases I'd been involved with had, I still found myself wanting to see the no-account, scum-of-the-earth murderer brought to justice. And having my usually reticent daughter interested in the case as well, and seeing her willingness to act as my partner in crime-solving, simply spurred me on and made me want to throw caution to the wind. I only hoped my fascination with the crime did not come back to bite me in the you-know-what, as it often had in the past.

CHAPTER 8

Before parting the previous evening, Wendy and I had made plans to meet at the little café centrally located in the Cozy Camping RV Park for a cup of coffee. We then planned to go for a walk around the park to admire some of the fancier rigs.

I had awakened feeling fairly refreshed, considering how I'd felt when I finally drifted off to sleep the night before. I dressed quietly and sneaked out the door of the motorhome so as not to disturb Stone, who was still snoring like a freight train. But to me, silence is deafening. I sleep with a noisy fan to drown out the sound of not only my sleeping partner's snoring, but everything else. Even a serial killer breaking the glass on the patio door wouldn't wake me. If a serial killer was going to make me his next victim, I could do perfectly fine without being aware of that fact in advance. I'd prefer to wake up dead than be an active participant in the crime.

Kylie smiled when I entered the café shortly after six, and said, "Greetings!"

"Good morning, sweetheart," I said, smiling back. "You sure do work long hours here, don't you?"

"Yeah, too long, I'm beginning to think."

"Don't let it affect your health," I told her. "Burning both ends of the candle soon leaves you with no candle left to burn."

"I know," Kylie replied. "Please don't mention it to the Harringtons, but it's one of the reasons I'm considering going back to Florida. It's only a seasonal job anyway, but after Ms. Finch's death—which I feel somewhat responsible for, by the way—I think I need to go back to my job at the hair salon."

"Honey, don't blame yourself for the woman's fate. It's not your fault. Whoever killed her would have most likely found a way eventually, you know," I said in an attempt to console the troubled young lady.

"I should have looked down into the pool before I locked the gate that night. Maybe it wouldn't have been too late to save her."

"Yes, it would have been too late, Kylie. The electrocution would have caused instant death, I'm sure. There was nothing you could have done. Fanny's death was inevitable, with or without you checking for bodies at the bottom of the pool," I assured her.

"Well, I hope you're right. Would you like a cup of coffee, Lexie?"

"Absolutely! Pour two because Wendy will be here any minute. Would you care to join us while the café is empty except for us?"

"I can join you for a few minutes, and then I'll have to start making some biscuits, sausage gravy and cinnamon rolls. I'm working the café today instead of the front counter in the office, which is fine with me."

"You must be a multi-talented gal," I said. "I cook for guests at our bed and breakfast and still worry about potential lawsuits for killing someone with salmonella. I almost bumped off my old boss that way.[4] I especially suck at cooking breakfast. I can't cook an 'over easy' egg to save my soul. I offer two choices at the inn: barely warmed over or hard as a hockey puck. I really hate to serve anything more complicated than a bowl of cold cereal and a pop tart."

"Hey, that's exactly what Emily told me about your cooking," Kylie said, with a teasing wink. "While I was in cosmetology school I worked as a cook at the local greasy spoon, so this is old hat to me."

Wendy walked in the door of the café just as Kylie was setting three cups of coffee down on the table, which had the rustic look of a table in a ski lodge. The tables fit perfectly with the cowboy paintings on the wall and the six-foot tall black bear statue that stood next to the cash register. The statue had been carved from a large log with a chain saw, Kylie told us. Hanging around the bear's neck was a sign that read, "Rude and unhappy customers will be properly seasoned and served up for supper."

"That's a little cannibalistic-sounding, don't you think? Hannibal Lector might feel right at home eating here, but I know reading that sign would make me think twice before ordering a meal in this cafe," I said jokingly.

"All I can tell you is to beware of the chef's special—the mystery meat omelet. When the meat used in an omelet is even a mystery to the chef, it's usually not a good idea to order it."

"Point taken, Kylie!" I said with a laugh. "But, seriously, the bear is incredible. I'd love to watch someone carve a statue like it with nothing but a chainsaw."

"You can, Lexie," Kylie replied. "A chainsaw artist

---

[4] *Just Ducky (A Lexie Starr Mystery, Book 5)*

will be giving a demonstration this afternoon at two o'clock in the pavilion next to the tent area. Harvey also sells some of his work after his presentation. He carved Yogi over there for the Harringtons last year, Stanley told me. Stanley is trying to learn the art now too, but he says it's a challenge because he has a tendency to saw off an ear, or some other vital part of the animal, leaving him with a deformed and not very appealing bear. He hasn't quite mastered the art of chainsaw carving yet."

We all chuckled at the idea of Stanley accidentally amputating ears on his chainsaw projects. When the laughter faded, Wendy asked Kylie if she or the campground owners had heard anything new about the drowning.

Kylie shook her head and answered, "Not that I'm aware of, but Emily did tell me that Avery Bumberdinger's ex-wife is in site C-26 in a small Airstream travel trailer. According to Emily, Cassie Bumberdinger, who apparently kept her married name after her divorce, told the investigators she and her kids are here to participate in a horseback-riding excursion at some ranch northwest of Cheyenne."

"Is it just me, or does that sound like an unlikely coincidence?" I asked. "The odds of Avery and his ex-wife finding themselves in the same RV Park in Cheyenne, Wyoming, on the very week Avery's new wife is murdered here have got to be slim to none."

"That's what I said to Emily," Kylie responded. "But Emily overheard Cassie being questioned the afternoon of the murder by detectives in the office. I was working in the cafe here at the time, but Emily told me that Cassie claimed to have had no idea Avery and Fanny would be here at the same time she and her kids were. She said she enjoys horseback riding at ranches all over the country. Says it's a fun way to bond with her young daughter who is training to be a barrel-racer. She said this trail-riding event in Cheyenne just happened to coincide with the rodeo. I guess it's possible, even though the chances seems remote to me."

"Yeah, me too," Wendy agreed.

I agreed with the two younger women, and said, "We will have to come up with an excuse to speak to Cassie Bumberdinger, Wendy."

"Emily told me about your success solving murders in the past, Lexie, and I admire you tremendously. But please be careful," Kylie said, gently touching the top of my hand, which was resting on the table. "I'd be afraid that anyone who would do something so horrific to Fanny Finch would not hesitate to do something horrific to you and Wendy, too."

"Trust me," Wendy said. "We'll be careful, Kylie. I'll be with her, making sure Mom doesn't do something rash and impulsive as she has in the past. I lack the apparent death wish Mom often appears to possess."

"Good. That's a relief." Kylie nodded before continuing. "I don't want to see your mom do something that might get her injured, or worse, because of a spur-of-the-moment decision."

"Hey! I'm sitting right here, you know," I said, wondering when I had supposedly left the room.

"Oh, yeah. Sorry about that," Kylie responded, as she and Wendy exchanged a look I didn't care to interpret. "But I am curious about this whole thing, so let me know if you find out anything interesting. If I didn't have so much work to do, I'd be joining you ladies in the hunt for the killer. Unfortunately, sneaking off to go horseback-riding doesn't get the bills paid."

Kylie drained her cup and excused herself to get

busy in the café's kitchen. She told us that around seven o'clock customers would begin streaming in and she wanted to be prepared for a busy morning.

Wendy and I decided to take our walk around the RV Park. After looking at some of the high-dollar rigs, we also hoped to locate site C-26 in the older section. Maybe we could find Cassie Bumberdinger sitting on her patio drinking her morning coffee. We headed for the expansion area that Emily had earlier referred to as "the south forty." The fenced-in area was located at the southern end of the campground and contained forty large sites with fifty-amp service.

Many of the beautiful motorhomes we saw were towing small vehicles, some with matching paint jobs. One even towed a trailer with two Harleys strapped onto it. There were a few Prevost motorhomes, and a Newell Luxury Coach with four electric slide-outs, which Stanley had told Stone cost well over a million dollars each. Some of the more elaborate units were purported to have granite countertops, built-in fireplaces, washer/dryer combos, and even dishwashers. They had a lot of customized features, including crystal glass cabinets, onyx bathroom lavatories, Italian art, mosaic tiled showers, and much more. After viewing the exteriors of these units, we were itching to see what they looked like inside.

On the way back toward the section where our three functional, but much less luxurious, rental motorhomes were parked, we found site C-26. The site, shaded by a massive cottonwood tree across from the pool area, was two sites down from the fenced-in dog park. Outside the dog park gate was a wooden bench where we sat down for a short break.

"Andy was talking to Stanley Harrington about Sallie yesterday while Stanley was weed-eating around the tent area," Wendy said. Sallie was a golden retriever Andy had inherited when he'd moved to the Midwest from the East Coast and purchased a small cattle ranch near Atchison, Kansas.[5] He'd instantly fallen in love with the sweet-natured pooch, and was thankful that Sallie got along well with Tank, the Mastiff puppy he'd later adopted. I listened as my daughter continued with her story.

"Stanley told him he'd constructed this dog park to encourage customers to utilize it when they took their dogs outside to do their business. Every morning he shovels up a bucket of dog poo from out of the dog park, but he said he'd rather pick up crap all day long than take it from customers who were upset that another camper had let their pet poop in their RV site and hadn't picked it up afterward. Stanley said that it was a chronic problem."

"Has the new dog park helped minimize the number of calling cards left scattered about the campground?" I asked.

"Somewhat, Stanley told Andy, but it hasn't been as effective as he'd hoped. He still hits piles of fresh dog poop with his weed eater, which he claims is not a pleasant experience."

"I can imagine it would be very aggravating for him. I think people who won't pick up after their pets shouldn't even be allowed to own one if they can't be responsible for it." This had always been one of my pet peeves, no pun intended. I'd had to deal with this issue every time I went for a walk in our nearby city park a couple of blocks from the inn. "It shows a total lack of consideration for others. The disrespectful pet owner would probably be the first one to complain if they stepped in a pile of dog doo-doo that resulted from someone else refusing to clean up after *their*

---

[5] *With This Ring (A Lexie Starr Mystery, Book 4)*

pet."

"I agree," Wendy replied. "It irritates me too. Andy and I always pick up after Sallie and Tank when we take them out in a public place, or even on the ranch. We don't want visitors, or even ourselves, to have to navigate our yard like it was a mine field."

After a few minutes, we continued on our walk. No one was stirring outside Cassie's rounded, silver-colored trailer, which was fairly small and obviously an older model. On the outside of the Airstream trailer there was a large sticker depicting the United States with about three-fourths of the fifty states covered with state-shaped decals, obviously indicating which ones the owner had visited. It looked like Cassie Bumberdinger was well traveled.

After Wendy had split off to head in the direction of her and Andy's site, I ran into Wyatt as he was leaving the men's shower house. His hair was still wet, and he held a damp towel over his arm. He looked to be in great spirits, as was usually the case with the amicable, easy-going detective.

"What's Veronica up to?" I asked.

"She's in the ladies shower house, but knowing it will be another hour before she emerges from it, I decided to head on back to our motorhome. After I drop off my soap and towel, I'm going over to the café to have some breakfast. Veronica said she wasn't hungry, but then, she rarely eats breakfast. You know, breakfast is the most important meal of the day, according to nearly every source. Unfortunately I can't convince her of that."

"I agree. Veronica is beautiful, but I worry about her dwindling weight. She's so thin she looks like she could blow away." I said this to Wyatt with genuine concern because his girlfriend seemed to be getting skinnier every time I saw her and was starting to look skeletal. I was worried about her health.

"Can I tell you something in confidence, Lexie? I know Veronica wouldn't want this to become public knowledge, but I trust you and need to have a sounding board if I ever need one."

"Of course you can tell me, Wyatt. It will go no further than me," I promised, and it was a vow I intended to keep.

"I know Veronica seems overly obsessed with her looks occasionally, but it stems from her childhood. Even her occasional rather vain remarks are nothing but false bravado, as if she's trying to convince herself she's attractive and not the ugly duckling she imagines. As a teenager, she was overweight, wore braces for severely buck teeth, suffered from bad acne, and was forced to wear large horn-rimmed glasses because her parents wouldn't put out the money for contacts, convinced she'd lose them within a week. Because of her looks, she was a victim of bullying throughout most of her growing up years, and a sense of not measuring up has become firmly ingrained in her psyche."

"Oh, my goodness," I exclaimed. "That poor girl. I hate to hear that, but I know how cruel children can be at times. There need to be stronger regulations that hold bullies responsible for their actions. Didn't her parents talk to the school officials about the bullying?"

"No. In fact, her mother actually ridiculed her. She told Veronica if she wanted the bullying to stop, she should quit eating so much, especially chocolate, which her mother claimed was also the cause of her acne. And her father, Horatio, was too wound up with his investments and career to pay any attention to her at all," Wyatt explained.

"But she's so gorgeous now!"

"Yes, but the names her classmates called her took a big toll, and created such a lack of self-esteem in her that she still sees herself as fat and ugly. Now she struggles with an eating disorder. Her only saving grace growing up was her grandmother, who always reminded Veronica she was a beautiful person, inside and out, and would one day be such a stunner, she'd make all her classmates jealous. She could see Veronica morphing into the gorgeous woman she is today, even though Veronica never could, and still hasn't, I'm afraid. I've been trying to boost her self-esteem and confidence, but it's tough because she's still haunted by the bullying."

"Thank the Lord for her grandmother. Is she still living?" I asked.

"Yes. Veronica visits her at the nursing home every Thursday. They're very close."

"Oh, okay, now I see. That explains why she bought trinkets for some of the residents of Rockdale Meadows," I said. "What a thoughtful gesture on Veronica's part. Wyatt, I'm so glad you shared this with me. If there's anything I can do to help, please don't hesitate to ask me."

I felt bad that I'd ever wondered about Veronica's obsession with her looks. Now that I was aware of what had prompted it, I'd be much more understanding. I wished there was some way I could help with the situation.

To change the topic of conversation, because I could see Wyatt's eyes tearing up, as I'm sure mine were doing also, I asked him if he'd had any ill effects from all the junk food he'd eaten at the fair.

"Not at all," he replied. "In fact, after we got home I heated up a frozen pizza to snack on because I was still a bit hungry."

Even as I'd asked Wyatt, I knew what his answer

would be. I had watched this man devour six plates of crab legs and two more of mussels and shrimp at an all-you-can-eat seafood buffet, and then stop at a McDonalds on the way home for a McRib and a chocolate shake to wash it down, because as Wyatt said, "it was only available for a limited time." He was a bottomless pit who could stomach anything he felt inclined to put in his mouth. Detective Johnston had the constitution of a Billy goat, but remarkably, Wyatt carried not one molecule of extra fat on his tall frame.

I told Wyatt about the chainsaw carving demonstration at two, and then headed back to my own motorhome to fix breakfast for Stone, if he felt up to eating anything after a rough night with a bellyache.

When I entered our rental unit, I found Stone lying on the couch, watching an old movie on a DVD that he'd borrowed from the selection in the office. In the movie, called *Indecent Proposal*, the billionaire character, portrayed by Robert Redford, offers another man a million dollars to spend one night with the man's wife, played by Demi Moore. The man, played by Woody Harrelson, who the billionaire made this offer to, and his wife, are in dire need of money and have to decide whether or not to accept the proposal. It was a movie Stone and I had both seen several times.

On the coffee table in front of Stone was a half-empty bottle of Pepto-Bismol. While he stretched out on the couch, groaning as only a member of the male species can over a little discomfort, I prepared some toast for him because he said that was all he'd be able to hold down. It was no wonder God had selected women to bear children. I would whine and moan less with two severed limbs than Stone would with a small splinter embedded in his finger. Still, his low tolerance for pain was one of the many things I found so endearing about him. As I spread butter on his toast, my husband of one year asked, "Would you sleep with Robert Redford for a million dollars?"

Without hesitation, I replied, "Of course I would—if we could afford it!"

It was not the response Stone had been hoping for, but he had to laugh at my instant reply to his question. After I assured him I would never consider sleeping with any other man, for any amount of money, he patted my knee, and asked, "Not even if we really needed the money and I begged you to do it?"

"Well, then, that's another story altogether. If it would make you happy, I would not hesitate to sleep with Robert Redford. I would never want to disappoint you, so I would bite the bullet and canoodle with Glamour Magazine's 'Sexiest Actor Alive' winner for the last two years in a row if you asked me to. I would step up to the plate and make the sacrifice—if you insisted, of course."

"So very admirable of you, sweetheart," Stone said, with a pat on my posterior. "That's just one of the many reasons I love you so much!"

With the Vex Vaughn concert on our agenda for the evening, we all chose to hang around the campground and take it easy until it was time to catch the shuttle bus to the rodeo grounds. The concerts were held in the same location where the rodeos took place, and our standing-room-only tickets would place us right in front of the stage down on the floor of the arena. Anybody with sufficient oxygen in their brain had a comfortable seat up in the stands where they wouldn't be jostled about and poked in the eye by cowboy hats for two hours. On the other hand, their chances of

catching a two-dollar guitar pick were next to nothing.
Oh boy, oh boy, oh boy!

After our bouts of *carnivalitis*, Stone and I had
sworn off buying any food from vendors at the fair. In
order to prepare for the evening, Stone planned to do
nothing more than lie on the couch and watch old
movies all day. Even the idea of watching a man carve
a bear out of a log with a chainsaw didn't appeal to
him.

Veronica had scheduled an appointment for herself
at a spa and salon on the north side of town. Wyatt
had made arrangements to borrow Stanley's F-150
truck to take her to the salon and wait while Veronica
had a manicure, pedicure, Brazilian wax, and
something she referred to as a "salt glow." Wendy
explained to me that a salt glow was a treatment
designed to exfoliate your skin, whereas, a Brazilian
wax was a treatment where you paid a licensed
cosmetologist, or an Esthetician, a significant amount
of money to torture you and make your *nether* regions
look like a peeled egg.

All I could say was that Wyatt must have the
patience of a chopping block, and his girlfriend must
have cojones like the bulls featured in the rodeo all
week. An Esthetician would have to *pay me* a
significant amount of money for me to let her do
something like that to me. I guess it was my age
showing, but I never imagined a woman shelling out
perfectly good money to have a specially trained
technician make them writhe in pain, or even that a
man would be turned on by that sort of thing. But
what did I know? I was way out of touch when it
came to anything in the "erotica" department. I
thought I was bringing sexy back when I bought a pair
of white cotton underwear that didn't cover up my
belly button.

With Stone, Wyatt, and Veronica's days already planned, that left Wendy, Andy, and me to attend the bear-carving demonstration at two o'clock. In the meantime, we decided to go for a long walk up the road in hopes of getting photos of the herd of antelope that Emily said frequented the fields on either side of the RV park.

Along the way, we discussed the possible motives Cassie Bumberdinger might have to kill her ex-husband's new wife. Although there were several possibilities on our list, none seemed worthy of murder. It had looked to me as if Fanny had been doing her best to wear out her welcome with her husband on her own accord, and Wendy concurred with my assessment.

Unlike his Uncle Stone, Andy was laid back and totally unconcerned about our interest in the murder, although he did seem a little surprised that his girlfriend had become involved in it with her mother. I was usually on the receiving side of Wendy's displeasure when it came to situations like this. I can only imagine the conversations they'd had about me when I wasn't within hearing range.

Luck was with us, and we were able to get photos of a small herd of the pronghorn antelope, including a doe with twin calves walking along beside her. Occasionally the calves would take off on a playful romp, darting here and there like bunnies on speed. They were amusing to watch, and we spent nearly twenty minutes watching the animals' antics until something spooked the entire herd and they took off like a bolt of lightning, and quickly disappeared from our field of vision.

We returned to the campground just in time to grab a sandwich at the café and get to the tent area before the woodcarving presentation began. A campground employee we'd never seen before waited on us at the café while the Harrington's college-aged daughter, Jennifer, took care of the cooking in the small kitchen behind the front counter. Our waiter told us that Kylie was working in the office for the rest of the afternoon and would be off all evening, because she too, had a ticket to the concert that evening.

Once we reached the tent area, we could see a man resembling Paul Bunyon setting up several tables to display his merchandise, which would be available for purchase after the show. I looked around for Babe, Bunyon's blue ox, but all I saw was an older model Dodge Ram with a bed full of wooden bears and other creatures. I spotted one I thought would be perfect to set on the front porch of our bed and breakfast in Rockdale, Missouri. I planned to purchase it if it wasn't too ridiculously expensive. The bear's paws were turned up, holding a wooden plaque that could be personalized with anything the buyer requested. I would have Harley burn a greeting into the plaque that said, *Welcome to the Alexandria Inn*.

We stood around for nearly half an hour as more and more campers gathered at the pavilion. Just before the demonstration began, I spotted Kylie speaking with an elderly man. I caught up with her just as she turned to go back to her post in the office.

"Hello again! I'm glad to see you made it," she said. "You will really be amazed by the demonstration. You will be shocked at how fast he can turn a block of wood into an adorable bear statue."

"Yes, I've already picked out the one I want to buy, if someone else doesn't beat me to it."

"Try to get in the front of the line then, because he tends to sell out fairly rapidly after every show," Kylie said. "Hey, Lexie, look over there next to the lilac tree. That's Avery's ex-wife, Cassie Bumberdinger."

"Seriously?" I asked. The gorgeous redhead was so stunning, she could have been a super-model. I thought she bore a striking resemblance to Angie Everhart. I recognized her as the redhead lounging at the swimming pool area a couple of days earlier. "Avery Bumberdinger gave up that woman to be constantly demeaned and ordered about by Fanny Finch? He must not have the sense God gave a banana peel."

"Yeah, crazy isn't it? But, you know what they say: beauty is only skin deep!"

"Yes, I know, but in the case of Fanny Finch, ugly went plumb to the bone."

Kylie laughed and slapped my shoulder playfully. "Lexie! You should be ashamed of yourself to speak ill of the dead like that!"

"I'm sorry. That slipped out before I could put the brakes on," I replied, with just a hint of contrition in my voice. "But if ever there was an unlikely pair, it'd be that piece of arm candy and Avery Bumberdinger. What could have possibly drawn Cassie to him?"

"Who knows? Evidently something did," Kylie replied. "Well, enjoy the show. I better get back to the office before I have customers lined up outside the door."

I quickly went back to where Wendy and Andy stood with their arms around each other's backs. Now that was a perfect pairing if I'd ever seen one, and I hoped their relationship would result in a marriage and several grandchildren for me to spoil and love.

I pointed out Cassie Bumberdinger to the couple, and they were as astonished as I had been. Andy shook his head, and asked, "Has Avery had a lobotomy? That bombshell could be the dumbest grape on the vine, and I'd still be hard-pressed to trade her in on someone like Fanny Finch, who looked to me like she'd fallen out of an ugly tree and hit every branch on the way down."

"Bombshell? Really, Andy?" Wendy asked him. "Besides, beauty is only skin deep, and Cassie could have a very annoying personality and be extremely difficult to live with."

"Now you sound just like Kylie," I told her. "She just said the same thing, and I know you both are right, but I just can't quite picture them as a couple."

Just then the roar of a chainsaw firing up distracted us. Without introduction or comment, Harley began shaving chunks off a large upright log in front of him. In what seemed like mere moments, a perfectly shaped black bear emerged, and the artist began burning definition into the statue with a small blowtorch. The crowd stood silently in awe as we watched the impressive transformation of the block of wood into a work of art. I was wishing I'd videoed the demonstration to show to Stone later on. He would have been impressed by Harley's talent and skill.

After the show, I was able to purchase the bear that had caught my eye and make arrangements to pick it up at the office the following day after Harley had personalized the wooden plaque for me. I handed him fifty dollars for the bear, knowing I'd really gotten a bargain. Wendy and Andy also purchased a bear to take home to their ranch that had a plaque which would read The Rocking V Ranch with a curved line below the V. The V stood for his last name, Van Patten, which I prayed would soon be Wendy's last name, as well. It would have been mine if I'd chosen to take Stone's last name when we'd married, but it seemed easier to me to leave things as they were, and Stone hadn't argued.

While the two of them were busy purchasing their bear statue, I walked over to the gorgeous redhead, who was now standing next to the pavilion. I was surprised to see two children standing with her; a strawberry-blonde girl, about ten or so, who was a miniature of Cassie, and a dark-haired boy who appeared to be a couple of years younger.

The young girl was engrossed in reading a paperback I'd earlier seen her pull out of a backpack she was wearing. The book had *Quantum Physics* printed on the cover. How, I wondered, would a girl her age know anything about that subject, or even care to know? I'd have expected her to be more interested in a Judy Blume novel. At her age, I was fascinated with Astrid Lindgren's *Pippi Longstocking.* To this day, I'd rather be reading a story involving the pigtailed, eccentric child with super-powers, than anything even remotely related to physics.

The boy was looking down, his hands in his pockets, dragging his right foot in a circular motion, stirring up a small cloud of dust. He had a forlorn air about him, as if the weight of the world was on his tiny shoulders.

To break the ice and initiate a conversation with Cassie, I said, "Isn't Harley unbelievable with that chain saw?"

"Yes, quite a talented fellow," she replied, without much enthusiasm. She didn't seem to want to continue speaking with me, but that was never a deterrent to me when I was trying to dig information out of someone.

"What brings you folks to Cheyenne?"

"You mean other than the famous annual rodeo?" Cassie asked, with a touch of sarcasm. A simple "duh" would have sufficed to make her point.

"Yes, of course."

"We're here to take in some horseback excursions at the Rolling Creek Ranch." Cassie now seemed more invested in the conversation. She threw her long red hair over her left shoulder, and continued. "After my divorce, I decided to take up horseback-riding as a new hobby, and I got my children involved with it, as well. My goal is for us to go on a horseback excursion in every state in the union, and after this week, we'll have nineteen under our belt. Brandi wants to be a barrel-racer one day, and Chace has shown an interest in wanting to take up calf-roping in a couple of years."

"How do you find the time to travel so much?" I asked.

"I'm a fashion model, but at my age, the modeling jobs are drying up as fast as my skin in the winter. Seriously, I buy moisturizer by the case. But I do have a part-time job, working as a claims adjustor for an insurance company, a lot of which I'm able to do on my computer when we're on the road. My boss, who's actually my Uncle Cole, is very accommodating."

"How nice it must be to have your Uncle Cole as your boss. I'm sure that's very beneficial when trying to arrange your schedule, and it's nice that it allows you to travel whenever you please. But doesn't that get expensive on your salary?"

"Well, yes, but I also make quite a bit on the side teaching children, and occasionally adults, to ride and care for horses."

"You certainly must keep busy. I'm sure the side job is one you really enjoy, as much as you like to go horseback riding. Speaking of which, the horseback-riding excursion tomorrow sounds like a lot of fun. I must say, you have very ambitious children. I'm so sorry about the death of their step-mother, but I'm sure they're excited that their father is here, as well."

It occurred to me the model may be pondering the fact I knew more about their personal life than I should, and be reluctant to continue the conversation.

So when Cassie just looked at me without responding, I changed the subject and continued, "My daughter and I are horse lovers ourselves, so we'll have to check it out."

I was actually scared to death of being within fifty feet of a horse. It's not that I didn't think they were beautiful creatures. It was just that every horse I'd ever been near had either thrown me, bit me, laid down and rolled over on me, or, on one painful occasion, kicked me clear across the barn at my late husband's parent's ranch. Now I was certain they could sense my trepidation whenever they approached me and felt they had to live up to my expectations of them.

However, I might have to face my fear and convince Wendy, who actually does love horses, to go on a horseback trek the following day. I knew it wouldn't take much arm-twisting, because she had inherited her love of anything equine-related from her father, Chester Starr, who had spent his youth growing up on a ranch that bred Quarter horses. Besides, she was as intrigued as I am with the family dynamics in the Bumberdinger clan, which might have a killer in the mix.

Before I could ask anything about her relationship to Avery and Fanny, and any possible involvement she might have had with the author's death, she bade me a quick farewell and ushered her children away from the crowd, which was beginning to disperse. Brandi walked alongside her mother without ever taking her eyes off the book she was reading.

I joined Wendy and Andy, and my daughter was delighted at the idea of going on a lengthy horseback ride the following day. Andy said it would work out splendidly because he and the other two men were planning to go trout fishing at a place Stanley had told them about on a stream, ironically called Horse Creek. The prime fishing spot was located about forty-five minutes north of Cheyenne. They had all purchased appropriate tackle and fly-fishing rods during our stop at the Cabela's in western Nebraska on the way to Wyoming, and were anxious to try them out. I encouraged Stone to get home before dark, because we gals didn't want to assemble a search party in the middle of the night.

Stanley had told them the brown trout were plentiful in Horse Creek, but to keep an eye out for rattlesnakes, which were also plentiful on the prairie. He'd also told them that if they didn't spray themselves down with insect repellent from head to toe, they'd be bleeding like butchered hogs by the time they reached the stream. Ironically, again, from horsefly bites.

The more Stanley had talked, the more Stone had considered just staying home and watching old movies again, but the itch to try out his new sporting good purchases was too much to resist. After listening to Stanley's warnings, I wanted no part of a search party combing an area riddled with horseflies and rattlesnakes at night.

"I think Wyatt told me once that Veronica liked horseback riding too, so it would be an ideal way for you three ladies to spend the day while we're fishing," Andy assured me.

My backside suddenly began to ache at the mere thought of the long trail ride we were to partake in the next day, and I was already regretting my impulsive decision. But as I have often said, No Pain, No Gain! First I had to get through a Vex Vaughn concert that evening, in the midst of a frenzied standing-room-only crowd. The very thought made my feet begin to throb in perfect harmony with my backside.

CHAPTER 9

As Andy had predicted, Veronica was thrilled at the idea of the horseback riding excursion the following morning. With Emily's help, I was able to make reservations for the ride. We were all sitting in lawn chairs on the patio, visiting and drinking coffee, while waiting to catch the shuttle bus to the fairgrounds. I was drinking cup after cup of strong brew, wishing I were gathering up my snorkel, beach towel, sunscreen, and latest Alice Duncan cozy mystery, to spend the next day lazing on a beach somewhere in the Caribbean, instead of the trail ride that was actually on my schedule. Veronica brought me back to reality with a thud when she reached over to kiss Wyatt on the cheek and squealed in delight.

"With the Vex Vaughn concert tonight, and horseback riding tomorrow, this is turning out to be one of the greatest weeks of my life," Veronica said. "Thanks so much for inviting us along, Stone. I really appreciate it."

"I'm glad you were able to join us, sweetie," Stone said, with a warm smile. Then he reached over and patted my knee. "We'll need to catch the next shuttle bus to get to the concert on time. Honey, are you sure you should be downing so much coffee? Finding a johnny-on-the-spot might be difficult in the standing-room-only section."

"No worries, sweetheart," I said with a smile. "You know I have the bladder of a camel."

Despite my show of nonchalance in front of the others, I had almost choked on my last gulp of the stuff. I'd been so busy concentrating on how much I dreaded the concert and the trip to the ranch the next day that I hadn't taken the availability of restrooms at the fairgrounds into consideration. I considered tossing the remaining coffee in my cup out onto the gravel, but that would contradict my comment to Stone. So, when I noticed there were only a few swallows left anyway, I finished what remained in one long gulp and walked my empty cup into the motorhome to set it into the kitchen sink. I used the restroom, just in case my camel theory didn't pan out, and then picked up my fanny pack and latched it into place around my waist.

Finally, I grabbed a sweatshirt off the back of the couch, knowing how cool the evenings were at this altitude, and rejoined the rest of my party out on the patio, where they were folding up the lawn chairs and preparing to proceed to the shuttle bus stop.

With the uneasy notion of not being able to locate a restroom if I truly needed one later on in the evening, I mentioned needing to take along a pack of Kleenex, which I'd actually already placed in my fanny pack, and rushed back into the motorhome to utilize the restroom one last time. I squeezed out exactly three drops of urine that hadn't emptied from my bladder ninety seconds earlier, and I'm not positive the third one wasn't a mere figment.

As expected, the shuttle bus was jam-packed.

According to the metal regulations plaque attached securely to the back of the driver's seat, I judged the mass-transit vehicle to be about two tons over its legal weight limit. The riders were in an excited state of anticipation because Vex Vaughn was the must-attend concert of this year's festivities. And to think, I'd never even heard of the performer until I'd met Fanny Finch. My age was showing more and more with each new artist who produced a hit song, and it wasn't a trend that was likely to get any better in the coming years. I normally only listened to the radio while driving back and forth to the grocery store or Wal-Mart, both of which were no more than a couple minutes away.

I would not have minded the lack of breathing space in the bus had I been on my way to a George Strait concert, or practically any other artist I'd ever heard of before. One consolation was that, because of the drowning death of Fanny Finch a couple days prior, I had to admit a curiosity about this singer she'd demonized in her tell-all bestseller.

Approximately forty-five minutes later we were being shuffled and herded into the standing-room-only section amongst a throng of young people who didn't seem to mind that they were being handled like a herd of Angus being led to the slaughterhouse. By the time we reached a place in the mob where we would stand to listen to Vex Vaughn sing for the next couple of hours, I'd had my feet stomped on a dozen different times by various cowboy boots. Listening to Vaughn sing would be the extent of my evening, because at five-foot-two, I couldn't see over the sea of cowboy hats in front of me.

Almost immediately, I began feeling the need to use the restroom. Apparently, those last three drops hadn't made a hill of beans' worth of difference in how soon I'd need to go again.

After what seemed like an eternity, the curtain opened up on the stage. I was craning my neck, trying to find an opening where I could get a glimpse of what was causing the crowd to erupt in pandemonium. I felt Wyatt grasp me around the waist and effortlessly lift me up just in time to watch a very handsome man in a Stetson walk out to greet the crowd. A glint flashed off his large silver belt as the bright lights shone down on the singer, who I estimated to be in his late forties. Like my favorite artist, George Strait, I'm sure aging had only made this man more attractive. I quickly indicated to Wyatt I'd seen all I needed to see because I felt a little foolish being hoisted up by the muscular detective as if I were a three-year-old child.

Veronica, who was half a foot taller than I, stood on her tiptoes and snapped at least a hundred photos of Vex Vaughn from practically every position she could catch him in as he entertained the crowd. By the expression on her face, I could tell she was in a state of delirium. Even Wendy seemed fully invested in the concert. Stone, Wyatt, and Andy were exhibiting admirable patience, even as their facial expressions made it apparent they were as anxious for the concert to end as I was.

As one song followed another, my bladder became increasingly more insistent. If I didn't empty it soon, I feared I was going to wet my pants. That would be a humiliating experience I might never live down. I could already hear my daughter jeering at my expense. *Hey, Mom, remember that time you peed all over yourself at the Vex Vaughn concert? I laugh every time I think about your remark about having the bladder of a camel. Good thing camels don't drink gallons of coffee before going to concerts, huh?*

As I imagined that scenario, I knew I had to find a restroom fast. I pulled Stone's ear down toward my mouth and shouted out my need to relieve myself.

"I had a feeling that was going to happen. Would you like me to accompany you?" He asked.

Always the gentleman, Stone would accompany me to the edge of hell if I asked him to, but I told him I'd rather he stayed behind. I knew he had his phone on vibrate, so I shouted to him that when he felt his phone vibrating in his pocket, I wanted him to wave his new cowboy hat in the air so I could locate the group and find my way back to them. He was hesitant, but agreed to my plan.

The easiest way out of the midst of the crowd was to head in a perpendicular direction toward the edge of the stage. Surely when I reached the opening, I'd find a security guard who could direct me to the nearest johnny-on-the-spot.

Pushing my way through the dense swarm of people was no easy task. It was now my turn to stomp all over other people's toes. As I trudged, I sounded like an old phonograph album that had gotten hung up on a scratch and continually repeated itself. "Excuse me, I'm sorry, excuse me, I'm sorry, excuse me, I'm so sorry, I didn't mean to make you spill your drink all over your girlfriend—"

When I finally reached the point where I expected to find a security guard to lead me in the right direction, there was no guard, just a cable stretched out between two metal stands to contain the crowd. Obviously, the cable was designed to keep people from crossing the barrier, which would lead them to the rear of the stage. In the condition I was in, I could see no option but to step over the cable and see if I could find a john behind the stage. The worst that could happen was for me to get booted out of the arena, which might not be such a bad thing. I could text Stone that I was waiting for them outside the fairgrounds by the shuttle bus pickup area. I knew I'd pass several restroom locations on my way there.

The problem was that I wasn't sure I could make it that far. My bladder was now practically throbbing in rhythm with the drums on stage. Although I knew it wasn't a promise I was apt to keep past seven o'clock the following morning, I vowed at that moment to give up my caffeine habit, once and for all.

Walking behind the stage, I realized I'd been gone from my group longer than I'd anticipated and Stone would soon be growing concerned about my whereabouts. Vaughn's band was so loud, though, that I didn't think I'd be able to carry on an audible conversation if I was even able to reach Stone on his phone. Besides, once he felt the phone vibrating, he'd begin waving his hat in the air, to no avail. My best bet was to hurry as best I could and try to limit my husband's worrying as much as possible. God knows I'd caused him enough anxiety already during our first year of marriage.

As I reached the rear of the stage, I could see nothing but the back half of the rodeo arena. There were no staff members, or any sign of a portable toilet in the area. Wouldn't the stage crew and musicians, even Vaughn himself, need a place to relieve themselves should the need arise? I wondered. With that thought in mind, I found an opening in the back of the stage and slipped in undetected.

It was quite dark behind the stage, but I could make out a set of metal stairs ahead of me. I climbed them blindly and it became nearly pitch black as I reached the top. I saw a flash of light ahead and walked toward it. I could hear a rumble of commotion in that direction and would surely come across someone who could assist me in finding a restroom.

I inched my way toward the noise, so as not to stumble over something in my path. Suddenly I froze as a large curtain to my left opened up and I discovered I was standing in the middle of the stage, surrounded by the band. Nearly everyone in the vast crowd was on their feet, stomping, shouting, and thunderously clapping. Vex Vaughn was holding a microphone and staring at me in surprise. I'm not sure what crossed his mind at that moment, but I'm sure the possibility of a crazed fan throwing herself at him was at the top of the list.

"What are you doing, lady?" He hollered at me to be heard above the roaring and applauding crowd, while glancing around, no doubt for someone on his security staff. "I'm almost ready to do an encore!"

"*I have to pee!*" I hollered back, in what had to sound like the most inane and ridiculous response Vaughn and his band expected to hear. As if on cue, the crowd had gone silent and a huge spotlight targeted me as I had screamed out my need to urinate. I noticed then I was standing directly behind a microphone on a metal stand. Had the entire crowd heard me? I wondered in horror. I was as flustered as Vaughn and turned away from the microphone to speak directly to the performer. As the sea of fans erupted into a frenzy again, I tried to be clearer in explaining my situation. "I desperately need a restroom and have been unable to locate one."

With a resigned expression on his face, the artist shook his head, and proceeded to pick up a tambourine and toss it to me. "Pretend to play it, lady. This is my last song, anyway."

As I stood there with a tambourine in my hand, the band began to play, and I suddenly wondered if Stone or anyone else in our group had recognized me up on stage. Even more humiliating, had they heard me shout out that I needed to pee? They wouldn't be expecting to see me up there so might not notice if I tried to blend in with the band.

For the next few minutes I attempted to hide behind Vex Vaughn. The fact that my bladder was about to explode inside my body never crossed my mind. The last thing I wanted was for Veronica to have a photo of me up on stage with her idol to pass around every time a party or gathering of friends needed a boost of amusement. And a wet streak trailing down my pant leg would make the photo even more titillating—worse, memorable. I could just see it going viral on YouTube if she was utilizing the video function of her camera.

With my mind racing, I didn't even realize I was banging the tambourine against my other hand in time with the music until the unfamiliar song ended abruptly, and I didn't.

"What part of 'pretend' didn't you understand, lady?" Vaughn asked me, obviously a little hot under the collar. He glared at me as the curtain came down to indicate the show was over. As a dozen men raced out and began to disassemble the stage and equipment, I tentatively handed the tambourine to him and began to babble nervously.

"I'm so sorry, sir. I truly am. You see, I was just trying to find someone to lead me to a restroom, because I really, really need to use one. I swear I had no idea I'd managed to find my way up onto the stage. It was so dark up here, you know. But, um, the concert was wonderful, and, um, I really enjoyed it," I said, hoping to temper his anger. "I'll find my way out of here. I really am sorry I disturbed your encore."

My pitiful apology seemed to soften the singer's attitude. "Oh, it's no big deal. I doubt anyone could make out a word of the last song anyway because of the crowd noise. And that's probably a good thing, because the lyrics to that song make absolutely no sense at all."

I didn't want to tell him I hadn't understood one word he'd sung all night, so instead I apologized one last time and turned to leave the stage.

"Hey, lady," Vaughn said. I began to walk away, my thighs squeezed together in an attempt to keep from springing a leak. "Would you like to use the john in my bus? My coach is right outside that side door, behind the curtains at the rear of the stage. There shouldn't be anyone in the bus right now. My driver is helping the stage hands load up the instruments."

"Really? That would be terrific! I can't tell you how much I appreciate this. My bladder's about to bust and I don't want to wet my pants!" In my surprise at his welcoming offer, I spoke before realizing what a personal and embarrassing statement I had just blurted out. But the surprisingly thoughtful singer, who was even more attractive up close, eased my humiliation with his next remark.

"Been there, done that, didn't like it! It was during a performance at last year's Country Music Awards Show, no less. Talk about bringing the crowd to its feet! Last time I downed a couple beers before a show though."

Vex Vaughn motioned for a big burly guy with a bald head and a long straggly beard to show me to his bus. Without saying a word, the large man led me to the steps of a beautiful motor coach, and then turned around to return to the stage. I was sure he had other responsibilities to take care of besides waiting for some silly old broad to use the bathroom.

The bathroom was small, but beautiful and functional. On the lavatory, there was a half-empty bottle of Ambre Topkapi Cologne, which I knew to be quite expensive. I wondered for a moment how it would feel to be able to spend money so lavishly. When I'd recently splurged on a forty-dollar bottle of Elizabeth Taylor's White Diamonds at Wal-Mart, I'd felt totally self-indulgent. I was only able to justify the expense by recognizing that the fabulous-smelling cologne was a gift to myself for the first anniversary of my marriage to Stone Van Patten. And how could I turn down a gift so thoughtfully given to me by myself without appearing rude and ungrateful?

After utilizing the toilet inside the bus, I glanced around at the luxurious features inside what I knew had to be a multi-million dollar unit. After having had a conversation with Wendy about wanting to see inside one of the fancier coaches, I was wishing she were with me to see the splendor I was observing at that moment.

With that in mind, I quickly took my phone out of my pocket and began snapping photos. I knew I would not be able to resist showing Veronica a photo of Vex Vaughn's bed, which was unmade and a messed-up tangle of bedding, including bright red silk sheets and a stuffed throw pillow that bore the likeness of the artist across the front of it. *Click!*

I spotted a pair of tighty-whities on the floor in front of me that could stand to be washed, or thrown away and replaced. *Click!* There was a well-worn edition of *Hustler* on his nightstand. *Click!* Right next to the magazine was an open bible with a *Miller Lite* bottle opener being used as a bookmark. *Click!* In an immodest salute to himself, Vex Vaughn had a poster attached to his closet door featuring himself in a provocative, and, I must admit, mouth-watering, pose. *Click! Click! Click!*

Just as I shoved the camera back into my jeans

pocket, the door opened and the subject of the poster I was just photographing stepped into his bus. He tossed his cowboy hat on a recliner, and asked, "Still here?"

"Yes, I was just leaving. Thank you for—"

"Were you taking photos? I thought I saw you put your phone in your back pocket when I stepped into the bus."

I was embarrassed to be caught snapping photos inside this man's personal space. I'm sure he'd feel like it was a serious invasion of his privacy if he'd known I had just been photographing his dirty laundry a few seconds ago—in fact, his skid-marked jockey shorts, for goodness sakes!

I started to express my sincere apologies, when his laugh caught me off-guard. "I don't care, lady. As long as you're not planning to publish the photos, that is. My entire private life is already on display in every bookstore in the country. And, besides, a few photos of the inside of my bus ain't nothing compared to all the lies some broad made up in her book about my life. Pardon my language, ma'am, but that's what Fanny Finch is—an insensitive bitch!"

"No, it's actually what Fanny Finch used to be," I replied.

"Huh?"

"Haven't you heard? She died a couple days ago."

"Huh?" Vaughn repeated with a look of complete shock on his face. "Are you serious, lady?"

"Very serious," I said.

"She's dead? Fanny Finch is dead? What happened to her? Was she killed? Did they catch whoever killed her? It surely wasn't one of my fans, was it?" He asked a string of questions and appeared shaken by the news.

"Somebody electrocuted her in a swimming pool at

an RV Park right here in town."

"Fanny Finch was here in Cheyenne?"

"Yes, for a book signing at the local bookstore."

"Humph! I'm sure with me headlining in a concert here, she had a lot of people wanting a signed copy of her unauthorized *Fame and Shame* book. Stupid title!"

"Well, yes, I hate to say there was quite a line of people at the bookstore."

"Aha! So, am I correct in thinking you were there to buy a book, too?" Vaughn asked. I detected a touch of bitterness in his voice, as if someone he'd so courteously lent his private restroom to had just stabbed him in the back.

"Oh, no, sir. I didn't buy a copy. You couldn't have paid me to buy or read one of her books, which, as you just said, was unauthorized and probably untrue. In fact, my daughter, Kylie Rue, and I made it clear to her that we thought it was despicable of her to even write the book. There was absolutely no way we'd patronize her by purchasing a copy. Kylie was particularly incensed and nearly came to blows with her."

"Kylie Rue?" He asked, with surprise etched on his face.

"Yes, she's a young woman who works at the campground. It was actually the three of us that discovered Fanny's body in the bottom of the pool."

"So, no kidding, she's really dead?"

"Very much so! Say, do you mind if I give my husband a quick call to let him know where I am? I'm sure he's worried about me."

"Sure, go ahead," he said. I noticed he wore an expression of delight. I tried to determine if he was truly surprised at the news of Fanny's death, or putting on a show for my benefit. Either option was possible.

I spoke to Stone, who, along with the others, was

frantically searching the fairgrounds for me. He expressed his relief and also his disbelief in seeing me up on stage with the famous artist and his band. I assured him I'd explain the situation when I joined them at the shuttle bus pickup area in just a few minutes. He told me the shuttle bus was not scheduled to depart for at least half an hour and cautioned me not to be late.

I thanked Vex Vaughn again for his thoughtfulness in letting me use his restroom and made a motion to exit the bus. He put his hand on my shoulder, and said, "Ma'am, I want you to know that most of the information in that book is pure hogwash. Yes, I've not been an angel by any stretch of the imagination, but I've only been arrested twice. Once was for driving while intoxicated, which I regret, and the other was for a trumped-up charge of assault and battery on a paparazzi photographer, which was dropped the next morning. I've only fathered one child, who I made sure ended up in a good home after the mother died during childbirth from a fluke complication. Most of the crap in that book is the result of the author using lenient creative license to sensationalize the information that she gathered from a whole slew of unreliable 'trusted sources.'"

"I can only imagine, Mr. Vaughn. I believe you completely, and I'm really sorry this happened to you. If it's any consolation, I had an aversion to the woman from the second I laid eyes on her. If I were you, I'd let it slide off me like water off a duck's back. Fortunately, in your profession, I'd think any kind of exposure can only help your career."

"Yes, I know. But ignoring it is easier said than done. My reputation is important to me. I don't like the idea that people think I'm some kind of wild-ass loser who treats others with such little regard," he answered. "Can I see your phone for a second?"

My initial thought was that the man was going to delete the photos I'd taken of the inside of his bus, in the event I might use them in some way that would adversely affect him. I'd have probably done the same thing had I been in his shoes. But, to my surprise, he turned the camera around, pulled me toward him with his arm around my shoulder, extended his arm and said, "Smile!"

Who'd have ever thought my very first "selfie" would be taken by, and with, one of the most popular entertainers on the planet? I'm sure he assumed I was a fan since I attended his concert. I thought it was kind of him to make sure I had a photo of the two of us together. It suddenly occurred to me that it might end up being Veronica who wet her pants when I showed her this photo on my phone! I only prayed that the ribbing, and possibly mild chastising on Stone's part, would be held to a minimum.

I thanked Vaughn one more time before exiting his lovely motor coach. I then hurried to the bus stop, not wanting to be responsible for all six of us missing the last scheduled bus ride back to the campground. I knew there was no way the other five in my group would leave without me, even it meant having to find an alternate way home. Even if there happened to be taxi service available, it would take two cabs to fit us all.

CHAPTER 10

As it turned out, rather than being the object of mockery, I was so envied by Veronica and Wendy that what few indignant remarks Stone was able to squeeze into the conversation were completely lost on me. He finally threw up his hands and laughed it off, as I knew he'd do once the sheer panic of not knowing where I was had worn off.

Huddled in a circle at the shuttle bus stop awaiting our ride back to the campground, I scanned through the photos I'd taken. Veronica squealed loudly at the photo I'd taken of Vex Vaughn's soiled skivvies, and I glanced at Wyatt just in time to see him roll his eyes and shake his head in amusement. He placed his arm around his girlfriend, and said, "Honey, I'd be happy to leave my dirty drawers lying all over the house if it would make you this excited."

"Don't even think about it, buster, or at least not until you have a hit song at the top of the charts," she retorted in a teasing manner. "Besides, when was the last time you even wore any?"

"Hey now, girl," he replied. "Don't give my friends the wrong impression of me. I only went commando a

few days that week we were waiting for the repairman
to come and replace the motor in the washing
machine."

"Really?" Stone asked the detective. "Would you
like to borrow a twenty so you can go buy a few spare
Fruit-of-the-Looms at Wal-Mart?"

Continuing the playful banter, Wyatt replied, "You
know I can't afford luxuries like extra underwear on a
cop's salary. And especially not when I have to keep
my lady in silk lingerie. Trust me, friend, I'm not
complaining one bit, because I am the appreciative
benefactor of all that frilly, sexy stuff."

As the entire group laughed at Wyatt's remarks,
Stone caught my eye and cocked an eyebrow. I knew
he was kidding, but I couldn't help but respond. "Not
in this lifetime, dear."

When the laughter died down, Veronica took my
camera out of my hand and continued scrutinizing the
photos inside Vaughn's motor coach. She was
somewhat disturbed by the photo of a beer bottle
opener being used as a bookmark in a Bible, but
nearly dropped my phone when she saw the close-up
of her idol snuggled up against me in the photo
Vaughn had snapped of us. In true drama-queen
fashion, Veronica lamented, "Oh, why couldn't I have
had to use the ladies' room too, so I could have been
with you at the time? Darn my efficient bladder,
anyway! If not for it, this photo would have been of
Vex Vaughn and me instead. Good Lord, he's even
more of a stud muffin close up!"

I wanted to say that it still could have been me in
the photo, but had to admit I'd probably been taking a
picture of Veronica draped all over the handsome star
instead of the other way around. After all, I was not in
total denial. All the lotions and potions Veronica
depended on had not failed to do their job in helping

her create a vision that any man—or woman for that matter—would admire. It seemed as if the young woman was trying to convince others of her worthiness, even though she wasn't believing it herself. If only someone could convince *her* that she was a beautiful human being and could stand to put a little meat on her bones.

Andy, who had contributed little to the conversation, which was not uncommon for the laid-back, soft-spoken young man, spoke up to announce that the shuttle bus was arriving. And because everyone had been delayed by waiting for me to find my way to the bus stop, it appeared as if we'd be the only six people on the last shuttle bus rotation of the evening.

I didn't know about the rest of the group, but I was ready to crawl into bed and call it a day. I needed to recharge my batteries in order to have enough endurance to get through the horseback excursion the next morning. I had a feeling, though, that even if I was Rip Van Lexie, there would never be enough shut-eye to sail easily through the coming adventure. My equestrian ineptitude would surely be evident before the day was over, if not my first five minutes at the ranch.

As it turned out there was very little shut-eye to be had for me that night. Visions of being kicked across another barn, at an age where brittle bones were becoming more of an issue, danced through my head all night long as Stone sawed logs in a blissful state of deep sleep.

"Good morning, ladies!" Emily said to Wendy, Veronica and me as we sat outside on the patio of my campsite, drinking coffee and preparing to drive out to the ranch for our morning trail ride.

"Good morning," the three of us returned in unison.

"Just wanted to drop the keys to my car off with you before I get busy in the office."

"We appreciate you lending us your vehicle," I told her, "but the men already took Stanley's truck to Horse Creek for their fly-fishing adventure. We'd hate to leave you without any wheels. What if something comes up and you need transportation?"

"No worries. I can always use Kylie's car in an emergency," Emily assured me, with a visible shudder. "The brakes are soft, neither the wipers nor horn work, and the gas pedal has a tendency to stick. But with any luck at all, it would get me where I was going without incident. Which reminds me, I forgot to tell you the bad news."

"Oh, my God! What now?" I asked in alarm. My reaction was maybe a little more dramatic than the situation called for, but occasionally the sub-conscious drama queen in me came out when I least expected it.

"Nothing that bad, Lexie," Emily said, with a laugh that sounded more like a snort. "No slain customers or anything of that magnitude. Kylie just informed me she's going back to Florida on Monday, the day after the rodeo ends. She told me she really enjoys the job, but misses her friends and family back home. I guess I can understand how she feels, but dang it, she was the dream employee. At least she's not going to leave me without office help during Frontier Days. The place empties out Sunday afternoon, and next week will seem almost boring in comparison."

"I can see where she's coming from too," I replied. I didn't want to tell her Kylie had told me about her plans the previous morning. Emily might be insulted I didn't go straight to her with the news. But in the event Kylie decided not to quit her job at the RV Park,

I hadn't wanted her to be affected by my spilling the beans. I also didn't want to repeat something the sweet young lady had told me in confidence. So I pretended to be surprised by Emily's remarks. "I'm sorry you're going to lose such a low-maintenance employee. With her bubbly personality and admirable work ethic, her position here seemed to be the perfect fit for her."

"I thought so too, but that's the way it goes, I guess. I'm sure I can find a workamper to fill the spot for the rest of the season. We close for the winter in mid-October. That's about when the first mention of the S-word shows up in the weather forecast. The word snow is like kryptonite for RVers. They head south like a flock of geese with a cold wind ruffling their tail-feathers."

"I'd be right in the middle of the flock if I were here," Wendy said, having been listening to the conversation between Emily and me. She asked, "What's a 'workamper,' Emily?"

"We occasionally get full-time RVers who want a break on their rent, and also men, like pipe fitters and welders, staying here in monthly sites while they're on temporary work stints at the oil refinery in town, or the chemical plant west of town. There's also a water treatment plant here that occasionally hires temporary workers."

"And how does that work?" Wendy asked.

"Well, a lot of times these men's wives travel from job to job with them, and are happy to have something to do to keep them busy. In lieu of monthly rent, they help out in the office, clean the shower houses, or whatever needs to be done. If they work more than a reasonable amount of hours every week, I pay them some salary, as well. It works out well for both of us. And, by the way, workamper is spelled without the 'C' because of the name of the magazine we advertise in when we need help."

"How nice to have a pool of possible employees amongst your customers," I remarked. "I might give that a thought when hiring help at the inn. I can offer room and board in exchange for a percentage of the employee's salary, like you do. That way someone will always be there, and I don't have to close the doors the way we did to come on this trip. I gave my housekeeper a week of paid vacation, but she had it coming, anyway. Colleen's exceptional help, and so is Janet, the gal who does most of the cooking and serving of meals at the inn. She had just been employed for a couple of weeks, but had requested time off while we took this vacation. She wanted to go visit her grandmother, who's on her deathbed in Glendale, Colorado. And, also—"

"You're rambling, Mom," Wendy stopped me in mid-sentence to remind me of the time. "We need to head out in a few minutes to get to the ranch on time."

I'd been chatting with Emily and drinking my morning coffee, and hadn't been paying much attention to the time. I think I was subconsciously trying to sabotage our plans, hoping we'd arrive too late to take the horseback excursion, but I would never have admitted it, even to myself.

"You girls have a great time today," Emily said, as she turned to walk back to the golf cart she'd driven to our site in. "I've already entered the address of the Rolling Creek Ranch on the GPS in my car for you. Follow the directions it gives you, even if it seems like it's leading you to the middle of nowhere, because the middle of nowhere is exactly where this ranch is located."

If Emily had not forewarned us, we would have turned around and headed back the direction we'd come, because we drove for miles without seeing any signs of human life. We did see plenty of antelope, a few jackrabbits, and a couple fox kits playing around a pile of wood. And once I saw what I thought was a rare albino peacock with its plumage fanned out.

"Stone is right, Mom," Wendy said, as both she and Veronica looked in the direction I was pointing and burst into laughter. "You need to make an appointment with your optometrist. Your 'rare albino peacock' is just a clump of white blossoms on some kind of shrub. Did the very notion of spotting a white peacock out on the high plains of Wyoming not seem a bit unlikely to you?"

"Well, yeah, now that you mention it. It's just that I'm getting a little concerned that we've taken a wrong turn along the way. This road seems to go on forever, and I've not even seen a house in miles. Are you sure we're even still in Wyoming? You know Cheyenne is only seven miles from the Colorado line."

"That's south, Mom, and we're heading northwest. Emily said this ranch was massive, so we're probably already on the Rolling Creek Ranch and just haven't gotten to where all the barns and the homestead are located. In fact, up ahead I believe I see what looks to me like a couple dozen horses."

I shielded my eyes from the sunlight coming in through the window. I sat in the driver's seat of Emily's car and couldn't see anything that looked even remotely like horses. I saw what resembled ink dots on a green canvas, though, and assumed they were the horses Wendy had pointed out. Since I didn't want my daughter to think she was riding with a legally blind driver at the wheel, I replied, "Oh, yes, of course. That must be our destination. The GPS indicates that the ranch is just up ahead a short distance."

Stone and Wendy were right about my deteriorating

vision, and I planned to schedule an eye exam with Dr. Herron when I returned home. The initial cost of the pair of glasses I was wearing had floored me, and I was hoping to make do with them for at least another year before having to replace them. I wanted to get new frames as well because, even though I liked the light weight and looks of my rimless glasses, they needed constant adjusting or repairing due to my habit of sitting on them at least once a week, whether I needed to or not.

We pulled up to a gate that a young ranch hand swung open. Driving slowly, we entered a field that was being utilized as a parking lot. There were about ten or eleven vehicles in the lot, most of them pickups and SUVs. Wendy pointed toward a red metal barn where people were gathering.

"There's Cassie Bumberdinger and her kids."

I noticed all three of them wore cowboy attire, complete with leather chaps. I had on a pair of jeans that were a size smaller than was comfortable. In my defense, I hadn't imagined I'd opt to go on a horseback excursion considering my history with horses.

Not to mention the fact I planned to start a diet after vacation ended. I didn't want to purchase an entire new wardrobe on account of a temporary ten-pound weight gain. After all, I had every intention of losing those extra pounds and fully expected these jeans to fit perfectly within a couple of weeks or so.

Of course, I also fully intended to learn how to speak fluent Italian and organize seven crates in the basement of the inn that were full of photographs dating back to the seventies. I hadn't gotten around to doing either one of those things yet either. Regardless, I just prayed the tightness of my denim jeans didn't become an issue. I was certain I'd have enough issues to address during the trail ride as it was.

We soon discovered there were seventeen people on the trail ride, including the three of us and the Rolling Creek Ranch guide leading the way. At my request, I'd been paired with a docile mare named Buttercup. Even her name sounded gentle, and I was pleasantly surprised at how comfortable I felt with her. I could sense she felt at ease with me as well, as she nuzzled my cheek with her warm nose. For the first time since planning this excursion, I felt confident the trail ride would be fun—a pleasant and relaxing adventure.

Mounting Buttercup was another matter altogether. My snug jeans didn't allow me the agility I'd witnessed in the others, including Wendy and Veronica, while mounting their horses.

"One foot in the stirrup, an easy swing of the other leg over the horse's back, then slide into the saddle, all in one fluid motion," Justin, the guide, repeated to me for the third time. Easy peasy, he assured me.

Easy peasy? Well, it might be for a cowboy who probably slid out of his mother's womb with his spurs on, but there was no conceivable way I was going to be able to swing my right leg up and over the saddle. I soon realized I'd have better luck scaling Kilimanjaro than I was apt to have getting to the top of this horse's back, which at the moment looked to be about twenty hands high. She wasn't actually that tall, of course, but she looked monstrous from my viewpoint on the ground next to her.

Justin finally lost patience with me and gave me a boost, practically tossing me up and over the calmly waiting Appaloosa. Listing suddenly to the right, as I tried to settle myself in the saddle, I nearly fell off the opposite side of Buttercup's back. My feeling of relief vanished like Stone in a lingerie store. I prayed this inauspicious beginning was not an omen for the remainder of the day.

CHAPTER 11

Once I was firmly seated in the saddle, Justin explained a few horseback-riding basics to me while the other sixteen riders sat quietly waiting. Although nobody voiced an objection, the audible sighing of the entire Bumberdinger clan indicated how impatient the group was becoming with the greenhorn. Even young Chace appeared to look displeased at being *saddled* with someone in the group who should have signed up for the "Beginners Horseback Experience" that was also offered, and not the "Advanced Horseback Trail Ride" package.

But little did the little brat know my only reason for signing up for anything horseback-related was to get to grill his mother about any motive she had to kill her ex-husband's new wife. If not for this potentially being my only chance to speak with Chace's mother, I'd have stayed and vegetated on the couch in our rented motorhome and let the younger gals do their own thing. I'd be snacking on butter-laden popcorn with my tight jeans unzipped and watching old movies on the DVD player. But, alas, instead of what I'd like to be doing, here I was preparing to begin an adventure I wasn't thrilled about.

I told Justin I felt confident I'd be able to keep up with no difficulty. He didn't look totally convinced, but he nodded and motioned for the group to follow him out through the gate the ranch hand was holding open for us. As we headed down a well-worn trail, Justin began to address us all with a litany of facts and information about our surroundings, as if repeating them for the umpteenth time.

"As most of you know, the Rolling Creek Ranch borders the Laramie Mountain Range, in what is referred to as the peneplain area. This flat area shows advanced erosion caused by water runoff from snowmelt and rain in the mountains. Most of this range is between 8,000 and 9,500 feet in altitude, except for Laramie Peak, which, at just over 10,270 feet, is the ninth tallest peak in Wyoming. Laramie Peak is further north of here than our ride is going to take us today, but we will have a good view of it later on if anyone would like to take photos of it."

As our guide spoke, I reached up to the front pocket of my flannel shirt to make sure I'd remembered to put my cell phone in it. I wanted to be able to take photos along the way. I was relieved to find it securely resting inside the buttoned pocket. There was no telling what kind of exotic animal I was apt to spot out on the prairie we'd be crossing on our excursion.

"For those of you who aren't from Wyoming, this is the tenth largest state in the union in size, but the least populated, with not much over a half million residents. In comparison, Denver, Colorado's capitol city, has about fifty thousand more residents than the entire state of Wyoming." Justin went on to recite interesting statistics and trivia about the area, and answered questions that his comments prompted. We listened to the guide as we headed up the dirt trail away from the corral and barns.

In true coroner assistant fashion, my necrology-fascinated daughter asked about the murder rate in Cheyenne. Justin assured us the murder rate was low, with no recorded murders so far for the year. He explained that the crime rate in general was low, with violent crimes averaging less than one hundred fifty per year, in a town with a population of just over sixty thousand. Wendy, visibly disappointed with those statistics, thanked Justin for the information. When the Q&A session withered out, Justin explained our schedule for the remainder of the excursion.

"In a couple of hours we will be stopping at a mesa along a stream where a chuck wagon will be cooking us up a 'cowpoke lunch' consisting of beans, flank steak, and fried potatoes. There will be coffee, water, and soft drinks available, as well. There's also a restroom station there, provided by the Medicine Bow National Forestry department, which I encourage everyone to take advantage of because it will be our last opportunity to use one until we return to the ranch."

Things were going smoothly so far, for which I was delighted. Buttercup and I moved as one at a leisurely gait alongside Wendy and Veronica and their mounts. Wendy's horse, a spirited Arabian, was named Riptide, and he fit his name perfectly. I was glad it was Wendy, and not me, who was riding him, because he definitely had a mind of his own. Buttercup, on the other hand, could not have been any easier to control.

I was optimistically hoping that the horseback adventure I'd impulsively signed us up for wasn't going to be the nightmare I'd anticipated. I could actually feel my courage being bolstered more and more with each step Buttercup took. I could see Cassie and her children riding right in Justin's wake at the head of the pack. Everybody else followed in groups of two and three, with Wendy, Veronica and me bringing up the rear.

Before I could finish mentally patting myself on the back for my self-proclaimed display of courage, the pace Justin had set picked up to more of a slow trot. I was sure I could adjust, but less certain I'd be able to make my way up through the pack to pull beside Cassie Bumberdinger so I could chat with her and feel her out on the death of Fanny Finch.

I knew Wendy and Veronica, both accomplished riders, were holding back for my sake, knowing I wasn't exactly at ease around horses to begin with. If they'd been allowed to by our guide, they would both take off at a full gallop across the prairie and be totally at ease and carefree, whereas I, even at a mild trot, could feel my stress level beginning to rise.

After a shorter time than I expected, I began to feel a little more comfortable with the pace Justin had set. My comfort level went up another notch when he said, "We are going to continue our ride at this speed to accommodate the less experienced riders."

As he spoke, Justin looked directly at me, and sixteen other pairs of eyes soon turned in my direction to stare at the novice in the crowd who was going to hold the rest of the group back for the remainder of the day. A chorus of cheers replaced the accusatory glares when he added, "But these horses know their way back to the feed trough with their eyes closed and will gladly lead you there if you'd like to ride at your own pace when we head back. They are also all trained to canter, and I promise they won't let you go astray on the ride back to the barn where our ride originated, no matter what speed you choose."

This was a "good news, bad news" announcement as far as I was concerned. I wouldn't have to feel responsible for ruining the day for the more experienced riders, but I also knew I wouldn't have an opportunity to speak with Cassie on the return trip because she and her children would be miles ahead of me. As long as Justin didn't ride off and leave me to fend for myself, I would also encourage Wendy and Veronica to let their mounts stretch their legs and run to their hearts' content. As for Buttercup and me, we'd be content to continue at the slow, steady pace we were already traveling.

As we approached the foothills of the mountain range, Wendy sidled up next to me and asked how I was doing. I assured her I was getting along just fine, and that Buttercup couldn't be any more of a joy to ride.

"That's good, because I know all about your past experiences with horses. It's a long list of bumps, bruises, and emergency room visits. But then, that pretty much sums up your life in general, doesn't it?" Wendy chuckled and reached out to lovingly pat my leg as she teased me.

"Easy, child. You're not too big to bend over my knee and wallop on like there's no tomorrow." Wendy, knowing I'd shoot myself in the sweet spot before I'd ever lay a hand on her, laughed at my lame excuse of a threat.

"Yeah, right, Mom! I'm shaking in my cowboy boots," she said, as she pulled her blue leather Tony Lama boot out of the stirrup and shook it at me. Along with a charm bracelet she had treasured, I'd purchased the boots for her on her twenty-first birthday, back when she was first showing an interest in learning to ride horses.

"As you should be, my child. I will admit, though, that I already regret wearing these old Levi's. I've discovered they're a bit too snug for horseback riding."

"Not to mention a bit too ancient to wear out in public. I need to take you shopping at the Legends to refresh your wardrobe. You still have a gift card to use, you know. We could look for new outfits that didn't go out of style two decades ago. And haven't you had that flannel shirt you're wearing since the turn of the century?"

"Yes, I've been wearing this shirt since way before Y2K. And, you're right, honey, I really do need a new wardrobe. I'd love for you to help me select clothes that are stylish, and would help flatter my figure. Well, as much as it's possible to flatter, at least. You know, last year Veronica got me started buying new shoes—"

"Which you need to stop," Wendy interrupted. "Your newly acquired shoe fetish is getting way out of hand. I know at least seventy-five percent of those new shoes in your closet have never even been removed from the box they came in. And I hate to say this Mom, but there are quite a few of them that should have been left on whatever clearance rack you found them on. When it comes to a woman's wardrobe, quality is more important than quantity. Just ask Veronica over there, if you don't believe me."

"No thanks, sweetheart. I believe you. I prefer being lectured to and humiliated by one *fashionista* at a time." I laughed to let my daughter know I was just kidding. I really did appreciate her offer to assist me on my next clothes-shopping spree. I had a new three hundred-dollar Chico's gift card that was burning a hole in the pocket of my already tattered, holey jeans. I'm fairly certain this anniversary gift from Stone was a subtle hint for me to spend it on more fashionable clothes, and not new bedspreads for the Alexandria Inn. I'm sure Wendy played a hand in his choice, since

Chico's was her favorite women's clothing store at the Legends shopping area in Kansas City, Kansas, which was about an hour south of Rockdale.

After my first husband had died unexpectedly of an embolism when Wendy was only seven years old, I'd pretty much stopped caring what anybody thought about my appearance. I was a single mother, working long hours to support and raise our daughter, and never even took the time to consider having another man in my life. Getting married again was not in my life plan during those years as a widow.

But life sometimes has a way of interfering with your plans. I met Stone on the east coast when I was delving into a cold case involving the murder of Wendy's husband's first wife—a previous marriage that Wendy knew nothing about.[6] The fact that Clayton Pitt hadn't shared this important information with Wendy concerned me. If he wasn't guilty, why would he hide his earlier marriage? If Clay was responsible for his first wife's death in any way, I didn't want my daughter to take the chance of becoming his next victim. So I fed Wendy some half-baked story about my upcoming trip, and left my home in Shawnee to head east to Schenectady, New York, in order to do a little digging into Clay's past on my own.

During my impromptu investigation, I'd met and fallen in love with Stone Van Patten. And now that Stone and I were celebrating our first anniversary, it was far past time to start caring about my appearance again. I owed it to my dear husband to make the effort to look like I hadn't acquired my entire wardrobe from a box of worn out clothing rejected by a homeless shelter.

---

[6] *Leave No Stone Unturned (A Lexie Starr Mystery, Book 1)*

In fact, I decided as we proceeded up a narrow trail into the mountains, I'd clean out my closet as soon as we returned home from vacation. I'd have sacked up and given everything in my current wardrobe to a charity to benefit the underprivileged, if not for the fact they weren't fit to donate. My Sunday best would be an insult to even those who were most in need.

I was starting to look forward to dressing a little more attractively, and thought I might even get a new, more chic hairstyle while I was at the Legends. I would go through my closet and throw away all but a few salvageable or sentimental items, and send a healthy check to our local Goodwill store, in lieu of a sack of cruddy, worn-out duds.

I was so deep in thought that I was startled when Wendy reached out and slapped Buttercup's rump to spur her to step it up a notch. "Wake up, Mom. You're starting to fall behind. By the way, I didn't get a chance to speak to you about your visit with Vex Vaughn last night. I was wondering if you got a chance to ask him about Fanny's death."

"Yes, as a matter of fact, I did," I replied. "He acted totally shocked at my news, as if it was the first he'd heard about it."

"Did you believe him?"

"Well, he appeared sincere and was a really likeable guy. However, it's hard to imagine that, with all his agents, managers, handlers, crew, and hangers-on, someone wouldn't have heard about Fanny's murder and brought it to his attention. After all, Vaughn would be personally affected by news of her death, since all of Fanny's wealth and notoriety had been gained at his expense."

"Yeah, I agree," Wendy said. I noticed with a sense of relief that she spoke in a soft tone so as not to be overheard by Veronica or anyone else. "I would think that news of Vaughn performing at Frontier Days the exact same week his nemesis was killed in Cheyenne would leak out to the press, or at least to someone in his inner circle. Wouldn't this long-shot coincidence make Vaughn a prime suspect?"

"You'd think," I said. I was hesitant to try to incriminate the man who'd spared me great humiliation by lending me his private privy, but Wendy's point was well-taken. I'd been thinking along those same lines myself. I listened closely as she continued.

"Did you know Vaughn has been cast in a bit part in an upcoming made-for-TV movie? He'll be playing himself in the movie, which has several well-known actors in it. And he's appeared in small parts in several other TV shows in the past, which I find quite significant."

"No, I hadn't heard anything about that, but Vex Vaughn's career was not one I would have ever bothered to follow, even if I'd known of his existence before this week. Why do you find this significant?"

"Only that he has experience in acting."

"And?"

"Could he have been displaying some of his acting skills while pretending to be hearing about Fanny's death from you?"

"Hmm," I said, thinking back to my conversation with the singer the previous evening. "I can't remember our conversation exactly, but I guess it's possible. You know, it seems to me I told him Fanny Finch had died, not that she'd been murdered, and he came back with a question about whether or not the killer had been caught. If he didn't know anything about her death, why would he automatically assume she'd been murdered? Statistically, wouldn't she have been more likely to have died of a heart attack, aneurysm, seizure, or some kind of fluke accident, like choking to death on her own words of self-proclaimed importance?"

"Ha, ha, Mom. In the case of someone like Fanny Finch, the statistics might be a little skewed, but, yes, you're right. Unless Vaughn knew more than he was telling you, it seems odd for him to instinctively sense she'd been the victim of a violent crime rather than a tragic accident or fatal health issue. Of course, it likely could have just been wishful thinking on his part. Still, I think he remains a viable suspect in this case," Wendy said. "Did anything else come up in your conversation that didn't seem quite right to you?"

"Not that I can think of," I replied. "He did seem to perk up when I mentioned Kylie Rue, though, as if he recognized her name or something. Of course, that might have just been a figment of my over-active imagination. As you can imagine, I was a bit flustered at the time."

"Well, I can certainly understand that," Wendy responded with a chuckle. "I'm thinking any kind of reaction to Kylie's name was a figment. You had to be in a state of bewilderment. After all, you'd just finished taking photographs of his dirty skivvies and other personal belongings. Besides, how could he possibly have any connection to a hair-dresser from Florida?"

"Yeah, you're right. The chances of that are too remote to consider. I wonder if he's been questioned by the homicide detectives yet. If Justin's right about the crime rate here, and the fact that this would be the first murder to occur in Cheyenne this year, I'm curious just how big the homicide department is, and how many resources they have? Wendy, can you think of any way we could contact them and run my conversation with Vaughn by them? If they haven't thoroughly investigated Vaughn and his possible motives and/or confirmed his whereabouts at the time of her death, maybe this will persuade them to do so."

"Possibly, I suppose. But other than walk straight into the police department and ask to speak to the Chief of Police, I don't know how we can voice our concerns," she replied. "And how serious are they going to take two out-of-state female tourists?"

"As I see it, the female aspect should have no bearing whatsoever. And you do work in a coroner's lab, even though it's in Missouri, Wendy. Maybe that will give us a little more credibility. After all, looking into the cause of death involving murder victims is right up your alley, and it's part of what you do for a living. That, and the fact that we were the ones who discovered her body, should be enough for the homicide detectives to at least hear us out," I reasoned.

"That's true. It might be worth a shot. You know, I don't know why I even care who killed the obnoxious writer, but there's something about this case that interests me and I just can't let it go."

"Yeah, don't you just hate when that happens?" I asked. "It seems to happen to me a lot these days."

"I admit, Mom, this murder does help me appreciate your commitment to the other cases you've been involved in," Wendy replied. "A case like this kind of grabs hold of you and won't let go, doesn't it? But still—just thinking back to some of the risky messes your determination to solve a murder case has landed you in is almost enough to make me want to just drop the whole thing. Besides, I don't think Stone and Andy are going to go along with our decision to speak to the detectives, Mom. After all the worry and angst you've put Stone through in the past, I have a feeling he's going to give us a big fat 'no' if we ask him about taking us to the police station in Stanley's truck."

"Who said I was going to ask him to take us in Stanley's truck? Emily's got a car, too. And I have a sneaking suspicion that she'd be more than happy to take us, or let us borrow her car again. I think she'd like this case solved as much as anyone, seeing as it happened in her campground. And after all, I'm doing this more for Emily than anything else."

"Yeah, right," Wendy said. Sarcasm was, unfortunately, one of the less admirable traits she'd inherited from my genes, but it still irritated me when she used it on me. "And how would we get away without telling the others where we're going?"

"Leave that to me. You're talking about something that's right up my alley now. This is the kind of delicate situation I excel at," I said, gloating just a bit too much for my daughter's sense of propriety. I could see her biting her tongue to keep from employing more of that inherited sarcasm I was just referring to. I had no intention of lying about where we were going, or what we planned to do when we got there. In fact, I had no intention of telling the others in our group anything. What they didn't know, wouldn't hurt them, *or* us, was my way of looking at it. I'm sure there was some perfectly good reason we needed to go into town with Emily. I just hadn't figured out what that was yet.

"Oh, boy," Wendy said with a long-suffering sigh. "I already have a feeling I'm going to regret this. If I've learned anything in my nearly thirty years of life, it's not to get involved in any kind of secret mission with you. I admire your moxie, Mom. I really do. But it's your nasty habit of throwing caution to the wind that scares the bejesus out of me."

"Don't exaggerate, honey. Okay, I admit, if the occasion necessitates it, I might be compelled to throw caution to a slight breeze, but—"

"A slight breeze?" Wendy interrupted. "It's more like hurricane force winds, sometimes, even when the occasion doesn't *necessitate* it."

Before Wendy could back out of joining me on a trip to the police station, I steered the conversation in another direction. "Darling, would you mind riding up next to Cassie and see if you can engage her in a conversation about Fanny's death? I still think she could be a prime suspect. She's got motive, for sure. She did make a remark about Avery dumping her for Fanny. And you know what they say. *Hell hath no fury like a woman scorned."*

"Yeah," Wendy said. "And they also say that love is blind, and I certainly think that applies in this case. I still can't picture slovenly old Avery Bumberdinger and Cassie together. She looks like she should be on the front of *Vogue Magazine* and Avery on the front of *Plumbers Digest."*

"Oh, he's not so bad, but I agree. Avery definitely married up when he hooked up with Cassie, and then in turn, married down when he divorced her and married Fanny. So, go on up there, honey, and see if you can strike up a conversation with Cassie. You can begin with asking her questions about the horseback-riding classes she offers, and her children's interest in being rodeo participants one day. You both share a love of horses and you can use that common interest to strike up a conversation."

"Oh, all right," Wendy said. I could tell she wasn't wild about the idea, but she pulled up beside Veronica, who was about thirty feet in front of her, and spoke briefly to her. Then she picked up Riptide's pace once again to a fast trot in order to catch up with Cassie and her kids. We had been riding single file through a narrow gap in between two rocky crevices. Our increasing distance from one another forced me to shout out my last comment.

"Don't forget to ask her about Fanny!" I hollered. I knew Wendy could be easily derailed from her purpose if she got involved in a discussion about something she was passionate about—like horses. I didn't want her to lose sight of her original goal.

Watching Wendy conversing with the pretty redhead a few minutes later, it occurred to me that my daughter had been right about Cassie and Avery being a mismatched couple. If opposites truly did attract, those two would have been a pair made in heaven. Could there have been something more to that marriage than met the eye? As far as I was aware, it was their union that had produced Brandi and Chace, so there surely had to have been some love connection between the two at one time. But the fact that it was Avery who had ended the marriage made me wonder if Cassie's beauty truly was only skin deep. Perhaps what lie beneath the surface wasn't quite as attractive. It was an intriguing relationship for sure, and I hoped Wendy could discover a little more to the story in her conversation with the widower's ex-wife.

About forty-five minutes later, Justin instructed us all to dismount and tie our horses to a hitching post next to a rippling stream in the middle of a lush meadow. The stream was named Rolling Creek, and was the ranch's namesake. The thick vegetation had been cleared in an area about fifty-by-fifty feet wide. Next to the hitching post were a half dozen picnic tables and two johnny-on-the-spots marked "Dudes" and "Dudettes."

When I hesitated to dismount Buttercup, in what could have only been an unceremonious tumble to the ground, Justin waved at me and said, "Be right there, ma'am."

With the guide's assistance, I was able to stick the landing with only a tiny step back. Had I been dismounting a balance beam in the Olympics, I'm sure I would have received at least an eight from the panel of judges. Then, with my new sense of self-confidence, I stepped forward and collapsed to the ground like a newborn giraffe taking its first step. I hadn't realized until that moment how sore my thighs had become. I'd never succeeded in staying on the back of a horse that long before. Usually by the time an hour had passed, I'd already been bucked off, kicked, rudely snorted at, and left behind in the horse's dust to lick my wounds.

When, due to cowardice, I hesitated to stand up again, Justin looked at me with a knowing smile. After giving me a second to compose myself, he gently helped me to my feet, and said, "Easy now."

Other than crumbling to the ground like an unbalanced stack of wood, which I'm sure everyone in the vicinity witnessed, I was quite proud of the way the morning had gone. I had sustained no bruises, welts, abrasions, or episodes of panic. Maybe my luck had taken a turn for the better when it came to horseback riding.

I was actually looking forward to the rest of the trail ride, after a welcomed cowpoke lunch, accompanied by a cup of strong coffee. I needed a boost of caffeine to perk me up. I still felt a little groggy from having slept poorly the night before. Every horseback riding mishap I'd experienced, and even worse ones I imagined, raced through my mind as I tossed and turned. At one point, I'd even moved to the couch so as not to keep Stone awake all night.

I utilized the privy before joining the line at the chuck wagon. The man spooning out beans, whom Justin introduced as "Cookie," was singing a song about a cowboy leading a bunch of "dogies" across the lonesome prairie. His voice was soothing, but had a forlorn tone to it. When I stepped in front of him, he tipped his cowboy hat, ladled some beans on my plate, and placed a raisin biscuit next to it. He stopped singing to ask me if I wanted some cow grease on my huckdummy.

"Um, well, I don't know, Cookie. Do I?" I asked.

Cookie winked, and replied, "Yes, ma'am, you do, ifin' you have a hankering for a little butter on that there biscuit."

I chuckled at the good-natured cook's remark, and played along with his bantering. "I'm thinking this old greenhorn does have a hankering for some cow grease on her huckdummy. In fact, load that there huckdummy plum up with cow grease, ifin' you would."

Wendy, who was ahead of me in line, turned around long enough to look at me as if she'd just found the idiot who had wandered away from the village. I shrugged my shoulders and stuck my tongue out at her. She shook her head at my silly gesture, turned back around, and stepped up to take a set of plastic silverware that was wrapped in a paper napkin out of a straw basket.

When I turned back to Cookie, who I guessed was about my own age, he had obviously sensed that Wendy was my daughter. He gave me a sympathetic smile, and said, "Kids! God must have given them to us to keep us humble, and it seems to work quite well."

"You think?"

Cookie winked again, and said, "Don't forget to get a piece of boggy-top for dessert."

When I raised my eyebrows at him, he replied, "It's a pie with no upper crust. Strawberry with whipped cream is on the menu for today. And, if I must say so myself, I make a mean strawberry pie."

"In that case, I will most definitely get me a piece of that there boggy-top, Cookie. It will go perfectly with a strong cup of joe, which I'm trusting is thick as axle grease."

"Wouldn't serve it any other way, ma'am."

As soon as I sat down next to Wendy, she leaned over and whispered, "Look at Veronica's plate. She doesn't have enough food there to keep a barnacle alive."

Even though I'd have liked to tell her about Veronica's struggle with an eating disorder, I didn't want to betray Wyatt's trust by telling my daughter what he'd shared with me in confidence, so I just shrugged my shoulders once again and began to eat.

With everyone sitting close to each other, I didn't get a chance to chat with Wendy about her conversation with Cassie Bumberdinger. As we ate our lunch, Cookie sang a number of cowboy songs in his rich, baritone voice. A short time later, I listened contently while I ate an ample-sized piece of strawberry pie, topped generously with whipped cream, which was as delicious as Cookie said it would be.

Also, as Cookie had promised, the coffee was thick and strong, more like espresso than coffee. More out of pure habit than anything else, I drank several cups in quick succession. As I was getting up to fill my blue-speckled tin cup one more time, Wendy grabbed my arm, and said, "Mom, did you learn nothing from last night? Justin warned us that once we resume our trail ride there would be no more opportunities to use the restroom until we get back to the ranch. Don't you think you had better pass on yet another cup of coffee? I know you like to compare your bladder to that of a camel, but that so-called camel bladder of yours let you down last night, and I don't think you want to put it to the test again today. You've already drank three cups that will probably come back to haunt you, as it is."

Have I ever mentioned how much I dislike being lectured to by my daughter? When she turned twenty-one, she had morphed from my respectful, obeying daughter, to my sometimes over-bearing and critical protector. I loved the fact she always kept my safety and best interests in mind, but I occasionally loathed the way she went about doing so. I'll admit it's mainly because her condescending attitude had a tendency to make me feel obliged to do the things she had advised, or frequently even insisted I not do. In nearly every case my act of rebellion came back to haunt me, just as she had suggested my stubbornness might do this time.

I prayed this would not be another one of those occasions, as I defiantly sipped on my fourth cup of coffee before Justin gave me a boost up into my saddle, and we fell into line to continue our journey.

CHAPTER 12

It didn't take long to realize my prayers were not on God's list to answer that day. Evidently, helping the ill and downtrodden, and saving people from life-threatening catastrophes, were given preference to miraculously increasing the size of some rebellious woman's bladder.

Gosh dang it! I thought. When exactly had my bladder, which I swear really was once the size of a camel's, shrunk down to the size of a gnat's? All I could do was tough it out and hope the ride back to the ranch would be quick and merciful. Bouncing up and down on Buttercup's back wouldn't help the problem any, but I'd let my bladder swell up and explode like a water balloon before I'd ask Wendy to help me find a way to rectify my precarious condition.

"Doing all right?" I heard Wendy ask, as she and Riptide pulled up behind me. This was the perfect opportunity to admit I'd been foolish to consume so much coffee. I'm sure after a chastising me briefly, she'd step up and assist me with my predicament.

"Yes, of course, I'm fine," I said instead. Bull-headedness is not a trait I'm proud of, but it was deeply ingrained in my nature. "Why wouldn't I be?"

"Just checking," she replied. "I know you aren't accustomed to long horseback rides. I was afraid your rump might be getting sore."

"No, not too much. A little extra padding in that department goes a long way, you know."

"Well, I don't know that you have all that much extra padding. Even I will be sore by the time we get back to the barn. I'm sorry I didn't think to warn you that your legs would be weak after a couple of hours in the saddle. I should have advised you to be extra cautious when you got off Buttercup for lunch break. But I think you're doing great and I'm proud of you."

I was tickled by Wendy's praise, but I could have smacked her for mentioning a sore rump. Until she'd mentioned it, I'd been so intent on other issues, I hadn't even been aware that my backside really was aching after several hours in the saddle. Now it was front and center in my thoughts, and I could feel it throb with each step Buttercup took. The only way I could think of to take my mind off my current state of discomfort was to distract myself. Not to mention, I was dying to know what she and Cassie had discussed in their earlier conversation.

"So, tell me, what did you and Cassie talk about?"

"Well, first, as you suggested, we talked about her children. Chace is still young and just getting serious about riding, but Brandi is already taking barrel-racing lessons and is showing great promise. She's won numerous ribbons in youth rodeo competitions. She's quite mature for her age, Cassie told me. As a matter of fact, Brandi turns eleven on my thirtieth birthday in August. We are birthday buddies."

"How nice!" I said. "So, what did she say about Fanny's death?"

"You really do have a one-track mind, don't you,

Mom?"

"Oh, sorry. Was there more you wanted to tell me about their equestrian hobby?" I asked apologetically. I really could be laser-focused when I was trying to determine who had the most incentive to want someone else eliminated.

"Not really," Wendy replied. "But your tendency to act like a dog with a bone when you're butting into a murder investigation can be a bit disturbing at times."

"Yeah, I know. And I guess patience is not one of my virtues, either."

"Now that's an understatement if I ever heard one."

"So what did she say about the murder? The suspense is killing me." It wasn't until later on that I realized the suspense might have been killing me, but it was also keeping my mind off my aching butt, and the fact that I had to pee like a racehorse—no pun intended. I pulled Buttercup closer to Riptide so I could hear Wendy's comments more clearly.

"When I was able to segue into the death of her ex-husband's new wife—or her children's wicked stepmother, as she liked to refer to her—she kind of clammed up and didn't respond much to my questioning. She mostly just replied with one-or two-word responses, and didn't offer up a lot of information or opinions. She seemed upset about the death, but not particularly upset that Fanny Finch was dead. In fact, the only real opinion she voiced was that 'the home-wrecking witch' got what she had coming to her, and that karma has a way of coming back to bite you in the ass when you least expect it."

"Well, at least she wasn't bitter about it," I said jokingly.

"Yeah, right," Wendy said with a chuckle. "But she made sure to mention she didn't know Fanny and Avery would be in Cheyenne this week, and that being in the same campground as them was entirely coincidental. She told me she was a fashion model, and due to upcoming assignments, this was the only week she and her kids could fit the vacation in without conflicting with her or Brandi's schedules. Brandi, she told me, had several barrel-racing events earlier in the summer, and one coming up in August."

"Hmm, I'm not sure I believe in coincidences on that scale."

Wendy nodded in agreement, and after a few minutes of silence, she pulled forward a few yards. At the beginning of our return journey, Justin had announced that anyone who wanted to increase their speed could do so, and if they chose to let the horses take the lead, they'd head straight back to the ranch, where they'd be rewarded with a bucket of oats and a rubdown.

"Don't let me hold you back, sweetheart," I said to Wendy. "Buttercup and I are perfectly content at this speed, and I'll let her take me straight back to the barn. You and Veronica go ahead and join the others up ahead. I really want you two to enjoy your trail ride experience. Please don't let me keep you from doing so."

"But Justin's up ahead with the lead pack and Veronica has already picked up the pace. I don't want you to be left alone back here, not with your lack of horseback-riding experience, and all. I don't mind staying back here with you."

I'm not sure what Wendy meant by "and all," but I felt completely confident that Buttercup would not lead me astray. And I intended to pick up the pace a bit also, in order to proceed as quickly as I felt comfortable doing. That way my gentle horse and I could return to the barn and join the others as soon as possible. Most importantly, I could use the restroom facilities located there if I could hold it that long.

"I'll be fine, trust me. You go ahead. Please, honey. If I run into any problems, I'll call you on my cell phone. If I don't show up eventually, it shouldn't be too hard to track me down. Just look up and head in the direction where the flock of buzzards is circling."

I was being ridiculous to let her know she was being needlessly concerned about my welfare. As I'd hoped, she laughed and nodded as she eased her horse into a canter. It didn't take long for her to speed up.

"Well, if you insist, Mom. See you back at the barn!" She hollered, as she and Riptide prepared to leave us in their dust. Buttercup made no effort to go faster, even as I gently tried to urge her to kick it up a notch. I knew prodding her gently in the side with my heels would do the trick, but she'd been so good to me so far that I didn't have the heart to do anything that seemed even remotely mean-spirited. I tenderly patted her neck and then reached back and patted her rump a little less tenderly. The mild-natured Appaloosa began to walk a little faster, but the increase in speed was barely discernible. I decided it was in my best interests just to let her take the lead and proceed at her own pace.

After patting Buttercup on the rear end, I noticed that mine was nearly numb, which was a good thing. Unfortunately, a numb bum does not make the bladder any gladder.

Fifteen minutes later, as I shielded my eyes from the sun and studied the horizon, I discovered the other sixteen riders were no longer within view. I experienced a moment of panic, but quickly reminded myself that Justin had assured everyone that our horses knew their way back to the barn. He had assured us that if we let them lead they'd take us straight home, where their reward for a hard day's work was awaiting them.

That didn't solve the problem of having to relieve myself, which had become urgent. Had I been Justin, Wendy, or even young Chace Bumberdinger, I could have hopped out of the saddle on to the ground, squatted in the meadow, as I would have normally been reluctant to do had the situation not been as dire. Then I could hop back astride my horse and commenced heading back to the ranch. Piece of cake for any of the other folks on this trail ride. *Easy, peasy*, as Justin would have said.

However, I was not Justin, Wendy, or even the snot-nosed little boy, who could ride circles around me. I was a middle-aged, still slightly apprehensive woman on the cusp of being a senior citizen, who was wearing a pair of jeans that were already stretched to their limit and were no doubt causing my thighs to chafe in a manner that would irritate me for the rest of our vacation.

I was practically to the point of crying in despair when I spotted a scrub tree with low limbs, growing right next to a decent-sized, flat-topped boulder, not more than a hundred yards ahead of me. With any amount of luck at all, I could slide off the horse's back and land squarely on the boulder. I could tie Buttercup's reins to the tree, and once I'd finished my business, I could hold onto a limb while standing on the boulder, and slip my leg right over Buttercup's back into the saddle. It was a well-devised plan, I thought, but whether or not I could carry it off was a whole different ballgame.

Without stopping to consider the risk of my "well-devised" plan turning into a train wreck, I thanked God for his act of compassion, and persuaded Buttercup to walk toward what I prayed was not just an apparition resulting from my having spent too many hours in the sun. At that moment, the only thing that could have appeared any more welcoming than the vision in front of me was, perhaps, a Starbucks. I guess it shows the depth of my caffeine addiction when, despite the fact that coffee was the reason I was in the plight I was in, I would have given my left hand—or at least my left pinky—for a cup of hot, steaming Columbian coffee.

As we approached the boulder, I was relieved to discover it hadn't been an optical illusion. It was ideal for my present needs, and I thanked God once again for his grace. I vowed to put an extra twenty in the offering plate at church the following Sunday, as a small token of my appreciation for the favor granted me. I was nearly giddy with relief.

I lifted my left leg over the horn of the saddle and slid off Buttercup's back onto the rock, awkwardly but effectively, and then did a face plant onto the hard surface of the boulder. I felt as if I'd broken my nose, but found no blood on my hand after swiping it across my face. When I tried to stand up, I collapsed into an ungainly heap again, as my legs refused to support my body.

Looking on the bright side, at least no one was around to witness my dismount this time, other than Buttercup. And by the look in her eyes, I'm not sure I'd want to know what was going through her mind at that moment. I gave myself a few seconds to regroup before gradually bringing myself upright and to my feet.

The distance between the bushy scrub tree and the large rock was greater than it had appeared from afar. Reaching out as far as I could, I was able to grasp a branch while trying unsuccessfully to avoid the menacing-looking thorns protruding from it. A thorn, nearly two inches long, buried itself deep into the palm of my hand. It stung like the devil as I held my breath and yanked it out.

Although the branch I'd grasped was not very substantial, I thought it would suffice to keep Buttercup immobile while I squatted next to the rock to relieve myself. In fact, I wasn't certain she'd move away from the boulder even if unrestrained, but I didn't want to take that chance. So I tied the reins around the branch, as best I could with a throbbing hand, pulled a small packet of tissues from my fanny pack, and crawled carefully down off the boulder.

How do I spell "relief?" With my back propped up against the boulder, I took care of business, which took a while since I was dispelling four cups of very stout coffee. After squatting for just the amount of time it took to empty my bladder, I found it difficult to stand up again. My legs felt as if they'd turned into rubber.

Only the thought of the embarrassment I'd have to endure if found in that less than enchanting position gave me enough incentive to power through it, grunting like a warthog in heat the entire time. I must admit that the swarm of red ants I spied about five feet from me might have enhanced my determination.

My sense of relief was overwhelming, but short-lived. I'd just been commending myself for coming up with such a well-devised plan, when I heard a loud snapping noise. You know what they say often happens to the best-laid plans of mice and men, don't you? Well, mine went awry in a split-second, when the inadequate branch I'd tied Buttercup to broke in two. Startled by the unexpected noise and recoil of the branch, my transportation bolted away from the scene as if her tail was on fire. I would not have guessed the laid-back horse could move that rapidly had I not witnessed it with my own, now watering, eyes.

Well, crap, I thought. *Crap, crap, crap*! What in the world was I going to do now? I should have known God was just playing with me, most likely reprimanding me for wasting his time with such a selfish, insignificant request, when children were starving and dying of preventable and curable diseases all over the globe.

Maybe it was that "karma" thing Cassie had mentioned to Wendy, coming back to nip me in the rear end for drinking coffee I knew I should have passed on. I should have heeded my daughter's advice when she only had my best interests at heart. How stupid I'd been to defy her and then pray that some divine intervention would rescue me from my self-inflicted predicament.

I crawled back onto the boulder and watched Buttercup racing away from me, enveloped in a cloud of dust. She would soon be rewarded with a relaxing rubdown and munching on a well-deserved bucket of oats, while I sat on a rock, wishing I could turn back the clock and resist the caffeine craving that had landed me in my current pile of doo-doo.

I unzipped my fanny pack, thanking God once again for creating cell phones, only to quickly discover there was no signal to be had out in the middle of Nowhere, Wyoming. My cell phone was suddenly as useless to me as a trombone would have been. Couldn't make a call on it, couldn't play a tune on it, couldn't mount it and ride it back to the ranch. In fact, I couldn't do a blasted thing with my phone but enable the camera feature on it and snap a photo of Buttercup's rear end, just seconds before it disappeared from sight.

"*Horse's ass*!" I shouted out in frustration, as I reviewed the most fitting digital photograph on the front of my phone. With the reality of my situation settling in, and with a now empty bladder, I would have seriously relinquished not only my left pinky, but the whole frigging arm, for a cup of coffee. I might have sacrificed even more bodily parts for the return of my transportation, Buttercup, if she returned with a step-ladder for me to use to mount her.

I would have put my face in my hands and sobbed if I'd thought it would help, but knowing it would be as pointless as making a wish on a falling star, I just sat there and stared off at the horizon, hoping that eventually somebody would realize I was missing and come find me.

CHAPTER 13

Although it seemed liked hours had passed, it probably was no more than fifteen minutes later when I saw a horse almost undetectable in a cloud of dust approaching me from the direction Buttercup had fled. I couldn't make out the rider yet, but I was certain it wasn't Justin or Wendy. The rider's head was barely visible over that of the horse's head as it bobbed up and down in its full-out gallop.

It quickly became apparent it was Brandi heading toward me. I was almost relieved to see it was Cassie's young daughter coming to rescue me, because surely the young girl would not be as judgmental about my situation as an adult rescuer might have been. However, I soon discovered the child, who read books about quantum physics for entertainment, was not the bundle of joy I'd hoped for.

"Hey, lady," Brandi said as she brought her horse to a halt in front of me. "Your horse showed up back at the barn by herself. What happened to you?"

"First of all, my name's Lexie. And second of all, I stopped here to relieve myself, and Buttercup got spooked when a branch snapped and ran off. I knew when she showed up alone, someone would come back for me."

"Yeah, I volunteered, because the adults were all sitting around talking and drinking beer. The barn is right down from the hill I just rode over. You really should have pulled yourself together and taken a little initiative. If you'd started walking in the direction your horse ran off in, you'd already be back in the barn by now, drinking beer with the rest of them." The precocious young girl spoke with the air of a Master Sergeant commanding a new batch of recruits at boot camp. I half expected her to insult my mother, just to try to raise my ire so she could then reprimand me for losing my cool. Instead, she said, "You should have used the restroom when we stopped for lunch, as Justin suggested."

"Well, I did, Brandi, but—" I stopped in mid-sentence. I didn't have to explain myself to this little brat. Besides, my justification sounded idiotic even to me. "Let's just head back to the barn. Okay? I'd like to put some Neosporin on the palm of my hand where I got pricked by a thorn on this scrub tree here."

"You didn't see those humongous thorns before you reached for the branch? The tree's called a Crataegus, by the way. It's commonly known as a hawthorn, which is a tree in the rose family. In a month or so, it will produce apple-like fruit, which helps provide food for a variety of wildlife species." Brandi spat this detailed information out as if she were an automated robot.

"How nice for the wildlife! How old did you say you were?"

"I'll be eleven on August 18th."

"Oh, yes, that's right. That's my daughter's birthday," I said. "She'll be thirty that same day. You are very mature for your age, aren't you, Brandi?"

"I'm gifted." The young girl said this as if saying she was cold. It was obvious she'd been told she was gifted from a very early age. She looked me straight in the eye and continued. "I'm a member of Mensa. Do you know what Mensa is? You have to have an I.Q. at, or above, the ninety-eighth percentile."

"Yes, I know what Mensa is, Brandi. Personally, I don't have an I.Q. in the Mensa range, but I haven't suffered an incident involving the absence of oxygen for an extended period, either. I still possess an adequate amount of brain cells to get by. In fact, I earned an Associate of Arts degree at a community college."

"A community college? Seriously, lady?" Brandi made it abundantly clear she felt a degree from a community college was akin to being held back a year in kindergarten for not being able to draw within the lines. "I've skipped several grades already. I'm on track to attend Harvard Medical School in five years or less—on a full-ride scholarship, of course."

"But of course." I turned away as I said this because I knew I'd be unable to keep from rolling my eyes as I did so. This girl might be brilliant, a genius even, but it didn't mean she wasn't extremely annoying. She was entirely too full of herself for my taste. Can you inherit that trait from a stepmother? I wondered, because Fanny had been pretty impressed with herself, too. "Aren't you a little young to be in Mensa?"

"Not at all," she replied. "There are over 2,600 members under the age of eighteen, with the youngest being less than three years old. My I.Q. was 162 on the Stanford-Binet scale the last time I was formally tested."

"Congratulations, that's very impressive. Is your brother, Chace, as bright as you are?"

"Chace is what gifted people like me refer to as an under-achiever. He used to have better focus, but he lost it when Daddy left, and now he makes no effort at all to maintain perfect grades. He and Daddy were practically inseparable before our parents' divorce, but now my brother just mopes around, showing little interest in much of anything. Chace actually received a 'needs improvement' mark on his last report card."

"Well, that's not so bad," I said in the boy's defense.

"I speak several languages fluently," Brandi continued as if I hadn't even spoke. "I am currently learning Italian, but Chace has yet to even master Spanish, and he's almost nine. I spoke fluent Spanish and Mandarin Chinese before I was seven. But Chace seems to have no ambition whatsoever."

"Slacker!" I meant this as a joke, but Brandi nodded her head in an exasperated manner. With a serious expression on her face, she replied, "Exactly! There's no excuse for it. It's just pure laziness on his part. He occasionally comes up with a spark of a good idea, but they're few and far between."

"Perfect grades may not be as important to him as they are to you. He's obviously no dummy, but perhaps he's content with not being perfect—scholastically at least. He may excel more in social interaction, athletics, or the arts, for example. We can't all be members of Mensa, you know, or the distinction would have no significance. Perhaps he doesn't need perfect grades, or to have the ability to speak multiple languages, to be happy in his own skin."

Brandi, with her mouth agape, stared at me as if I'd just told her that perhaps her younger brother didn't need oxygen to be content with his life. She shook her head in disbelief, so I'm sure she thought she was wasting her breath talking to someone who didn't have the sense God gave a grape, not to mention a sub-standard AA degree from a lame, almost comical excuse of a college.

"Let's just go. Get up on Titan, lady, right behind me, and hold on. I'd already removed the saddle so you'll have plenty of room," Brandi instructed me.

I stood up on the boulder, and tried to raise my leg up over Titan's back, to no avail. With my leg lifted as high as I could possibly lift it, it was still a foot shy of reaching the top of Titan's back. Little Miss Einstein shook her head again and asked with great impatience in her voice, "Don't you own a pair of jeans that would've been more appropriate for horseback riding? Those look like they've been applied to your legs with a paintbrush."

"Your smart-aleck remarks are not necessary or appreciated," I said. "You told me the ranch is just over the hill, so why don't you go on now and I'll walk back by myself."

"I'll walk with you, or my mommy will be upset with me for leaving you behind." She sounded as excited about walking back with me as I felt about walking back with her. "I don't like it when Mommy is unhappy."

"Swell."

She nonchalantly hopped off Titan and we began walking south toward the barn. Although the saddle had been removed, there was still a bit in Titan's mouth, so Brandi held the reins in her hand and the solid black horse followed us. Like Riptide, Titan was a spirited and muscular stallion, and Brandi, with her amazing equestrian skills, had no difficulty in commanding his compliance and obedience. There was a mutual respect between the two that was impressive to me, considering my lack of experience with horses.

Brandi and I walked side-by-side in total silence for several minutes. When we came across a fresh pile of excrement that had been deposited in the middle of the dirt trail, Brandi said, "There's a mountain lion in the area."

"Mountain lion?" I asked, swallowing hard. Had I been aware of that fact earlier, I'd have been a nervous wreck. Peeing my pants would have been inevitable, brought about by unimaginable fear, but it would have been the very least of my concerns. The potential of becoming a mountain lion turd myself would have been moved right to the top of my priority list.

"Should we be concerned?" I asked, shaking my head to clear my mind of the disturbing vision. For the first time, I welcomed any knowledge she might have to share with me about our chances of being eaten alive by a nearby flesh-eating creature.

"No, it won't bother us," she assured me. "Besides, we're not far from our destination. Did you know that you can identify nearly any animal by its scat? Scat is another term for poop, by the way."

"Yes, I know. Seriously, young lady, I am not down to my very last brain cell." I was pretty sure I really *was* down to my very last nerve, however, and she was trampling all over it.

Brandi continued expounding on animal scat, as if she felt it was necessary to flaunt her intelligence. "Most can be identified by observation alone, such as the size, shape, color, and consistency of the scat. For example, this scat is about five inches long, with a blunt end, and has hair and bone fragments in it. The fact that there are scratch marks around it, which is evidence the animal tried to cover its excrement, is also indicative of a mountain lion. Did you know the science of scat is called scatology?"

"No, I didn't, because, I'm happy to say, I've never

been obsessed with poop, as you appear to be. You read a lot, don't you, child?" I asked in amazement.

"Yes, almost constantly," she replied in a matter-of-fact tone. "Everyone says that I have an insatiable curiosity, and an incredible thirst for knowledge."

"Do you have plans of becoming a scatologist when you grow up?" I was teasing when I asked the child this but, apparently her brain was so crammed with facts, figures, and intricate details about an untold number of subjects, that there was no room left in it for a sense of humor.

"Of course not," she replied, with a huff. "I'm going to be a scientist in the medical field. I intend to find a cure for cancer one day."

"Personally, I'd like to find a way to create world peace. But I've no doubt you'll succeed in accomplishing your goal before I do," I replied. My comment about creating world peace was in jest, because we all know war and terrorism wasn't going away anytime soon. I knew the teasing aspect of it would never register with this serious, no-nonsense child. Besides, even though her desire to cure cancer was a lofty goal, I couldn't deny it was possible. With Brandi's intelligence and fierce determination, if a cure was ever found, it would most likely be an individual like her who'd be responsible for discovering it.

"And then again, I might be a world champion barrel-racer instead."

I had to laugh. It was the first evidence I'd seen that even though Brandi was intelligent way beyond her years, she was still a child. "I've no doubt you could be both if you set your mind to it."

"That's true," she replied. An overabundance of modesty was not an issue for the child, either, I noticed.

As we walked, I occasionally reached down to massage the inside of my thighs, which felt as if they'd been rubbed raw. I was massaging, trying to alleviate the soreness, when, without even turning to look at me, Brandi said, "That wouldn't have happened if you weren't too fat for those jeans you have on."

"Excuse me?" I responded, appalled at her rudeness. Obviously, this young brainiac was missing a sensitivity chip.

"I noticed you had a large piece of strawberry pie at lunch, with whipped cream on top of it, no less. That dessert probably elevated your caloric intake to more than you should be consuming in an entire day, particularly considering you really need to lose a few pounds. You won't find a grain of sugar in our home. Eating healthy is a priority in our household, and not just because my mom is a model and staying slim is critical to her career."

Good for Miss Twiggy, I said to myself. Yes, it was true that Cassie had a face that would stop traffic. However, healthy diet or not, I didn't find anything attractive about bony shoulders, arms and legs that looked like broomsticks with blue veins protruding from them, or a ribcage that could be used as a washboard if the Maytag shot craps. Veronica was the only person I knew who made Cassie look bloated in comparison. At least Cassie wasn't scary-thin like Veronica, but she didn't need to lose any weight, or be overly obsessive about digesting a grain of sugar on occasion either.

And, yes, I knew I could stand to lose a few pounds. As I've said numerous times before, I had every intention of working toward that goal after we returned home from our vacation. I didn't need some pint-sized freak of nature bringing it to my attention, or lecturing me on what I should or shouldn't be eating, or wearing, for that matter. To be honest, I felt perfectly comfortable in my own skin, with or without those ten extra pounds.

I was too flustered to respond, but Brandi only seemed to be warming up. She continued, in her droning, monotonic manner. "Sugar is also detrimental to your teeth. Sugar can cause decay, and decay can cause infection, which, in turn, can adversely affect your entire system. Do you still have your own teeth?"

I nodded woodenly, my mouth hanging open in astonishment. If I'd had dentures, they'd have probably fallen out already.

"Well, then, don't get too attached to them, because you probably won't have them much longer if you keep eating things like that strawberry pie they served at lunch."

"Has anyone ever told you that you can draw more flies with honey?" I asked, finding it hard to believe I was having such a mature—and, I might add, depressing—conversation with someone not yet eleven years old, *gifted* though she might be. I would have been happier discussing Lalaloopsy dolls and how annoying boys could be with the youngster.

"Huh? Why would I want to draw flies?" Brandi replied, without a clue what I was talking about. "Now that's just gross!"

"Never mind. I'm too tired to explain the meaning behind that old adage." I could feel my temper starting to rise, and I didn't want to unleash it on a young girl who probably had no idea her remarks had been offensive and inappropriate.

It suddenly occurred to me that the tragic loss of her stepmother might have emotionally affected her demeanor. After all, I had no way of knowing how close the two had been. Before Brandi could think of more clever ways to demean and insult me, I decided to change the subject and offer her my condolences. My bruised and battered ego couldn't take much more abuse from the little snot.

"By the way, I'm sorry for your loss, sweetheart."

"My loss?" She asked, confused. "What loss are you talking about?"

"You know—the death of your stepmother."

"Her death is no big loss as far as I'm concerned."

"Well, dear, it's got to be a little hard to accept the fact she's been so brutally and abruptly removed from your life. She did play a part in your life, didn't she?" I asked.

"Not really. The only part she played in my life was to break up my family. Now I hardly ever see my daddy anymore. But it's my mom, more than me, who's been a complete wreck since Daddy left us. She's just not the same anymore. She cries all the time and refuses to let me spend much time with Daddy. She told me she doesn't want me to be influenced by his new wife—or didn't, I should say. But I really don't want to talk about Fanny," Brandi said. I could tell I'd put a damper on her mood, which hadn't been exactly cheerful to begin with. I felt bad about bringing up a sore subject. But feeling bad, or not, it didn't deter me from probing deeper.

"Okay, I understand. I just want you to know that I feel bad for you, and I'm sorry about the whole situation with your parents."

"Thanks."

"Do you know if your mother has any idea who might have electrocuted Fanny, or any suspicions about the killer?"

"I'm pretty sure she knows very little about the murder. Why do you ask?"

"My daughter and I are kind of looking into possible suspects' motives and alibis, in hopes of being able to assist the detectives in tracking down the perpetrator. I've helped our local police back home solve a number of murder cases. I'm quite good at it, actually. In fact, not long ago I was awarded a Certificate of Appreciation from the police department for my help in solving the murder of our local librarian," I boasted.[7]

"Really! No kidding, lady?" Brandi asked. The girl might not have much of a sense of humor, but I'm sure I detected a healthy dose of sarcasm in her four-word response. Granted, a letter of appreciation from a small town's police department was hardly a Pulitzer Prize for single-handedly discovering a cancer-cell-killing medication, or a Medal of Honor for saving an entire platoon of soldiers from being ambushed by the enemy—or even a Doctorate Degree from Harvard, which I had no doubt she'd be awarded before she could legally purchase a beer. Still, I felt my achievement demanded a little more respect than Brandi had extended to me.

A sense of melancholy had settled over both of us, as if a thick cloud had dipped down into the valley we were meandering through. We walked the rest of the way to the barn in silence. I was relieved to see a smile return to the young girl's face when her mother met us at the entrance to the barn. I could hear Wendy and Veronica talking and laughing animatedly inside the barn. I patted Brandi on the shoulder.

"Thanks for coming to my rescue, sweetheart. I wish you only the best in the future, one I know will be bright, like yourself. I'm certain you'll be successful in whatever path you choose to follow."

---

[7] *Just Ducky (A Lexie Starr Mystery, Book 5)*

Brandi thanked me politely, as did Cassie, who asked me if I'd had fun on the trail ride.

"Yes, very much, Cassie. I appreciate you telling me about it. I know Wendy and Veronica had a wonderful time, as well. Enjoy the rest of your stay here in Cheyenne."

"Thanks. You too. We head home Friday afternoon. I have a photo shoot for a magazine cover on Monday, and want to be well rested so I don't have bags under my eyes. Not to mention, these photo shoots can be long and tedious—much more than people who aren't in the fashion industry could possibly imagine. And a model my age needs a long time in the makeup chair before the shoot can even commence."

"Don't cut yourself short, honey. I'm certain that even at your age, which I still consider to be 'spring chicken-ish,' and with your looks and physique, you are still in high demand. Best of luck with your upcoming photo shoot. In the meantime, I hope we run into you and your kids around the campground before we leave. We're heading home Saturday morning, since we don't have tickets to the rodeo finals on Sunday and we want to beat the mass exodus out of town."

"Spring chicken-ish? Ha-ha. I wish! But thank you for the kind words. Sad to say, but that's one of the nicest compliments I've received in a while," Cassie replied. Then Cassie told her daughter to go on into the barn and get herself and her brother a sugar-free soda. Afterwards, she'd meet them at their car to head back to the campground.

I bade Cassie goodbye and walked into the barn, mentally going over how I'd explain to Wendy why I ended up needing to be rescued by a ten-year old. An extremely intelligent and mature ten-year-old, I might add, but a ten-year-old, nonetheless.

* * *

As I walked toward the corner of the barn where Wendy and Veronica were chatting with one of the other female riders on our excursion that day, I thought I detected paleness in Veronica's expressionless face. Studying her intently as I approached the three women, I saw her knees begin to buckle and I moved faster than I'd have ever guessed my fifty-one-year old, worn-out body, with every muscle screaming in agony, could move. I reached out my arms and cushioned Veronica's fall just as she toppled over face-first in a dead faint.

A loud gasp echoed around the room as people realized what had just happened. Shortly after their initial reaction, they all rushed to offer assistance. The olive-skinned woman with whom Wendy and Veronica had just been conversing shouted out to her husband, who, as luck would have it, was a trauma nurse at their local hospital in Idaho.

Veronica regained consciousness fairly quickly, but we were all concerned about what had prompted the fainting incident. Wendy explained to the male nurse about how little her friend had eaten at the cowpoke lunch earlier in the day, and he agreed the lack of nourishment had most likely been what had caused her to pass out. The nurse pulled a candy bar out of a pocket of his windbreaker and handed it to Veronica. When she shook her head to refuse it I felt I had to speak up.

"Take the bar and eat it! And I mean right now, Veronica! You need the energy and sustenance it will provide, and I am not going to let you die of malnutrition on my watch!"

The still shaken woman looked up at me in bewilderment, as if trying to recall who I was. Then she snarfed the candy bar down like she'd been stranded on a desert island without food for a month. The poor confused girl was literally in danger of starving herself to death, I realized.

After Veronica had regained enough strength to get up and walk under her own power, we thanked the nurse for coming to her aid, and prepared to leave the ranch. Not surprisingly, with Veronica's fainting spell at the forefront of our minds, nothing was said about my little "incident" on the trail ride as we drove back to the campground. I gave a great deal of thought on how to approach the nutrition issue with Veronica without making it obvious I'd spoken to Wyatt about her.

"How are you feeling, honey?" I asked as I studied her face in the rear view mirror. Wendy was sitting in the back seat with her so she could keep an eye on her and respond to an emergency if one arose.

After she weakly replied she was fine, I said, "Veronica, I've been noticing your weight dwindling over the last year or so, and I'm concerned about your welfare. You just don't look well to me."

Even though I'd kept Wyatt's concerns to myself, Wendy jumped right in with concurrence, and said earnestly, "I agree with Mom. You know, Veronica, a year ago I thought you were the prettiest woman on the planet, as I'm sure Wyatt, and everyone who's ever laid eyes on you, did too. But now as the pounds are melting off your body, so are the gorgeous features that impressed me so much. They are being replaced by sunken cheeks, dark shadows under your eyes and skeletal limbs. Even your once lustrous hair is being adversely affected. You are much too thin— unhealthily so, as today's fainting episode proves. If you have body image issues, please, for your and Wyatt's sake, get some help before it's too late. You have beautiful features, Veronica, and they'd only be enhanced by a healthy-looking physique. "

Veronica's head hung down, in embarrassment I'm sure. Her chin nearly touched her prominent breast bone. I knew my daughter was speaking from the heart and had no intention of hurting her friend's feelings. She was as concerned as I was about the emaciated young lady. I didn't want to humiliate Veronica, so I added, "Honey, we aren't trying to beat you down in any way. We care so much about you that we're afraid of what might happen to you if you don't start eating better, and hopefully put a few pounds on your thin frame in the process."

"I know, and I appreciate your concern," she replied, as I saw Wendy reach over and put her arm around Veronica's shoulders. "I promise I'll try. I know Wyatt is worried about me too. I've been battling demons from my past for several years, and he has been helping me in my attempt to overcome them. Please don't tell him what happened today. I don't want him to be angry with me."

I was thinking I didn't want her boyfriend to be angry with me either, and he surely would be if I didn't share today's health scare with him. I'd been on the wrong side of Wyatt's good nature several times before, and had no desire to be there again.[8] So, instead of promising to keep my lips sealed, I replied evasively, "We don't want him angry either, but we all are concerned. And we're here for you—always—to do whatever it takes to get you well!"

We rode in silence for a while until I asked Wendy about her conversation with Cassie Bumberdinger. As Wendy and I discussed the Bumberdingers, Veronica listened to tunes on her iPod, with an ear bud in each

---

[8] *Pretty much every Lexie Starr mystery involving Detective Johnston*

ear. She dutifully munched on a pack of peanut butter crackers I'd had in my fanny pack. In contrast to Veronica, I was never without some form of snack in my possession, and it didn't take a fainting spell to encourage me to indulge. In fact, it took great willpower not to.

I listened now as Wendy spoke. "Although she didn't have much to say about Fanny's death, she did make a remark that kind of threw me for a loop. She said, kind of under her breath, 'This just wasn't the way Avery and I planned it.'"

"I wonder what she meant by that?" I asked. "Did she expound on her comment at all?"

"Well, when I asked her, she just kind of hemmed and hawed, and said she was referring to the way they'd planned to spend their lives together after she'd gotten pregnant with Brandi."

"Hmmm...interesting."

"I told her I couldn't quite see what there was about Fanny Finch that would have attracted her ex-husband, and she told me there was more to Fanny than met the eye. When I prodded her to continue, she explained that Fanny's father, who was critically ill with terminal kidney cancer, was the owner of a huge trash hauling company, a company that included five massive dump sites, hundreds of trash trucks, and thousands of employees. Apparently, there's a lot of money to be made in trash removal, and Fanny was the sole heir to a small fortune. In fact, Cassie told me that ownership of the Vandersnoozeski Waste Management Corporation had already been transferred over to Fanny when her father became too ill to run the company and she took over as the CEO. It was basically a figurehead position, with a board of trustees handling the day-to-day operations of the company."

"Did she think Avery had an eye on Fanny's money?" I asked.

"She didn't say so, but she kind of inferred that might be the case, because, like all of us, she couldn't imagine what attracted her husband to an overbearing woman like Fanny. In any event, it was obvious there was no love lost between her and Avery's new wife. Do I think she might have been involved with Fanny's death? I don't really know. But I think she definitely had an ax to grind with her and is not overcome with grief about her replacement's untimely death."

"It doesn't appear as if anyone is exactly overcome with grief. Brandi doesn't consider her stepmother's death to be much of a loss, either," I said.

"Cassie told me Brandi is extremely intelligent, and that the girl's so mature for her age that Cassie often forgets she talking to a child when she's discussing a grown-up matter with her. She said Brandi's what is known as—"

"Let me guess," I said, interrupting Wendy in mid-sentence. "Gifted, right? Brandi refers to herself as gifted as most kids would refer to themselves as being bored, completely matter-of-factly, as if she's been reminded of it a zillion times."

"Exactly," Wendy replied. "What was she like when you were with her today? By the way, did I not caution you about drinking all that coffee at lunch?"

I decided to ignore her last question, and answer the first one instead. "Brandi's an enigma, let me tell you. Conversing with her is like chatting with R2-D2, the Stars Wars robot. She was almost stoic while she expelled facts and figures as if she was reading from a text book. Saying she's extremely intelligent is an understatement if I've ever heard one."

"Does Brandi have a pleasant personality, even though she's smart?" Wendy asked.

"Not just smart, but one of the youngest certified members of Mensa kind of smart," I said. "And, no, I wouldn't call her personality pleasant. More like severely and offensively grating. But I feel sorry for the child. She can't possibly have very many friends. When most girls her age are spending their time together playing with dolls or watching cartoons, Brandi would be more apt to invite a friend over to memorize the "H" section of her Funk and Wagnall's. On a really fun day they might even contact the publisher to question the accuracy of some of the material in the reference book."

"Oh my goodness," Wendy said. "That bad, huh?"

"That bad. And she's definitely lacking in the social graces department too. But when I asked her about losing her stepmother, she showed no emotion at all. She made it clear her mother holds Fanny Finch totally responsible for the breakup of her family. She said Cassie cries a lot, and just hasn't been the same since her father left them. I'd say her mother probably wanted revenge against Fanny, but I don't know how far she'd go to get it. Cassie seems nice enough, and was quite pleasant when we spoke after the trail ride."

"I'm thinking she deserves further consideration though, don't you?" Wendy asked.

"Most definitely."

"I just don't want us to get so involved in the case that we find ourselves in a fix. You know, kind of like the fixes you've been in every single time you've gotten involved in a murder case."

"Don't be silly, sweetheart," I replied. "That will never happen. We really have nothing riding on the outcome of this murder investigation. It's more of just satisfying our curiosity about who killed Fanny Finch."

CHAPTER 14

I was straightening up inside the motorhome when I heard my husband laughing as Stanley dropped him off at our campsite. When I spoke to Stanley through the rolled-down window, he was animated and in great spirits. I could tell his day had gone smoother than mine had. I heard him open up an outside compartment and slide his rod and tackle box into a storage area underneath the belly of the unit.

Not surprisingly, I'd already brewed a fresh pot of coffee and poured a cup for Stone when he came inside. Always the gentleman, he greeted me with a kiss and an inquiry about how my day had gone.

"Interesting," I replied. "How was yours?"

"We had a blast! Since the list of reservations due to arrive today was manageable for Emily and Kylie to handle without him, Stanley decided to join us. All four of us caught our creel limit of brown trout, and Andy and I each caught a nice brook trout as well, which we released. I had one hooked that was a real monster, but I lost him as I tried to net him. He really gave me a tussle too. I fought him for a good ten minutes before I got him to the net, only to have him spit the fly out at the last second. I swear he stuck his tongue out at me as he swam away. Stanley told me it was a Palomino Rainbow, a very rare albino trout that's not even native to Wyoming. Dang it, I wish I hadn't lost that one."

"Yes, I'm sure," I said with a smile. Stone's grin was so contagious, it was impossible not to flash one of my own. "But just think of 'the one that got away' fish story you can tell now."

"That's true, darling. And you can bet that Palomino Rainbow is going to increase in size with every telling of the story."

"If you are any kind of fisherman at all, that trout will weigh fifty pounds and have battled with you for three days by the time we return to Rockdale. By the way, why do your arms look so red and puffy?"

"Horseflies! Unrelenting horseflies the size of hummingbirds. We didn't see any rattlesnakes, but Stanley sure didn't exaggerate about the flies. I was afraid I'd need to go to the hospital for a blood transfusion before I caught my limit of trout. And I was lucky—you should see Wyatt. He was like a fly magnet out there. He was occasionally so covered with them it looked like he had on a long-sleeved black turtleneck sweater."

"Didn't you guys spray yourselves with some kind of repellent?" I asked.

"Yes, but I think the stuff Stanley sprayed on us was actually drawing them in from miles around. It was as if it contained some kind of catnip for horseflies that they couldn't resist. I'm not sure Stanley wasn't holding out on us, though. The flies didn't seem to bother him at all. I doubt he got bit twice all day. But other than the flies, the fishing trip couldn't have been any more fun."

"Oh, good," I said sincerely. "I'm so happy you guys

had such a fun day. Ours was nice too."

"How was your horse? I know you're a little uncomfortable around them."

"Buttercup was a sweetheart. She couldn't have been any gentler, and I felt very comfortable with her, or at least until she ran off and left me."

"Huh? What happened?"

"And then there was Veronica's fainting episode that had us scared half to death for a few minutes."

"Huh? What happened?" Stone repeated, with even more concern in his voice.

"Long story. Let's get some salve on your arms and then we'll talk over a cup of coffee. Wendy, Veronica and I decided to take the shuttle bus downtown to eat at a little Mexican restaurant that Emily recommended. Kylie Rue worked all day in the office, and since she has the evening off, we invited her to join us."

"It sounds like a plan to me," Stone said. "Now where's that salve you were talking about?"

"I'll try the enchiladas," I told our waiter, Todd. "And make them both cheese and onion, please."

"Anything to drink?" Todd asked.

"Decaf coffee, black, and a glass of water with lemon." With nothing on the agenda after supper, I could consume as much coffee as I wanted, as long as it was of the unleaded variety. After my lack of sleep the night before, I didn't need a caffeine overload keeping me awake all night tonight, as well. And after a full day in the saddle, I was almost too tired and weary to lift a fork to my mouth. Almost, but not quite.

Just relaxing over coffee and conversation with friends bolstered my energy, and snacking on the chips and salsa the waiter had brought to our table didn't hurt either. Whatever energy I'd acquired from our cowboy lunch had been spent before Buttercup had abandoned me and left me to fend off mountain lions and whiz kids on my own. I think I'd have fared better with a cougar than I had with Miss Smarty-pants. At least the big cat wouldn't insult me while it was tearing into me.

As the rest of my party was placing their orders, I glanced around the restaurant admiring the decor when I noticed a couple of ladies waving at me from across the room. The room was dimly lit, and my eyesight couldn't be trusted to tell the difference between a wild boar and a five-gallon bucket. I waved as if I knew for certain who I was waving at, and whispered to Wendy. "Are those the wanna-bes waving over there?"

Wendy looked up, and with a friendly wave, whispered back. "Mom, you shouldn't call them that, not even in jest. It tends to make you sound as insensitive as Fanny. But yes, it's Sarah and Norma in the flesh. Funny how they each believe the other could be a murderer, yet it doesn't stop them from sticking together like glue. I think if I seriously thought my dinner partner had recently electrocuted another colleague, I'd have begged off with other plans for the evening. Wouldn't you?"

"Yes. In fact, I'd already be in my RV, putting as many miles between us as I could. I probably should go speak to them, out of politeness, you know. And I promise I won't offend them in any way."

"Yeah, sure," Wendy replied. I could tell a wise-crack remark was on the tip of her tongue, begging to be verbalized. Instead, after a few moments of consideration, she said, "And I suppose it would seem rude of me not to join you in greeting them, too, after all the helpful advice Norma gave me about clipping coupons."

It occurred to me that Wendy was beginning to turn into her mother. It was an observation that, although amusing would have scared the living crap out of her if I'd mentioned it. Probably the only comment someone could make that would alarm her more was that she was beginning to look like me, too. *Egad*, I thought with a snicker.

We excused ourselves and walked over to greet the two authors, who seemed delighted to see us. I patted Sarah on the shoulder and asked, "What brings you two ladies out this evening?"

"Just treating ourselves to a night out," Norma replied. She and her dinner companion slid over on their bench seats to allow Wendy and me to sit down next to them. They'd just placed their orders as we had, and were sipping on glasses of iced tea.

"Same thing we're doing," Wendy said. "The three of us spent the day riding horses on a trail ride excursion on a ranch northwest of town, while our men spent the day fishing. We all needed to kick back and have a nice meal cooked and served to us tonight."

"I can imagine. It sounds like you all had a busy, fun-packed day," Norma said. "We've had a very quiet, relaxing day at the campground. Was your trail ride the same one Cassie Bumberdinger went on today?"

"Why, yes it was, as a matter of fact," I replied. Although her question took me off-guard, I knew they'd probably discussed various aspects of Fanny's personal life since they'd known her so well. And those discussions might have included any involvement she'd had with her husband's ex-wife, who claimed Fanny was the primary cause of the breakup of her and Avery's marriage. But to be privy to Cassie's daily agenda indicated they'd had a recent conversation with her, or with someone else who knew Cassie's plans. "Do you two know Cassie well?"

"No, not well," Sarah said. "She did call me a couple of months ago to inquire about the date of our book signing event here, for some reason. But we also know a lot about her from things Fanny mentioned regarding her husband's ex. We've always been amazed Avery dumped her for someone like Fanny Finch, but we ran into her in the office this evening and exchanged some small talk with her. She was having a discussion with that young blonde who works at the campground about the possibility of getting a refund if she left a couple of days early."

"She was speaking with Kylie Rue?" I asked Sarah, more to keep her talking than anything else, since Kylie was the only young blonde currently working at Cozy Camping.

"Yes, I believe that's her name. Oh, in fact, that's her over there at your table," she said as she pointed.

"Yes, she had the evening off and we invited her to join us," I replied.

"Anyway, since we were there to ask the same question, we were interested in listening to Kylie's response. She said, that according to the park's policy, during Frontier Days every customer is responsible for the days they reserved, so no refund was in order. So, as the three of us left the office, we were discussing amongst ourselves the unfairness of that policy. One thing led to another and Cassie mentioned that following the trail ride they'd participated in today, they'd accomplished all they'd planned to do in Cheyenne. She said they were ready to head home."

"It makes sense that she'd be ready to leave early," I said. In loyalty to my friends, Stanley and Emily, I added, "But I can see the reason behind that policy.

Everyone would book the entire week and then take advantage of the Harrington's leniency and decide to cut their stay short at the last minute. It would be a scheduling nightmare for the owners, not to mention a costly and not very smart business practice. Those sites would stay open, when they could have been reserved by others who'd been turned away due to the park being fully booked."

"Yeah, whatever," Sarah replied, in obvious disagreement. "In my opinion—"

"So, ladies," Wendy interrupted Sarah in mid-sentence. She had been nodding throughout my comments in defense of the Harringtons' cancellation policy. Sensing an argument brewing, she quickly changed the subject back to the two authors. "Why were you two wanting to cut your stay short and leave before your original day of departure? Aren't you enjoying all the festivities going on in Cheyenne this week?"

The expression of indignation faded from Sarah's face, and both ladies perked up at the opportunity to talk about themselves. Norma, who'd been relatively quiet, spoke up first.

"Yes, our time here's been very pleasant, and we're looking forward to the Thunderbirds' air show tomorrow morning, but our funds are running short. Eating out tonight was the one extravagance we've allowed ourselves all week."

"What about the money you made selling your books at the bookstore on Saturday?" Wendy asked.

Both authors laughed at the question. It was Sarah who replied. "You've got to be kidding. For us, book signings are a deductible business expense, not a profitable undertaking. Including the books your mother bought, we each sold a grand total of two copies each. That's hardly a windfall, by any stretch of the imagination. Our profits on the sale of two books didn't even cover the sandwiches we had for lunch that day, much less any travel expenses we've incurred. A lot of people assume that any author who gets a book published is rewarded with a lot of money in royalties. But the truth is that very, very few books ever turn a profit, and even fewer authors make a significant amount of money from one they've written. Fanny was a rare exception, and then only because of the curiosity aspect of her book and the popularity of her subject. It's the exact same kind of crap that sells those gossip magazines you find on racks at nearly every check-out stand these days."

I don't know what it was about Sarah's attitude that made me feel obliged to speak in defense of Fanny, who was an egomaniac I had disliked from the second I'd first laid eyes on her. But I found myself doing it anyway. "I'm sure Ms. Finch's writing skills paid a role in her success, as well."

Both ladies looked at me as if I'd just said the reason *Fame and Shame* had become a *New York Times* best-seller was because the world was flat, and that both Fanny and I sacked up kittens and threw them in the river for our own amusement.

"Are you nuts, Ms. Starr? Fanny Finch's, or, rather, Claudia Bumberdinger's, success is in no way the result of her writing skills. Norma and I exhibit more impressive writing skills while making out our grocery lists. It was fortunate for Fanny that a good editor could mask the fact she thrived on butchering the English language. That woman could dangle participles with incredible regularity, almost as if she were trying to prove she could dangle anything she darned well pleased, whenever she darned well felt like it. Her grammar was absolutely atrocious."

"Well, Sarah, you two are in a better position to

judge her writing prowess than I am. I've no doubt I dangle participles at every opportunity myself, with little regard for my lack of grammar skills. I've even been known to throw around a double negative or two, and you'd be appalled at how often I erroneously end a sentence with a preposition. But I understand where you two, as master wordsmiths, would be able to detect all of Fanny's writing inadequacies with no trouble at all."

I flinched as I felt the tip of my daughter's left boot make contact with my shin under the table. She was reacting to my deliberately stinging remarks, which, as far as Sarah and Norma were concerned, fell on deaf ears, or were just not blatant enough. They both beamed as if I'd just offered up a highly flattering compliment and they were basking in their glory. I found their attitudes almost nauseating.

Before her insensitive and offensive mother could embarrass her by making another inappropriate remark, Wendy said, "We better get back to our table. I think I just saw our waiter carrying the taco salad I ordered. It's been nice chatting with you ladies. I hope your supper is delicious and the remainder of your stay in Cheyenne is pleasant, as well."

"Thank you," the ladies said in unison. As we got up to leave, Norma asked a question that made me sit back down instantly.

"Do you know if Cassie has been cleared as a suspect in Fanny's murder?"

"I don't know, Norma," I said, with renewed interest in the conversation. "Why do you ask?"

"It seems to me she has a strong motive, and it's obvious she despised the woman who broke up her marriage. When I asked her earlier if she was at the campground when Fanny's body was discovered, she said she'd taken a sleeping pill the night before and was practically unconscious until ten that morning. She'd heard about the murder from a couple in the fifth wheel next to her later in the day."

"And you think that somehow makes her a likely suspect as the killer?" I asked.

"Not that in itself, of course. It was her next remark that makes her a likely suspect, in my opinion anyway."

"And what remark was that, Norma?"

"She said the sleeping pill she took is known to make people do things during the night that they have no recollection of the next day, such as sleep-eat, or sleep-drive. Then she laughed, and said, 'Gee, I wonder if the pill turned me into a sleep-killer?' Cassie said it as a joke, but I'm not sure it was one, because before she walked away she laughed again and said, 'Doesn't really matter, though, because either way, she's dead.'"

We returned to our table where the three men, along with Veronica and Kylie, were all laughing at something Wyatt had just teased his girlfriend about. Veronica was playfully punching Wyatt in his upper arm as Wendy and I sat back down in our seats.

I didn't see a waiter carrying a taco salad over to the table and realized Wendy had used that as an excuse to drag me away from Sarah and Norma's table. She often said I could be relentless when I was determined to make a point, or pry information out of people not willing to spill their guts on their own. I couldn't argue with Wendy's assessment of me, nor could I change my inborn nature and morph into a milquetoast, either.

From the gist of the next few comments in their conversation, they'd also been discussing the murder of Fanny Finch. Veronica, who was an accomplished cook, as any partner of Wyatt's would need to be, poked fun at herself by saying, "I can guarantee you, the last two things I'd be apt to sacrifice by throwing them into a pool to electrocute someone, would be my hair dryer and my electric skillet."

"I can vouch for that," Wyatt said.

Kylie cut in with a remark of her own. "As a cooking catastrophe waiting to happen, I'd gladly toss any cooking apparatus I owned in the pool, but the hair dryers I used as a licensed cosmetologist cost too much to deliberately destroy."

Not surprisingly, as everyone was laughing, they all turned to look at me. I knew what they were thinking, so I spoke for the whole group when I said, "I can certainly relate to your cooking catastrophe comment, Kylie. I once came close to burning down the Alexandria Inn with an over-nuked potato."[9]

"And she nearly killed both of us, along with her new boss at the library, with a bacteria-laden under-baked chicken,"[10] Stone added, for Kylie's benefit, who was the only one at the table unaware of some of my finer moments in the kitchen.

The restaurant was packed, and service was slow as a result. But, kicking back, sipping on our beverages, and enjoying the camaraderie of friends, no one seemed to mind the long wait. Even Wyatt seemed content with just digging into the bowls of tortilla chips and salsa the waiter had just refilled for the second time.

To everyone's amusement, Kylie told a few stories about her own cooking mishaps, including the disastrous first meal she'd cooked to impress her latest

---

[9] *The Spirit of the Season (A Lexie Starr Mystery, Holiday Novella*
[10] *Just Ducky (A Lexie Starr Mystery, Book 5)*

ex-boyfriend. She explained to us she'd roasted a small turkey with the bag of giblets still inside the bird and served it with a broccoli-rice casserole she'd made with regular rice instead of the minute rice the recipe had called for. She hadn't realized the rice would still be hard as tiny bricks when eaten. To make matters worse, she'd deep-fried some hush puppies in peanut oil, unaware of her boyfriend's nut allergy, and they spent the remainder of the night in the emergency room as he was being treated for anaphylactic shock.

"Can you believe that after I spent three hours with him at the hospital, the ungrateful jerk never asked me out for a second date?" Kylie asked with an exaggerated pout. After the laughter died down, she continued. "I'm just kidding. Jason and I actually dated for several more months, even though my mom and dad couldn't stand the sight of him. And they were right, of course. He turned out to be as worthless as they'd warned me he was. It was probably the only time I ever showed any kind of rebellion against them, because they couldn't have been any more loving or supportive than if they'd been my biological parents."

"It sounds to me like you were one lucky girl," Stone said. "I think I speak for all of us in saying I think they were lucky to have you in their lives, as well."

"Thanks," the smiling young lady replied.

"Do you have any kind of relationship with your biological parents?" I asked.

"No, but I hope to have one with my real father, whose identity I have only just recently been able to discover. My biological mother was sixteen when she gave birth to me, and shortly thereafter died from a complication resulting from my birth. I was immediately put up for adoption by my father. I don't hold that decision against him because I'm sure he realized I'd have a better life with more mature, and financially sound, adopted parents."

I thought her father made the right decision and that it was quite a sacrifice for the sake of his newborn child, and I said as much to Kylie. "Have you ever met him?"

"No, but I would have thanked him had I had the opportunity to meet him. I'd always assumed my mother just didn't want to be tied down with a kid to take care of when she was really still a kid herself. Unfortunately, in my research, I discovered she'd died of a rare complication immediately following my birth. That's something that's weighed heavy on my mind. But it was that knowledge that made me step up my attempts to locate my father. With the help of my adoptive parents—I call them Mom and Dad—we were finally able to get a lucky break and locate my biological mother's mother, and learn the identity of my father. I have recently met my maternal grandmother, who still lives in Nashville where I was born, and we are getting to know each other now."

I was going to ask her about her father's identity, but decided she'd tell us more about him if she wanted to. As it was, our waiter approached our table with an armful of plates at that moment, and the conversation quickly changed to whose plate was whose.

I was happy to see Veronica order a beef burrito with beans and rice on the side, a meal that might seem average for most folks, but for Veronica it was akin to a Thanksgiving feast. I was happier still to watch her finish off everything on her plate except for half the serving of beans, which, if they affected her like they occasionally did me, might have been in order to limit the potential of gassing her boyfriend out of the motorhome later on that evening.

When Veronica caught me gazing at her, she flashed

me a shy, somewhat timid, smile, and I responded with a warm smile of my own. I wanted to convey to her that I was proud of the effort she was making. I had no unrealistic illusions that conquering her demons would be easy, or without setbacks.

The cheese enchiladas I'd ordered were either the best I'd ever tasted, or I was so hungry I could have eaten under-cooked Rocky Mountain oysters and been just as satisfied. With a full belly, a body as limp as a rag doll, and the rhythmic jostling of the vehicle on our ride back to Cozy Camping RV Park, it was all I could do to keep my eyes open. I knew I'd be as unconscious as Veronica had been earlier that afternoon within minutes of our return to the motorhome. I was sure I'd sleep soundly that night, and even if I were hooked to an intravenous caffeine drip, I could not have stayed awake for long.

CHAPTER 15

As I knew would be the case, I was so zonked all night that a super-sonic jet, breaking the speed of sound fifty feet above our RV could not have awakened me. When I opened my eyes at ten minutes to eight, I saw Stone waving a cup of coffee back and forth underneath my nose.

"Good morning, my little chickadee," Stone said good-naturedly. "I tried shaking you, turning the TV up to a deafening level, and every other thing I could think of short of slapping you awake, and nothing seemed to faze you. So, to wake you up I had to resort to a no-fail method, at least as far as you're concerned."

I guess even though coffee—even massive amounts of it—rarely ever kept me awake, the smell of it could wake me from the nearly dead when nothing else did the trick. Frying bacon was my go-to method when trying to get Stone out of bed. I smiled up at him and said, "Good morning, honey."

"I thought you should get up if we're going to catch the shuttle bus down to the fairgrounds for the Thunderbirds' performance at ten," Stone said, as he lovingly ran his hand up and down my left leg, which was sticking out from under the covers. "You still want to go, don't you?"

"Yes, of course. I heard the annual air show was really awesome."

"Good," he replied. "Why don't you grab a shower while I make the bed and prepare us something for breakfast? I make a mean omelet, you know. How does that sound this morning?"

"Delicious," I replied. "I think I'll go to the shower house this morning, rather than squeeze into the tiny shower in this rig. I'll make it quick and be banging my silverware on the table in twenty minutes."

Fifteen minutes later, as I was standing at one of the lavatory sinks in the shower house, brushing my teeth and running a comb through my damp hair, an older lady using the basin next to me asked, "Say, aren't you the one who found that author lady dead earlier this week? My husband and I hurried up to the pool area when we heard a gentleman in the trailer next to us hollering to another camper that someone had drowned."

"Yes, my daughter and I had gone up there for an early morning swim and were horrified to discover her body on the bottom of the pool."

"I thought dead bodies floated." The sixty-some year-old lady exclaimed.

"They do—eventually—but not until after the body has bloated with gas, or so my daughter explained. She's an assistant coroner back home. It hadn't been long enough for the body to rise to the surface, Wendy told me."

"Oh, that's interesting. I'm Rapella, by the way."

"I'm Lexie Starr and I'm happy to meet you, Rapella. My husband, Stone, and I are out here on vacation, celebrating our first anniversary. This is our first experience in an RV."

"It's an interesting lifestyle," Rapella said. "My husband and I are full-timers. We've traveled all over in our thirty-foot trailer and have stayed in RV Parks in nearly every state in the union, but we've never seen anything like this before. We did see an old fart choke to death on a bone from one of the chicken wings he was shoving in his mouth like nobody's business, and we've seen a couple elderly RVers keel over when their tickers shot craps. We've never seen one get their ticker stopped for them like this poor unlucky sucker did, though."

"Yes, it was shocking, wasn't it? Especially to my daughter and me, as you can imagine," I said. I was wishing Wendy were with me right then so she could hear what "insensitive" and "offensive" really sounded like.

"Oh, my goodness. I'm sure it was an unbelievable sight. Congratulations to you both on your first anniversary. Rip and I have been hitched for almost fifty years. Tied the knot when we were both just eighteen and right out of high school. Reason be, I got knocked up and my pappy would've tarred and feathered old Rip if he hadn't put a ring on my finger," she explained with a cackle. "My husband has always gone by Rip because his last name was Ripple, and he hated his given name of Clyde. After we got married, everyone started referring to me as Rap, and we were collectively called Rip and Rap. The nickname stuck, but to his dying day my pappy called us Riff and Raff, grudgingly at first, but with affection later on."

"Sounds like your pappy was a real pistol," I said.

"That he was. I was wondering if you heard if that woman's killer has been arrested. We've heard nothing about it since they hauled her carcass off in a body bag."

I tried not to laugh at the this lady's callous but amusing way of turning a phrase before responding in the negative. "No, as far as I'm aware, the murder's still under investigation and the killer is still on the loose. My daughter and I have actually been kind of meddling into the case a bit ourselves, but without much success so far. Our interest, of course, stems from the fact we feel personally involved, having discovered her body."

"I'd feel exactly the same way, Lexie. You and your hubby need to stop by and meet my old man when you get a chance. Rip and I are in the site directly across from the office, under that big oak tree."

"Do you mean that chartreuse-colored travel trailer with the yellow sunflowers painted all over it?" I asked, amazed. We'd all shaken our heads in disbelief every time we passed the outlandishly-painted rig as we pulled into the RV park. At her enthusiastic nod, I replied, "That's quite a cheerful-looking trailer, Rapella."

"Yes, it is, isn't it? We got bored one weekend and decided to spruce the old thing up a bit."

"Well, I must say, you accomplished your goal. I'm originally from the 'Sunflower State' of Kansas. You'd fit right in there. Now we live right over the Kansas border in Rockdale, Missouri, where we own and operate a bed and breakfast in a refurbished turn-of-the-century Victorian mansion called Alexandria Inn."

"I believe Emily has mentioned your name on several occasions. She told me she and Stanley stayed with you around the holidays last winter. Sounds to me like you're a real sparkplug with a lot of spirit, which I find to be a breath of fresh air. We'll have to stop by there some day when we're passing through the Midwest. We've been to both states numerous times. Rip and I spent several summers working and staying at a park in the Ozarks. Believe it or not, we fit right in with them toothless boot-legging hillbillies 'round there," Rapella said, with a deadpan expression.

"We would love to have you stop and visit us at the inn. We're located not too far north of I-70. Is this your first time to come to Cheyenne Frontier Days?"

"Oh, no. We're here nearly every year at this time. Emily Harrington is my cousin on my mother's side, so we're always able to snag one of the premium sites. And my cousin gives us a sizeable discount—as in we pay zip for our site—and Rip and I clean the two shower houses every morning in exchange. In fact, Rip and I work as what's called 'workampers' at RV parks all across the country. Campground owners advertise for helpers like us in a 'Workamping' magazine and online site. It works well for us and allows us to travel and live cheaply."

"Emily told us about hiring workampers. It seems like a win-win situation for both the RVers and the RV Park owners. Sounds like a fun lifestyle too! As first-timers, we're really enjoying ourselves," I said sincerely.

"We've always loved it, too. We usually go south when it's cold and north when it's hot, kinda like a pair of monogamous snow geese. Just like Rip and me, they mate for life. Only in Rip's and my case, it's because no one else would have us," Rapella's laugh, complete with a couple of spontaneous snorts, was infectious. I could tell humor was an important aspect of her personality, and I adored that in a person. Suddenly she realized she'd gotten off our original topic of discussion. Her expression turned serious again as she asked, "Just curious, but had you met the stiff before her death?"

After blanching a bit at her rather crudely asked question, I briefly told Rapella about my impression of the self-centered, overbearing woman, and about her unsanctioned tell-all biography of the popular singer. She asked me a few questions and I responded with what little knowledge I had about the case. "My daughter and I are planning to visit the police station today, just to pass on what little information we've been able to garner."

"Good for you! It's been a pleasure to meet you, Lexie. If you hear anything, or make some kind of breakthrough yourself, will you stop by and tell Rip and me about it? We're in our late sixties and have nothing better to do than stick our noses in other people's business." Rapella laughed, as did I, since I could strongly relate to her last comment. "I'd like to meet that new hubby of yours, and introduce you to my old one."

Rapella Ripple was immensely charming and I would have liked to talk to her longer, but I suspected I had an omelet growing cold in the motorhome. "I promise I'll let you know if anything interesting develops. I've been known to occasionally stick my nose where it doesn't belong, too. It was nice meeting you too, Rapella. I'll try to make sure we hook up again before we head home."

An hour later, the six of us were walking through the turnstiles at the entrance to the fairgrounds. The air show could be seen from nearly anywhere in town, but we decided to view it from the fairgrounds. It was a stop on the shuttle bus schedule, and we could walk around and look at what the various vendors had to offer.

I still wanted to pick out a souvenir to take home to my best friend, Sheila Davidson, and I knew Wendy and Veronica hoped to find souvenirs of our trip to take back home to a couple of their friends, as well. Stone, Andy, and Wyatt probably had their hearts set on another loaded chili dog.

At exactly ten o'clock, a squadron of six jets flew in formation over our heads to signal the beginning of the air show. After discovering the U.S. Air Force Thunderbirds performance had been an annual part of the Cheyenne Frontier Days festivities, I'd googled them on the Internet to do a little research before leaving on vacation.

I found out that the Thunderbirds were based out of Nellis AFB in Nevada, and the F-16Cs they piloted were called Fighting Falcons. The pilots were an elite group, and would be flying at speeds approaching seven hundred miles an hour during their display of amazing maneuvers. More astounding was the fact they'd begun performing during Cheyenne Frontier Days in 1953, a few years before I was born. I shared this information with the rest of the group.

We all stood in a state of awe with our necks craned back to look at the sky, watching the highly skilled pilots maneuver their powerful jets with incredible precision. Just the sound of their engines was thrilling to me. I could not imagine the total concentration the pilots must possess in order to execute such dangerous stunts, which allowed for no margin of error. Their very lives hung in the balance with each stunt they performed for the enjoyment of the crowd. I, for one, appreciated their bravery and the untold hours of practice they'd endured to earn the prestige of becoming a Thunderbird pilot.

Stone was as impressed as I. I heard him speak to Wyatt in a low voice during a lull in the action. "Talk about having balls of steel."

Being the gentleman that he is, Stone then turned to

me, and said, "That would take way more courage than I could ever muster up."

"You and me, both," I replied.

Stone must have been doing more extensive research about the Thunderbirds on his iPad than I had. He informed our group that the formation they'd just completed was called the *Five Card*, and any time now, they'd be performing their signature *Bomb Burst* maneuver, which was usually toward the end of their routine. It involved four jets going straight up from the *Diamond* position and breaking off into separate directions, while a solo F-16 goes straight up between them and executes aileron rolls until they're three miles above the ground, concluding with all six aircraft rejoining in a formation called the *Delta*.

One of the first things that had attracted me to my husband was his ability to retain a lot of facts and figures about a vast number of subjects. As always, I was impressed with the information about the Thunderbirds he was sharing with us that morning, even though he'd lost me at *Five Card*. I'd been proud of myself just to remember what state they were based in, and that I hadn't mistakenly referred to them as the Blue Angels, the Navy's aerobatic flying team.

When the show ended, we clapped and cheered along with the rest of the observers. We all decided to walk around for a while, visiting various booths and vendor stands before grabbing a bite to eat for lunch. My legs were still stiff from the trail ride, and all the walking helped loosen them up.

Following lunch, we'd catch the shuttle home. Stone had acquired six tickets to the concert that evening through Emily Harrington when he made our reservations. We decided to kick back and rest during the afternoon before heading back out to the fairgrounds and arena where the nightly concerts were held. I was thankful to discover we'd be sitting in seats up in the stands, with the "normal" people, and not relegated to the crazed throng of screaming fans in the standing-room-only section.

Even though finding a restroom from that vantage point would surely be easier, I vowed to myself not to have a sip of any beverage after lunch. I didn't want an encore performance during the concert that evening. For one thing, the performer was one of my all-time favorites, and I didn't want to miss a single song.

After the men branched off to look at some handcrafted knives at a display they'd heard about on the opposite side of the vendor area, we gals walked over to the Indian Village area reserved for Native American artwork and crafts. I found a leather belt with silver studs and stitching that I knew Sheila would love. Wendy bought some jewelry for herself and her friends. Veronica spent an inordinate amount of her own money on a warm Indian blanket for her beloved "grammy" and a leather jacket for Wyatt, with which he was enthralled when she gave it to him a few minutes later after we'd met back up with our men. He and Veronica returned to the Indian Village for a short spell while the rest of us sat on a bench and did some people-watching, which was entertaining in itself.

When the love struck couple returned from the Indian Village, Veronica showed off an elaborate, and shockingly expensive, Navajo squash blossom turquoise and coral necklace that she had admired earlier. Wyatt had been delighted to return to the Indian Village and purchase it for her.

It occurred to me then that there'd likely be two upcoming weddings I'd want to look my best for in the near future. I would use that as incentive to step up the after-supper walks that Stone and I tried to fit in our schedule. We normally walked a two-mile route, but increasing it to a three-mile route wasn't beyond our capabilities.

I had muscles that needed firming and toning before they turned into the consistency of Jell-O, and not necessarily that of Jell-O that had set up yet. I could squat down for the length of time it took me to dust the lower shelves of the four bookcases in the little library at Alexandria Inn, and then would have to pop an Ibuprofen or two the next morning just to climb down the stairs to the ground floor without groaning in pain from the soreness in my thigh muscles.

I could count on one hand the number of dated, but tasteful, dresses in my closet. All were currently a size too small, like the jeans I'd worn on the trail ride the previous day. I was sure I'd feel compelled to buy a more stylish outfit for each wedding, but it would still be comforting to know I could choose to wear one of the dresses I already owned if I wanted to. Dresses which, quite frankly, neither Stone nor Wendy would be likely to allow me to wear to Pete's Pantry to pick up a loaf of bread, much less to a wedding ceremony as the mother of the bride.

I always hated the pressure of having to find the perfect outfit. I could walk into my favorite women's clothing store with a three-hundred-dollar gift card and be unable to find one article of clothing I liked. But if I walked into that same store with less than five bucks in my pocket, I'd find dozens of items I couldn't live without. I'm sure it was a psychological thing, but I found it to be a remarkable phenomenon.

After we'd finished our shopping and polished off our various carnival-food lunches, we decided to walk around the perimeter of the park on our return to the shuttle bus waiting area. Wendy and I had decided to see if we could take Emily's car to the police station while the rest of the group chilled out in the campground that afternoon to re-energize and refresh for the concert that night. I was going over in my mind what I wanted to say to the detectives or chief of police if we were allowed to speak to him, when Veronica said, "Hey, isn't that Kylie Rue over there walking into that fancy big bus?"

We all looked in the direction she was pointing and saw Kylie walking up to the bus in question, which was parked in a roped-off exclusive section of a big open area behind the fairgrounds. It took me awhile to recognize her, as I really did need an updated eye examination, but I recognized the custom-painted Prevost coach immediately. As the only one out of the six of us to have seen the exterior of his Class A motorhome, I quickly pointed out that the coach belonged to Vex Vaughn. It was definitely the one in which I'd utilized the bathroom facilities Monday evening after the concert.

We all watched silently as Kylie walked up and knocked on the door of Vaughn's bus. After speaking with the entertainer briefly, and exchanging a lengthy embrace, she was led into the Prevost with his arm around her shoulder.

"What's that all about?" Andy asked.

"I don't know," I replied. "But Kylie did mention recently finding her biological father last night, even though she didn't offer up his name, or anything. Could there possibly be a connection there?"

"The age difference fits," Wendy said.

"I think there's a facial resemblance too," Stone agreed. "They both have the high cheek bones—"

"And blue eyes," Veronica added.

"The hair color is a lot different," Wyatt said. "But if Kylie's anything like Veronica, she hasn't worn her natural hair color since she turned eighteen."

"I'm pretty certain Kylie's a natural blonde," I said. "But, now that I think about my interaction with Vex in that bus, they do have some of the same mannerisms. But if he is her biological father, why wouldn't she have mentioned it to us? She told us she was going to his concert, but never showed any indication of her connection to him. I find that odd."

"Me, too," Wendy said. "I wonder why she'd want to keep something like that to herself. If it were me, I'd post it on Facebook for everyone I know to see, although I'm sure there's any number of reasons she might want to keep their relationship private."

Everyone nodded in agreement, and we continued on our way to catch the shuttle bus, scheduled to arrive in less than fifteen minutes. As we walked, I couldn't help but mull over the possibilities regarding Kylie's connection to the popular country and western singer. I knew she could be doing it to protect his privacy. After all, with the release of *Fame and Shame*, Vaughn was already a prime target of the paparazzi and gossip magazines. Still, there was a thought in the back of my mind that there might be a remotely sinister reason Kylie was keeping their connection to herself. I didn't want to even entertain the idea that Kylie could be involved in anything as horrible as murdering someone in order to exact revenge on them. I tried to push the notion away, but it kept coming back like a stray cat you'd put milk out for.

CHAPTER 16

About an hour later, Stone was snoring loudly as he napped in the recliner of our rental motorhome. I sat at the dinette table, engrossed in a cozy mystery on my Kindle and snacking on a pack of chocolate-covered pretzels. A soft rap on the door broke my concentration just as I was about to find out who the killer was.

I let Wendy inside, put my finger up against my lips, and pointed to Stone. Wendy nodded and whispered, "Are you sure Stone doesn't have sleep apnea? I could hear him sawing logs from the other side of the Bumberdinger's fifth wheel."

"He told me he'd been tested for it and was assured he didn't need a C-Pap machine."

"Yes, Mom, but he also told you he was allergic to pet dander when you wanted to bring home a couple of kittens. Andy told me Stone's first wife had cats before she died, and he'd never reacted adversely to any of them. He said Stone just wasn't a 'cat' person, and didn't like litter boxes in the house."

"And I can understand his aversion to them," I whispered back in his defense.

"My point being," Wendy continued, "you're not the only one allowed a little white lie on occasion when you feel it's necessary. A lot of people don't fancy the idea of having to sleep with a mask on, but like them, Stone would adjust to it after a while. Sleep apnea can be fatal, you know. That's what killed Reggie White, the NFL Hall of Fame football player."

"Jeez, I didn't know that. Okay, I'll talk to Stone about it again. Are you ready to go to the police station if we can borrow Emily's car?"

"Yes, like his uncle, Andy is asleep in the recliner, so it's a good time to sneak off. I left him a note on the table that just said you and I went into town for an hour or so to look around."

I left a note similar to Wendy's on the table for Stone, and we began walking up to the office to speak to Emily. Before we could walk twenty feet, we were stopped by Avery Bumberdinger.

"Good afternoon, ladies," he said.

"Good afternoon," Wendy and I replied in unison.

"How are you doing, Avery?" I asked.

"As you can imagine, I'm still in a state of shock. I feel totally lost without Claudia."

"Claudia?" I heard Wendy ask.

"That was Mrs. Bumberdinger's real name," I explained. "Fanny Finch was her nom de plume. As a writer, she thought her pen name sounded more suitable than Claudia Bumberdinger. I guess I forgot to tell you she used a pseudonym for her writing."

"Yes, she's right, dear," Avery said to Wendy. "Her maiden name was Vandersnoozeski and—"

"Enough said," Wendy responded with a grin. "If I had to pick between Claudia Vandersnoozeski and Claudia Bumberdinger, I think I'd choose Fanny Finch, too. I doubt it's a good idea for any author to have the word 'snooze' on the cover of their novels."

We all laughed at her remark, even Avery, who'd looked quite despondent when we'd first seen him sitting in his lawn chair on the concrete patio outside his fifth wheel.

"How long will you be staying in Cheyenne, sir?" Wendy asked. The respect she showed her elders, aside from me of course, was something I'd instilled in her at an early age. I was happy to see she still maintained that courtesy.

"While the investigation into Fanny's death is going on, her body is being held at the morgue here. I don't know how long it will be, but I'm staying here for as long as it takes. We had our ups and downs, and occasionally a real dustup, but I cared for Claudia, and I'm not leaving without her. I'll go home when I can take her with me." His expression had returned to one of deep sorrow. We'd witnessed one of the couple's "dustups" the night of our arrival, but even if he and his wife didn't always see eye-to-eye, I couldn't picture this soft-spoken man harming her in any way. Like my husband of one year, Avery seemed to have a very gentle nature.

"And where's home?" Wendy asked him.

"Spring City, Tennessee. I want to bury her next to her mother in the cemetery there."

"And do your kids live there too?"

"No, but reasonably close. Only about five miles away, actually."

"What an odd coincidence that they're here in the same campground as you this week. Don't you think?" Wendy would make a good investigator, I realized, as she asked him questions that hadn't even occurred to me. It was a reminder of how nice it was to have her on board during this current meddling episode.

Avery shook his head, and said, "No coincidence. When Chace found out his stepmother had a book signing here this week, he talked my ex-wife into coming here to go on a trail ride they'd wanted to go on one day soon, anyway. Cassie arranged to stay in this RV Park so I'd get a chance to spend some quality time with my kids—Chace in particular, who has taken my absence hard. I don't get to see them very often, you see."

Wendy had a puzzled expression on her face, as she asked, "Didn't you just say they lived only about five miles from you? Seems to me you'd see them pretty regularly."

"Claudia's schedule has kept us pretty busy. We'd been crisscrossing the country on her book-signing tour since right after we got married, which was about eight months ago. But I was able to spend yesterday with my kids, taking carnival rides down at the fairgrounds, and I'd gotten tickets for us all to go to the daily rodeo, as well. Both my children have aspirations about participating in rodeo competitions in the future, so I knew they'd enjoy our day together."

Wendy's puzzled expression returned, as she said, "Yesterday was the trail ride at Rolling Creek Ranch. Cassie, Brandi and Chace all spent the day with us northwest of town."

"Oh, dear," Avery said, with a shake of his head. "You're absolutely right, pretty lady! It was Monday that we spent the day together. Yesterday I spent a great deal of the day at the Cheyenne Police Station, answering questions and all. I guess my memory's not what it used to be."

"Neither is mine, Avery," I said. "By suppertime tonight, I'm apt to forget we even went to watch the Thunderbirds perform this morning. It's a small wonder you don't have to re-introduce yourself every time our paths cross. Well, Wendy, we need to get up to the office. And Avery, I hope a perpetrator is arrested soon so you'll be able to take your wife home to Tennessee."

"Thank you."

Even though it was none of my business, I was curious about something Cassie had mentioned to Wendy that I knew my daughter was too respectful to ask about. She'd paid close attention when I'd been teaching her how to treat her elders, which was more respect than I often showed my own elders. I knew there were exceptions to every rule, and I repeated that to myself twice before asking Avery, "What is going to happen to the Vandersnoozeski Waste Management Company now?"

Avery showed no reaction to my question, nor did he seem surprised I knew about Fanny's interest in the company. He didn't even seem annoyed that I'd inquired about its fate. "It will pass into the hands of Claudia's nephew, as stated in my wife's last will and testament. And thank God for small favors, because I wanted no part of that cesspool of lawsuits and personnel problems. That's why I insisted on signing a pre-nup before we got married. In the event something like this were to happen, I didn't want that nightmare dropped in my lap. Just last month an employee was backed over by a trash truck, and now, as a paraplegic, he's suing for ten million in restitution. I feel he deserves every penny of it, but I don't need that kind of stress in my life."

"I don't blame you, Avery. Life's too short to be burdened with something you had no interest in to begin with. Well, have a nice day. Wendy and I need to get going, but it was nice to see you," I said.

"It was nice to talk with you ladies, too."

As we continued our walk to the office, Wendy asked, "It doesn't look as if Avery had any designs on getting his hands on Fanny's money. But doesn't it seem odd to you that he couldn't remember which day he spent with his children?"

"Yes and no. It seems to me if you're under as much stress as he's under, your days truly might all run together. And, I know from experience, our memories start to get a little fuzzy after we hit that half-century mark. But what really seems more suspicious to me is that Kylie told me that Emily told her that Cassie told the—"

"Whoa." Wendy stopped me mid-sentence. "How many degrees of separation is this hearsay going to be?"

"Okay, then let me rephrase it. According to a reliable source, Cassie *supposedly* told the detectives that she had no idea her ex and his new wife were going to be in Cheyenne this week. And Avery just told us he and Cassie worked the logistics out together specifically to give him and their children some time to spend together."

"Then one of them is lying, huh?"

"It seems so," I said. "I'm beginning to think there's a fox in the chicken coop as far as those two are concerned. But I'm leaning toward Cassie rather than Avery as being the sly predator in this instance."

"Me too," Wendy replied in agreement.

As it turned out, there were four of us paying a visit to the police station. Emily thought her presence would give us more credence, since the incident took place on her property, and she was a citizen of Cheyenne. Her cousin, Rapella Ripple, whom I'd met earlier that day in the shower house, had developed an interest in the case after conversing with me and asked if she could accompany us. I'd been enchanted with her at our first meeting and was delighted to have her along.

We walked as a group into the police station at two fifteen and approached a woman sitting behind a desk. There was a banner behind her that read, "Protecting the Legend." When I asked the receptionist if we could speak with the detective in charge of the Fanny Finch murder investigation, she looked at me as if I'd asked to pop in on the Pope. "I assume you have an appointment, ma'am?"

"No. I'm afraid we don't. But we have some information we'd like to share with him, or someone else assigned to the case, that might be of some benefit in apprehending the perpetrator. We only need a few minutes of his time."

"Are any of you a member of law enforcement?"

"No. I own and operate a bed and breakfast in Rockdale, Missouri," I replied. As far as having credentials to be involved in a murder case, it sounded lame to even me as I said it. I didn't think "assistant librarian" would impress the receptionist much, either.

"I see." The expression on the woman's face told me she thought I had as much business bringing "beneficial information" about a murder case to the detectives as I had trying to stay atop a raging bull for eight seconds at the rodeo event that afternoon. She sighed and asked, "Well, in that case, are you a member of the deceased's family?"

"No, but I was somewhat familiar with the victim."

"I'm sorry, ma'am," she replied, obviously having lost her patience with me. "The investigating team doesn't have the time or resources to chase down every tip and random theory suggested by citizens with no law enforcement affiliation, or at least some form of connection to the case."

"My daughter, Wendy—who is an assistant coroner back home in Missouri—and I were the two who discovered her body, which gives us a connection to the case," I said to the snooty receptionist with a heavy dose of resentment in my voice.

As she was pondering the validity of my statement, two police officers walked out of what appeared to be a break room. Rapella, bless her heart, said, "Hey, officers, these two women here have vital information about the murder that just occurred in this other lady's RV Park. Which detective in your department do they need to talk to about it?"

When both men turned to look at the receptionist, as if to determine who was responsible for letting four ditsy nutcases into the building, she shrugged and shook her head. I wasn't certain if the information I had to pass on to the detectives would be considered vital or not. But I had to admire Rapella's spunk in taking the bull by the horns and out of the hands of the receptionist, who was about to send us on our way without giving us an opportunity to speak with anyone, even the janitor mopping the entryway.

The older of the two officers said, "The lead investigator assigned to that case is out interviewing suspects at the moment."

I was itching to ask who he was interviewing, but knew my question would go unanswered. Detectives weren't keen on offering up information regarding a crime to just any bed and breakfast owner or library assistant who walked in with inquiries, which I found very rude.

"Do you know when he'll return?" I asked instead.

"No, but if you want to step into the C.I.D. room for a few minutes, Detective Harrison can take the information from you and hand it over to Detective Colmer when he gets back."

"The C.I.D. room?" I asked, as the four of us were ushered down a narrow hallway by the younger cop.

The police officer ignored my question so Wendy

replied, "It's just an acronym for the Criminal Investigations Department."

The young officer introduced us to Detective Harrison, a handsome black fellow with a very serious demeanor, and explained to him that we had information about the Finch case. As the four of us shook hands with the detective and told him our names, I noticed a hand-held hair dryer in a large plastic bag on his desk. Shiny silver with red accents, I recognized it as the one that had been instrumental in taking Fanny Finch's life.

"Isn't that the—" I began.

"Murder weapon? Yes, it is." Detective Harrison picked up the bag holding the evidence and dropped it into the deepest drawer in his desk, as if he didn't want us to look at the melted hair dryer that I'd pointed out to the detectives to begin with. He retrieved two chairs from another desk so we'd all have a place to sit. "Detective Colmer set it on my desk after examining it one more time. He still found no trace evidence or fingerprints on it. I was just getting ready to take it back to the evidence locker. This model, the Hair Blaster 2410, is way beyond a police officer's salary. Who would pay over two hundred clams for a hair dryer, anyway?"

"Not me," Rapella said. "My model is called the Air 24/7, and it's free."

As we all, except the stone-faced detective, chuckled at Rapella's remark, I studied her hairstyle, and realized she probably had not been kidding. It definitely had a wind-blown quality to it. When the laughter died down, I began to tell Detective Harrison about my impromptu meeting with Vex Vaughn, and my conversations with Avery, Cassie, and Brandi Bumberdinger, as well as the two authors who'd participated in the book-signing on the morning of the victim's death.

I told him about Vex Vaughn asking me who had killed Fanny Finch when I'd only said she'd died and hadn't elaborated about her death being a homicide. I told how he'd acted as if it was the first he'd heard of the tragedy. In reaction to my comments, Harrison picked up a broken toothpick off his desk and used the tip of one end to clean underneath his fingernails.

I was surprised when the detective made a comment about Detective Colmer going to the campground that afternoon to speak to Sarah and Norma. Throughout my long-winded and detailed summary, with occasional input from Wendy, Harrison said very little and asked no questions, not even to have us clarify something we'd said. He wrote down approximately eight words on the pad of paper in front of him, and I'm pretty sure five of them were, *Pick up milk after work.*

It was evident Detective Harrison considered nothing "vital," or of any relevance whatsoever in the information we'd related to him. It was also clear we weren't being taken seriously, as if we were four busybody gossipmongers trying to stir up a hornet's nest for our own entertainment. The detective even had the gall to patronize us as we stood up to leave. "Now don't you all worry your pretty little heads about this case. We're very good at our jobs, tracking down criminals and getting the bad guys off the streets. We take great pride in our ability to protect nice folks like you from harm. Go on home to the RV park now, ladies. Your time would be better spent piddling around the campground. Paint your nails, watch a couple soap operas, and leave investigating the bad guys to the professionals."

We left the station with a bad taste in our mouths, feeling as if we'd been chastised for our helpful observations and genuine concerns about the case. We'd just wasted an hour of our time. I was certain Detective Harrison would have already tossed his notes into the trashcan if not for the fact he didn't want to disappoint his wife when he arrived home without the milk she probably needed for their children.

After we'd piled into Emily's car and adjusted our seat belts, I said, "Well, that was a futile effort, wasn't it? I'd have liked to kick the chair out from underneath that buffoon when he told us to go home, paint our nails and watch soap operas."

"I'd have been happy to bust that cop's chops if you'd have only asked me to," Rapella said, in a totally serious tone. Judging by the look of annoyance on her face, I didn't doubt her sincerity.

"I would have done just that, Rapella, if I didn't think our husbands would have been irked about having to come down to the police station to bail us out," I said with a smile. "But I do think we can eliminate Sarah and Norma from our suspect list."

"I agree," Wendy said. "I think most of what they said to us on the Ferris wheel was pure hogwash, and perhaps fodder for a future novel. Having an active imagination is practically a necessity for an author, I'd imagine."

"Not to mention the fact I can't see either of them purchasing a two-hundred-dollar hair dryer. Eating out last night, a meal that probably cost less than fifteen bucks apiece, was their big splurge of the week. If they had purchased a hair dryer that expensive, I can't see them sacrificing it, even as a means to kill a rival they despised."

Vex Vaughn could easily afford the high-priced Hair Blaster 2410, and wouldn't hesitate to purchase it, as was evidenced by the expensive cologne I'd seen on his bathroom sink. As much as I detested considering Kylie Rue as a suspect, I said, "Also, there's Kylie, who made a living as a hair stylist. She admitted that she bought expensive professional-quality hair dryers, as I suspect most hair-stylists do. As we've discovered, she has some connection to the subject of Fanny's incriminating book. If Vex Vaughn is truly her biological father, as we suspect, couldn't she conceivably want to seek revenge on his behalf?"

I went on to tell Emily about spotting her young employee entering Vex Vaughn's motor coach at the air show earlier that morning. Emily was astonished, having had no idea Kylie had ties to the entertainer. "Could that have something to do with why she applied for this job not long before Frontier Days, and then announced this morning she's returning to her home in Florida on Monday after the conclusion of Frontier Days?"

"Could be," I said. "Kylie's an extremely likeable young lady, but Ted Bundy was an extremely likeable young man, too. Enough so that he was able to entice multitudes of women to go out with him. It's possible Kylie's friendliness is a ruse, and we're all being duped. She appeared genuinely upset by Fanny's death, but it could have just been a reaction to the realization she'd taken another human being's life. Or maybe she was just improvising. I almost hate to say this, and I pray I'm way off base, but Kylie is starting to look like the most likely candidate to be Fanny Finch's killer, with Cassie Bumberdinger a close second. A fashion model might own expensive hairstyling tools, too. After all, Cassie's entire livelihood is based on her looks, and being in her early thirties now, she's aware she's in the waning years of her modeling career."

Everyone agreed with my assessment, and we

headed back to the campground. Emily was still steaming at the patronizing way we'd just been treated. She was speeding and weaving through traffic like a Nascar driver on the final lap of the Daytona 500. She said the traffic was ten times heavier than normal with Frontier Days in full swing, but I think her erratic driving was more a result of the way we'd been dismissed by Detective Harrison.

Like me, the other three ladies seemed to feel a little deflated by our humiliating and underwhelming experience at the police station. It was time to begin getting ready for the concert anyway. The entertainer we'd be watching that evening was one of my longtime favorites, Reba McEntire, who had many number-one hits dating back to the late seventies. But it was nice to see the younger women traveling with us were also excited to be attending the legendary singer's performance.

Not surprisingly, Rapella had never heard of Reba McEntire, and when questioned by Wendy, had never heard of Pink, Lady Gaga, or Rihanna, either. However, she said, she'd almost worn out her Eminem CD. Her eccentric personality was just one aspect of her charm that I found so endearing. I hoped it wouldn't be the last opportunity I had to spend time with Rapella Ripple. I was anxious to meet Rip, just to see if her husband was as intriguing as she.

CHAPTER 17

Sitting at the motorhome's dinette table, which could magically be turned into an extra bed if needed, Stone and I were eating French toast for breakfast. I'd also heated up some pre-cooked sausage in the microwave, which was surprisingly tasty. I was mentally patting myself on the back. Wanting Stone to join in on my self-congratulations, I said, "Looks like my diligence in not drinking any beverages after lunch yesterday paid off. No bathroom emergencies all day."

"Congratulations, you've really outdone yourself," Stone said, rather mockingly. "But your 'diligence' in avoiding beverages did answer a question I've had since I met you."

"What's that?"

"I've wondered if your body was so accustomed to boatloads of caffeine every day that you couldn't function without it. And you've now proven that theory to be so."

"What do you mean?" I asked.

"Honey, you fell asleep at the concert last night before the second song ended, and didn't wake up again until the middle of the encore. I'm beginning to think you need caffeine to keep going like the rest of us mortals need blood coursing through our veins."

"I was pretty wiped out last night from the events of the last couple of days," I said in an attempt to justify my napping during the concert.

"I was a little disappointed that you didn't get to really experience one of your favorite singers' performances, but it was nice to see the kids all enjoying it. Watching their reactions was more entertaining than watching the musicians on the stage, wasn't it?" Stone asked, before teasing me with his next remark. "Oh, I'm sorry. You wouldn't know, would you? You slept through the whole damn thing."

"Laugh it up, buster. The next time you—"

A sharp rap on the door stopped me in mid-sentence, which was a good thing, because I had no idea what I was going to say, anyway. I opened the door to find Emily standing there. She'd parked her golf cart on our patio next to the picnic table. I opened the door wide and said, "Come on in. What brings you here so bright and early?"

"I wanted to tell you what I just learned from Detective Colmer, who is the lead detective on the murder case," she added for Stone's benefit, who didn't seem to question how Emily and I knew his name. She recovered before she let the cat out of the bag about our true activities the previous afternoon. "He was here yesterday while we were messing around downtown."

"Has there been a break in the case?" I asked anxiously.

"He felt Stanley and I deserved to know what our guards, Jack and Mike, were doing the night of Fanny's death, since we were paying them a good wage to watch over the campground throughout the night while we got some sleep."

"Oh, goodness," I said. "What were they doing?"

"Well, not what they were being paid to do, that's for sure. If nothing else, we at least found out we need to hire different guards next year. No telling what's been going on at night this last week. It can get pretty crazy during Frontier Days. There's occasionally a little too much partying and carrying on, and we try to control it by hiring night guards. We enforce a 'quiet time' for the sake of our customers who are trying to get some sleep."

"Go on, go on," I urged her, impatient for her to get to the point. "So what were they doing that night?"

"Detective Colmer notified them to meet him here at two-thirty so he could question them after he spoke to Norma and Sarah. He wanted to see if they'd witnessed anything unusual or suspicious. They'd been questioned before and were very evasive with their responses, so this time the detective grilled them and put the fear of God in them. They finally opened up after being threatened with jail time for obstruction of justice and some additional trumped up charges the detective came up with. They began to sing like canaries, which would have been beneficial had they known anything to sing about."

"I'd be spilling my guts too if I were them, whether I knew anything or not," I said.

"The detective also got their attention with a comment about how all their hard work at the gym would make them real popular with their cell mates. It didn't take them long after that to start answering Colmer's questions as truthfully as they could. They claimed they didn't recall seeing anyone pull in the gate besides the shuttle buses and other folks returning from the night show Saturday around eleven-fifteen. Neither did they recall seeing any vehicles parked near the pool area, or even any foot traffic near the pool. But they confessed they couldn't be certain something like that didn't occur, because they couldn't see the front gate or the pool area from their vantage point."

"Why not?" I asked. "Weren't they patrolling the park on their golf carts?"

"No, they were sitting behind the trash dumpsters, in their carts of course, smoking a couple of joints, playing games on their cell phones, and texting their girlfriends. For that kind of service, I was paying them each twenty bucks an hour, and this is the third year we've employed the lazy creeps," Emily explained with a grimace. "According to Detective Colmer, when he inferred that the two of them were prime suspects in the murder of Fanny Finch, they couldn't get the truth out quick enough. Imagine, using incompetence as an alibi."

"Good grief," Stone said. "I'll bet Stanley wanted to throttle those two."

"We both did," Emily replied. "I also spoke with Kylie. I told her you all had seen her walking into Vex Vaughn's motor coach. I hope that was all right for me to tell her."

"Sure, no problem. What did she say?" I asked, feeling a bit uneasy about telling the young woman's employer something she'd obviously wanted to keep to herself. On the other hand, I felt the Harringtons had a right to know the truth.

"She told me she'd discovered Vaughn was her biological father just a few weeks ago, by tracking down and contacting her grandmother on her mama's side, just as she told you guys at dinner a couple of nights ago. Kylie knew he was a prime target of the media, and was under additional scrutiny due to Fanny's book right now, so she didn't want to take the chance of causing him more problems by releasing his identity. She was afraid he'd want nothing to do with her if news of her existence got out, especially at this most inopportune time of his life and career."

"I can understand why she'd feel that way," I said.

"Yes, so can I," Emily agreed. "Then I asked her why she wanted to go back home to Florida so soon. She told me that when she spoke with Vaughn, he was very gracious to her. He seemed truly happy to see her and to know that she was doing well. But, for the same reasons Kylie didn't want her relationship to him to be released, Vaughn didn't want the news to be made public either. He promised to keep in touch with her, if she promised to keep their connection a secret. But visiting with him made her realize how lucky she'd been to be adopted by the very parents she would have chosen had she'd been able to pick them out herself. And she told me she really missed her folks back home in Longwood."

"That's a touching story. Was Kylie aware from the beginning that Fanny Finch was the author of the book vilifying her father?" I asked, wondering if the gal could have been resentful enough to murder Fanny in order to avenge her biological father. It had been blatantly obvious she had no use for the author. In fact, Kylie had practically snarled at Fanny in the office on Saturday morning for penning such a disrespectful book with no regard for the lives of the people who might be affected by it.

I described the confrontation in the office that morning to Emily, who hadn't been present at the time. After I finished my story, she said, "Kylie was a little vague about whether or not she recognized Fanny Finch when the woman walked into the office to register for her site, or if she knew in advance Fanny had a reservation here. I didn't want to press the issue, because I didn't want to give her the idea that I or anyone else suspected she might have been involved in the woman's death."

"That was probably a good decision on your part," I said. "And I appreciate you coming over to fill me in on the details. I'm anxious to pass them on to Wendy."

I looked at Stone as I spoke. He just shook his head and rolled his eyes before stabbing another sausage patty off the plate in front of him.

After I cleaned up the kitchen and washed our breakfast plates, I decided to walk over to Wendy's site and tell her what I'd learned from Emily. We had nothing on our agenda for the day, and had planned to rest and relax around the campground until suppertime.

While the four youngsters, as Stone and I refer to them, spent the evening at the Lady Antebellum concert, Stone and I would be treating our hosts, Stanley and Emily, to supper and cocktails at the Little Bear Inn a few miles north of Cheyenne. Emily had described the place as a former brothel with plenty of history behind it and said it was a longtime personal favorite of theirs. She raved about their lobster tails, and Stanley loved their steaks. I was looking forward to visiting with them over a meal and drinks.

Just as I approached Andy and Wendy's site, Brandi and Chace Bumberdinger met me coming from the other direction. I acknowledged them with a pleasant greeting. Without any unnecessary small talk, I asked Brandi if they were managing all right after the loss of their stepmother. After she replied affirmatively, I asked, "Weren't you shocked to find she and your father were staying here when you arrived?"

"No, we planned it that way so my brother and I

could spend some time with Daddy. He took us to the carnival and rodeo a couple of days ago. This afternoon he's taking us down to Rocky Mountain National Park for lunch and to view some wildlife, like elk, bighorn sheep, and maybe even a moose if we get lucky."

"Now that sounds like a fun day to me," I said sincerely. I had always been interested in wildlife photography and wish we'd had time to visit the park, too. "I could have sworn your mother told the detectives she was unaware your daddy and Fanny were going to be here at the same time as you three."

"She did. When I asked her why she told them that, she told me she didn't want to look as if she were stalking them, or anything else of that nature. I'm not sure I even understand why a person would stalk another human being, but that's what she told me. Why are you asking me about that, anyway?"

"My daughter and I are doing a little delving into the murder case, and we're trying to tie up loose ends. As I told you before, I've actually been instrumental in solving a number of murder cases in the recent past. So we were just curious about the discrepancy in her statement to the police. Thank you for clearing that up for me. We wanted to assure ourselves we had the right killer pin-pointed before we went to talk to the cops. Do you remember what your mother did the evening of Fanny's death?"

"No, I can't recall anything about that night," Brandi replied defensively. I knew this young girl would do anything to protect her mother, and I admired her loyalty. I listened as she went on to say, "But I'm sure my mommy didn't hurt Fanny. We have to go now. We told Daddy we'd be at his trailer by nine o'clock, and it's two minutes to nine already."

"I don't want to hold you kids up, so you better get

going. I hope you see a whole slew of moose, lots of elk, a herd of bighorns, and other amazing animals as well!" The stalking part of Brandi's remarks sounded feasible, but I would bet my last dollar Brandi had lied about not recalling what their mother did the night of the murder. This baby Einstein could remember all the distinguishing features of a mountain lion's turd, so she surely wouldn't forget seeing her mother sneak out of the house with her hair dryer late in the evening.

"A group of moose are called a herd, not a slew, as are multiple elk, and a group of sheep are referred to as a flock, unless there's a large number of them, and then it's—"

"Okay, okay, Brandi," I said before I had to listen to the entire list of what groups of animals were officially called. "I only meant to say I hope you have fun."

I had pulled Brandi's string and she wasn't about to miss an opportunity to put her vast knowledge on display. With her hands on her hips, she asked, "Did you know that three or more crows is called a 'murder?'"

"How interesting, Brandi," I replied. "Does that make two crows an 'attempted murder' then?"

The young girl looked befuddled as the children walked away. I'd forgotten Brandi lacked a humor chip in her DNA makeup.

Stone and I sat with the Harringtons at our table near the bar at Little Bear Inn, sipping on our drinks and waiting for our meals to be brought to our table. I'd taken Emily's advice and ordered the lobster tail. Stone and Stanley ordered porterhouse steaks. If my lobster was as good as the Tequila Sunrise I was drinking, I'd be more than satisfied.

One drink led to another, and before I knew it I was

draining my fifth glass of strong tequila with barely a splash of orange juice. The drink contained just enough grenadine to make the concoction look like the bartender had sliced his finger cutting a lime into wedges and dripped a few drops of fresh blood in it.

I was pretty much looped before my supper arrived, and was thankful to have something to soak up the alcohol. I think at one point I told the young man who waited on us that he had the sexiest little butt I'd ever seen, but I can't be certain I said it out loud. However, he'd looked at me as if he were on the verge of throwing up after some old blitzed broad had just hit on him, so I'm guessing I did verbalize the observation. The look Stone threw my way was not one of amusement, but more one of concern about my behavior.

I saw our waiter make a short comment to another male waiter crossing his path with two full plates of food in his hands. I couldn't read the young man's lips, but I'd guess his remark was something like "Cougar Alert—Table Four."

As we took our time savoring our meals, Emily and I exchanged slurred, nearly incoherent thoughts and theories about the death of Fanny Finch as the men discussed fishing for salmon in Alaska. They were talking about the four of us booking a trip to Homer, Alaska, next summer. One of the top things on Stone's bucket list was to catch a big halibut, which was likely to happen in that area, since several halibut charter companies were located on the four-and-a-half mile peninsula of land called "The Spit." He'd always wanted to experience what had been described to him as "like reeling in a garage door."

The food was exceptional, our conversation lively, the camaraderie between friends was enjoyable, and overall, it was a wonderful evening. Stone won the battle over the bill, as he had been determined to do come hell or high water, and he left a healthy tip for our charismatic and finely built waiter.

On the ride back home, sitting in the back seat of Stanley's truck with Emily, I fought to keep my eyes open. I eventually lost the fight, but I remember thinking that I hoped the youngsters' evening had been as nice as ours. It crossed my mind, right before I dozed off, that a trip to Alaska with the Harringtons would be a fun vacation, and also that I should have bypassed the last two Tequila Sunrises I'd practically chugged.

CHAPTER 18

Early the next morning, I was sitting in the recliner, drinking a cup of strong coffee, of course, when I heard a light rapping on our door. It was a quarter to six, and Stone was still in bed. I opened the door quietly to hear Wendy whisper, "You up?"

"No, what you see standing here with a cup of coffee in her hand, is a very detailed figment of your imagination, my dear. Of course, I'm up, silly girl. Come on in, but keep your voice down because Stone is still asleep."

"I don't need to come in and take a chance of waking him," she replied. "I only wanted to see if you were interested in an early morning swim. Kylie opens the gate at six, and we'd probably have the pool to ourselves. We might even get an opportunity to ask Kylie some more probing questions to get an idea of how far she'd go to defend her father's reputation."

"Yeah, that does sound appealing this morning. But why don't you come in and have a cup of coffee while I get my suit on."

"I've already had two cups, Mom, but I guess I could handle one more."

I quickly changed into my skirted one-piece suit, the most modest one I could find at Kohl's, and left a note on the kitchen table to let Stone know where I was. After we both finished our cups of coffee, Wendy and I headed to the swimming pool. The campground was so quiet, it felt like we were the only two stirring at six in the morning.

The pool gate was already open and despite what Wendy had expected, we weren't the only ones up for an early swim. I was delighted to see Rapella Ripple already executing a backstroke while doing laps the length of the pool, which I estimated to be about forty feet long. We exchanged pleasantries. She told me she always liked to get in a little water aerobics before cleaning the shower houses.

I wasn't completely surprised to see the senior citizen wearing a purple and white polka-dotted two-piece that looked amazingly good on her. I hadn't realized how toned and youthful her body was for a woman her age. In comparison, I felt dumpy, lumpy, and now grumpy, for being so totally out of shape. Rapella and Wendy had clicked immediately at their first encounter the previous day, and engaged in a lively conversation about Lady Antebellum, the popular singing group.

Apparently, the Ripples had also attended the concert the previous night, which I found a bit surprising. Rapella said, "We don't normally throw away good money like that, and even though we'd never heard of the lady before, we try to attend at least one concert every year while we're here during Frontier Days. It helps broaden our horizons and keeps us in the loop. We don't want to get so completely out of touch that we can't even converse with the younger set."

"What a wonderful attitude, Rapella. I take it you all

had a pleasant evening?" I asked. I didn't bother to tell her that Lady Antebellum was the name of a group, and the female singer's last name wasn't "Antebellum".

They agreed it was a great concert, and fun was had by all. All three of us were standing in the middle of the pool in water up to our chests when Brandi Bumberdinger walked in through the pool gate and said, "I saw you walking past our trailer in your swimming suits and carrying beach towels, so my little brother and I came down to speak to you."

Brandi was alone, so I greeted her by saying, "Well, good morning young lady. I trust you had a good time with your dad yesterday and spotted all sorts of wildlife. Where's Chace, by the way?"

"He'll be in here shortly," she answered, with no inflection in her voice. The foliage on both sides of the fence surrounding the pool was so dense it provided complete privacy from anyone outside the pool area. I couldn't see her brother, but I heard a low humming noise. I listened with a feeling of uneasiness as Brandi continued to talk.

"Of course we had a good time with daddy yesterday. I told you before that Chace and I miss seeing him and hate seeing our mommy upset all the time. If not for Fanny Finch, we'd still all be together, and a happy, loving family—"

"Not necessarily, honey—" I began.

"Yes, we would!" The ten-year-old said with a great deal of vehemence in her voice. Wendy, Rapella and I stood there in stunned silence, chest-high in water, as the young girl continued, "So, when we saw that woman going into the pool area alone late Saturday night, my brother and I decided to eliminate Fanny Finch from the picture so we could have our family back together. Like I said before, I don't like it when

Jeanne Glidewell

my mommy's unhappy. Mommy had taken a sleeping pill, as she's had to do every night since Daddy left, and was sound asleep. We knew she'd just put her hair dryer in the trash because it would only run on high and she liked to dry her hair on low so she could style it at the same time. The three of us went into town to purchase a new one at a beauty supply store she located on her computer. She bought the exact same model, since she'll be reimbursed for it by the manufacturer. She is the model in all of their magazine advertisements."

Wendy was staring at the child with her mouth open, apparently finding it hard to believe what she was hearing. Rapella looked shell-shocked, as well. Dreading the answer to my question, I asked Brandi, "Are you telling us it was you and Chace who killed your stepmother?"

"Yes, and I was afraid you might have accidentally figured it out for yourself, since you were snooping around asking questions. That's why my brother and I decided we need to eliminate you, too. It was actually his idea to kill Fanny, and now you, after I told him about water being an ideal conductor of electricity. It was one of those rare, but genius, ideas he occasionally comes up with. Chace's the one who actually threw the hair dryer in the pool next to Fanny. Unfortunately, Ms. Starr, the other ladies with you will be collateral damage."

"Collateral damage" is not a term one would expect to hear from a ten-year-old, even one with an incredible I.Q. such as hers. Hearing it come out of the child's mouth in reference to my daughter and new friend sent chills down my spine. Before we could make a move toward the ladder, Chace came through the gate with a running hair dryer in his hand, which was covered with a latex glove like one his mother might have had under the sink with her cleaning supplies.

That explained why no fingerprints were found on the first hair dryer. I'm sure the gloves had been Brandi's idea. The murder had been pre-meditated and she hadn't overlooked many details. This one was also attached to a long industrial-sized extension cord, just as the hair dryer that killed the author had been. I was certain Stanley had replaced the ruined electrical cord with a new functional one after Fanny's death. I froze in place, thinking we might be more successful in trying to talk the kids out of executing their plan than trying to get out of the pool before the young boy threw the dryer into it.

"Brandi, do you know how unhappy your mother will be if you ruin her new hair dryer?" I asked the girl, who, like a sense of humor, seemed to be lacking the compassion and emotional genes in her DNA makeup, as well. "You'll have to explain to your mother what happened to the brand new one she just purchased a few days ago, you know."

"This is my hair dryer, a cheap one she bought for me at Wal-Mart a couple of years ago. I rarely ever use it anyway, so Mommy will probably never even realize it's missing."

"If your mother finds out you're behind Fanny's death, and now the deaths of the three of us, as I can almost guarantee she will, she'll be even more upset about her two children being thrown in prison for the rest of their young lives than she's ever been about your father leaving her for another woman. And you know how much you hate seeing her unhappy," I said, trying desperately to make her decide to scrap the notion of letting Chace heave the running hair dryer into the pool and taking another three lives. I knew I sounded desperate when I asked, "Did you know they don't let people read books in prison?"

"Oh poo! I'm not an idiot, you know. Besides, they wouldn't lock us up for the rest of our lives," Brandi replied. "Did you forget that I'm gifted? We'd probably end up in a correctional center for kids for a couple of years and then be released, and that's in the unlikely event they discover who's responsible for the murders. After all, who would suspect two kids our ages? And even if we are caught, it's extremely doubtful they'll try to charge Chace as an adult for murdering his stepmother. After all, she's the woman who tore apart our family."

Before I could think of another tactic to save Rapella, Wendy, and me from suffering the same fate as Fanny Finch, Brandi turned to her brother and said, "Go ahead, Chace. We need to get this done and get out of here before anyone else comes near the pool area."

I saw the boy's arm go back in order to get better momentum on his throw, and then saw the hair dryer being released from his hand. All three of us in the pool gasped in horror. But to our immense relief, just as the dryer started its descent into the water, directly above our heads, the lights went off, and the entire park became eerily—but blissfully—quiet.

As if frozen in place, Brandi and Chace stood still, as the three of us in the pool made a mad dash for the ladder. It appeared as if Brandi's usually lightning-quick mind had screeched to a halt. She stood there expressionless and speechless for several long seconds as we exited the pool. I doubted she'd thought ahead to a Plan B if Plan A failed to pan out. Personally, I never wanted to come near this pool again, and getting into any other swimming pool in the future didn't look too likely either.

Just as the three of us made it out and away from the

pool, Kylie rushed through the gate, an expression of deep concern on her face, and asked, "Are you ladies all right? What's going on in here?"

Wendy and I stood in front of the gate, blocking it to keep the young perpetrators from exiting the pool area, and explained to Kylie what had just taken place.

Kylie shook her head and said, "Oh, my God. I'm so glad I happened to be coming this way a few moments ago. When I unlocked the gate earlier, I was going to test the alkalinity, PH, and chlorine levels of the water, but discovered the little canister of test strips was empty. I was irritated by that at first, but now I think it might have been a matter of divine intervention."

"Amen to that!" I said.

"So anyway," Kylie continued, "I walked over to the maintenance shed to get a new canister and as I was walking this way, I saw the young boy standing outside the gate with the hair dryer. Considering what happened Saturday night in this pool, I was alarmed. I ran back to the maintenance shed and opened the electrical box as fast as I could. I saw a large toggle switch marked "Main" and just yanked it down, rather than try to figure out which circuit breaker controlled the power to the pool area. I could tell when the lights in the entire park went off that I'd pulled the right one. When the kids electrocuted Fanny, they must have unplugged the cord from the electrical outlet before retrieving the hair dryer from the bottom of the pool by reeling in the cord attached to it."

"Thank God you turned off the power when you did, and not a second later, or we'd be toast right now!" Wendy said as she wrapped her beach towel around her waist. Cheyenne mornings were usually cool, even in late July, and we were all shivering from the combination of nearly being electrocuted and the weather. After a violent shudder, Wendy said, "I can't recall peeing in a pool since I graduated from elementary school. Excuse my language, but I can honestly say that this was the first time I've literally had the piss scared out of me."

"It's nice to hear I wasn't the only one to suffer a bladder crisis on this vacation," I said, knowing it was probably that third cup of coffee I'd convinced Wendy to drink that had caused her incontinence in the grip of fear.

"No worries," Kylie said with a broad smile. "That's why God created chlorine—to kill bacteria. I'm just relieved you three ladies are okay."

"Thanks to you," Wendy said. "Thank God for you, or we'd all be lying at the bottom of the pool like Fanny was when we discovered her body Sunday morning. You saved our lives with your quick thinking, and we are infinitely grateful. It's hard to put how I feel into words right now, because my heart's still racing and my knees are shaking. And not just because I'm chilled to the bone."

Rapella told Kylie she considered her an angel sent from heaven to save us, and that she appreciated her realizing something wasn't right and shutting down the power in the nick of time. I was thinking Rapella must be a tough ole bird, as she hadn't even wrapped her towel around her to block the cool air.

I thanked Kylie in turn, with an overwhelming sense of regret. How could we have ever suspected this young lady of such a vicious crime as murder? She was our savior. I wanted to find her a special gift as a token of our appreciation. Instantly, I knew exactly what I'd get for her. I'd heard her gush over Wendy's Tony Lama boots more than once. I'd go downtown to the Wrangler western wear store that afternoon to find a pair as similar to Wendy's as I could. The cost of the boots was inconsequential. It was the least I could do.

Then, as Kylie instructed Brandi and Chace to sit down in two chairs located by the fence, I walked over to my little pile of belongings and picked up my cell phone, looked up the number online and called the police station.

"Detective Harrison here," said the baritone voice on the other end of the line. I knew I should ask for Detective Colmer, the lead detective on the case, but I had a bone to pick with this detective. He'd left a nasty taste in my mouth that was still stuck in my craw, and I wanted to return the favor.

"Hello, Detective. This is Lexie Starr."

"Yes, can I help you?" I could tell he didn't recognize my name, but that was not too surprising, given the fact he'd paid no attention to our names when we'd introduced ourselves to him on Wednesday.

"I'm one of the 'pretty little ladies' you verbally blew off in your C.I.D. room a couple of days ago. We might not be professionals like you and your detective buddies, but if you send a squad car out to Cozy Camping RV Park, we'll turn over Fanny Finch's killer and his accomplice to you, so you can get back to protecting nice folks like me from harm." I wasn't proud of the sarcasm that practically dripped off my tongue, but as often happens, I couldn't hold it back.

"What? You've got the perp who killed the author lady? Are you serious?"

"Of course I'm serious. Would I phone the police to joke about something like this? You need to come on over now, because I can't keep them corralled here forever. Their mother's going to get worried about their whereabouts."

"What? Their mother's going to do what? Are you telling me you have them apprehended?" He asked again with a hint of skepticism.

"You could say that," I replied, as I glanced over at the two children sitting restlessly in the lounge chairs beside the pool. They should have looked nervous, scared, apprehensive, or even ticked off, but they didn't seem to realize they should be anything but bored. I could think of a dozen different people I wished were sitting there, ready to be turned over to the police instead of the two young mixed-up children who were merely grieving the fact their father didn't live at home with them anymore.

"Yes, ma'am. We're on the way," Detective Harrison said after a long pause. I wondered if he'd been mulling over the possibility we might have some innocent citizens lashed to a tree.

"Well, don't waste time piddling around the station, Detective, because I'd like to get my nails polished before *Days of our Lives* comes on."

"Um, yes, ma'am."

Before I could tell him it was unnecessary to bring the entire task force to take the perps into custody, he ended the call. As I stowed my phone back into the pocket of the terry cloth robe I'd thrown on over my bathing suit, I couldn't help feel a sense of satisfaction at being able to toss a few of the detective's patronizing remarks back in his face.

On the other hand, I was incredibly disturbed that a couple of young children could perpetrate such an unimaginable act of violence. I imagined they'd be tragically scarred by the crime for the rest of their young lives. It had left its mark on me too. I knew I'd have to think twice before ever immersing myself into a murder case again.

EPILOGUE

We'd gotten off to an early start Saturday morning, heading home to Rockdale. Sitting in the passenger seat as Stone drove, I was still shaken from my near-death experience the day before. Discovering Fanny's life had been taken by two young children, who'd also attempted to kill Wendy, Rapella, and me, was something I'd never get over.

I'd been involved in other disturbing murders, but the fact the perpetrators in this case were just misguided kids shook me to the core. Like all of us, unfortunately, I'd heard stories about children killing others in episodes of violence. But this was the first time I'd been personally involved in such a case, and it was a bitter pill to swallow. As I started to cry at the thought of what Brandi and Chace's futures might entail, Stone glanced at me.

"You okay, baby?" He asked. "I talked to the detectives, and they assured me the circumstances and ages of the kids would be taken into consideration. Detective Harrison agreed with Brandi's assessment of what their punishment might entail. He said they'll probably spend a number of years in a rehabilitation center for young offenders, with abundant visitation time with their parents. They would ultimately be released when they reached adulthood, as long as they appeared to pose no further threat to society."

"Yes, I know you're right," I said. "But it's such a sad situation. I felt so sorry for Cassie and Avery, who were devastated by the turn of events. I'm glad the EMTs were there to give Cassie a sedative to calm her down."

Stone nodded and said, "After I spoke with Harrison. I heard Cassie tell Detective Colmer that she and Avery had known there was something unusual about Brandi at an early age, and she'd been mistakenly diagnosed with autism at age two. Because Brandi was so far advanced compared to the other children her age, she was a loner, practically an outcast. The lack of interaction with friends had resulted in her failure to learn social skills."

"Yes, that was clear to me the first time I had a conversation with her," I agreed. "Even though intelligence is usually considered a blessing, I can see where in some cases, like Brandi's, it could also be a curse."

"Yes, and that's such a shame," Stone said. "Say, did you see the warm embrace between Cassie and Avery? I saw him kiss her forehead several times, and hold her in his arms for a long time as they consoled each other. It was rather touching."

"I noticed that too. Makes you wonder, doesn't it? Even though their children went about it in the worst possible way, maybe their ill-fated plan to reunite their parents might actually prove successful."

"I hope you're right, Lexie. I hate to see any marriage fall apart, especially when children are involved. And these two kids will need a lot of parental support as they are forced to face the process of being dealt with by the justice system and, of course, the punishment that will ultimately be meted out."

"I hope I'm right, too," I agreed, as something along the interstate caught my eye. "Hey! Pull over, Stone! I'm pretty sure I just saw a bear right off the shoulder of the road back there a little ways. I'm certain Andy and Wyatt will pull over behind us. Surely one of the kids saw it, too."

"Was it a black bear or a grizzly?" Stone asked in a serious voice. I wondered why he wasn't slowing down.

"I couldn't tell because we were moving too fast and I barely got a glimpse of it."

"Being that we're in the flat plains of Nebraska, and bears wouldn't normally stand that close to a busy interstate, it could just as likely have been a polar bear or a koala."

"Are you suggesting I didn't see a bear at all?" I asked, slightly hurt by his mockery.

"No, I'm not suggesting it—I'm flat out saying you didn't see a bear back there. I'm not going to have all three of these motorhomes pulling over and backing down the shoulder on I-80 to look at what is probably nothing more than a tree trunk or a dark-leafed bush. Sweetheart, I'm calling your optometrist to make you an appointment when we get home."

"Humph," I muttered. "No need for you to do that, my dear. Yesterday afternoon after we got back from our trip downtown to purchase Kylie's new Tony Lama boots—which she was over the moon about, I might add—I called and made an appointment with Dr. Herron for next Thursday."

"Good. Oh, I almost forgot to tell you. Wyatt told me that Veronica has agreed to seek therapy for an eating disorder she's battling. He said you and Wendy convinced her it was something she needed to do, for her sake as well as his."

"Ah, that's music to my ears. I know it's not going to be easy for her, but I'll be praying for her to succeed. At first I was kind of skeptical about having her along on this vacation, but now I'm so thankful to have gotten the chance to get to know her better."

After a couple of minutes of silence, I brought up the possibility of Wendy and Andy marrying in the near future. Stone said, "It's supposed to be a secret, but if you promise not to say anything, I'll let you in on it."

"Tell me! Tell me! My lips are sealed. I promise!"

"Well, all right then," Stone said, as if still debating whether to spill the beans to someone who thrived on gossip. "Andy told me he's going to ask Wendy to marry him on her thirtieth birthday. He's having a ring designed for her right now."

"Oh, my gosh! That's wonderful news. I've got an idea to make the occasion even more memorable. We can throw Wendy a surprise birthday party at the inn."

"Okay, great idea, sweetheart. You can start planning it as we head home. But remember to keep it to yourself. We don't want to ruin the surprise."

I then thanked my husband for the memorable anniversary trip, and asked, "What would you like for your anniversary gift?"

"Just a promise you'll cut me some slack in the future. I love you dearly, but worrying about you has taken ten years off my life in just the first year of our marriage."

The look of sincerity in my husband's eyes made me realize how much I'd put him through when I put myself in harm's way while investigating murder cases. So I promised to try my best to not put more stress on my husband's overflowing plate. I didn't want to take any more years off his life because I loved him dearly too. Having the bejesus scared out of me every time I turned around was getting tiresome, as well. I'd had so many close calls that I felt the odds were turning against me.

Besides, Stone was right. It was time I stepped aside and let the homicide detectives do their jobs while I settled into the second year of my marriage to the love of my life. I had a party to plan, a wedding to prepare for, and hopefully grandbabies to spoil in the near future. Because, frankly, as cute as they were, baby alpacas were just not doing it for me.

"Now that we've taken care of that, could you go back and pour us each a cup of coffee out of the thermos? I need something to keep me alert, and I think your caffeine level must be dipping dangerously low. You are imagining highly unlikely wildlife alongside the interstate and agreeing to back off your tendency to get smack dab in the middle of murder cases. Obviously, something's desperately wrong with you."

I didn't know if there was any truth to his statement, but you should know me well enough by now to know I almost never turn down a cup of coffee.

THE LEXIE STARR MYSTERY SERIES

Leave No Stone Unturned
The Extinguished Guest
Haunted
With This Ring
Just Ducky
Cozy Camping
The Spirit of the Season (a novella)

SPOILER ALERT
To be read *only after completion* of Cozy Camping

Dear Readers,

I realize the outcome of this fictional story may be a bit shocking, and I sincerely apologize if any of you find it offensive because that was never my intention. I wanted the Lexie Starr series to end with a bang. I also wanted to give Lexie a very compelling reason to want to retire from the amateur sleuthing business, and I had to step outside the box to do it. Although this kind of tragedy is rare, thankfully, it does happen on occasion and that's just a sad fact of life.

I'd also like to express my sincere gratitude to all of you who have spent time and money reading one or all of my Lexie Starr mysteries. I am spinning off a new crossover series and excited about creating new, and hopefully entertaining, characters. I wanted to do this before I got so tired of my main characters that I was tempted to have a meteorite drop on the roof of the Alexandria Inn and wipe them all out. I wanted to have a surprise ending to the series, but not quite that surprising! Like Lexie, I never like to make a promise I can't be certain I'll keep. So, it's always possible Lexie might find an urge she can't resist and end up knee-deep in a murder investigation again sometime in the future.

I hope you will enjoy my new series. An excerpt from A RIP ROARING GOOD TIME, book one in the Ripple Effect cozy mystery series follows.

Happy Reading!

Jeanne

Turn the page for an

excerpt from

A
RIP ROARING
GOOD TIME

A Ripple Effect Cozy Mystery

Book One

Jeanne Glidewell

"We ain't getting any younger, you know. Aren't you about ready to hit the road?" I asked Clyde "Rip" Ripple, my husband of nearly fifty years.

"Don't get your bloomers in a bunch, my dear. All I need to do is get the jacks cranked up and the antenna cranked down and we'll be ready to roll. We have plenty of time to get to the Alexandria Inn in time for the party."

"Well, get to cranking, buster. I'm anxious to get the Chartreuse Caboose on the road." I had nicknamed our RV this after we'd hand-painted it that color one weekend in a fit of boredom. We'd highlighted it with a few scattered yellow sunflowers for a little added flare. If nothing else, it was easy to locate in a crowded campground.

We'd already eaten breakfast and as usual, I heard a chorus of snap, crackle and pops before I'd even poured the milk on our cereal. It was just part of being a senior citizen, as was the prune juice we drank to wash down the whole-wheat toast that completed our morning meal. Bacon, eggs and pancakes loaded down with butter and maple syrup had gone by the wayside when our cholesterol levels achieved "walking time bomb" status. They were just a fantasy now, as were a lot of other things we'd always enjoyed in our younger days. Even our sex drives were more often in "park" than not. Still, for both being sixty-eight years old, we felt we had a lot more active lifestyle than most folks did at our age. We made sure there was never any room on our schedule for bingo and potluck dinners, staples of many senior citizens' social lives.

Rip and I, Rapella Ripple, are full-time RVers, crisscrossing the country in our thirty-foot travel trailer. We both retired at sixty-two years old, the earliest we could draw our social security benefits. Rip spent his entire career in law enforcement, first as a beat cop, then as a detective, and finally as Captain in our south Texas hometown of Rockport.

I, on the other hand, have had a vast array of full- and part-time, positions involving dozens of different occupations. It's not that I'm a high-maintenance, incompetent, or difficult employee, it's just that I bore easily. I've quickly tired of doing everything from pitching magazine subscriptions, where I made random phone calls and was rudely hung up on ninety-nine out of every hundred calls before I could even spit out a full sentence, to working as a clerk at a stained glass art gallery, where the "You break it, you buy it" policy applied more often to me than the customers.

My favorite occupation was short-lived—a taste-testing job at a local ice cream factory, which I was forced to quit when I developed both lactose intolerance and a double chin. But lest you think I'm flaky or unreliable, of all of the many jobs I've had, I've only actually been fired once. And that was due to an unpleasant customer I was serving at a local restaurant who took it personally when I referred to her rowdy young son as an obnoxious spoiled brat who should be put in time-out until he graduated from college. Let's face it, some people are entirely too sensitive.

We found retirement to be less than it was cracked up to be after a full year of sitting on the couch staring at a TV, speaking to each other only briefly during commercials. Fortunately, we could watch the same shows every other month and not remember whether or not we'd ever seen them before. The most excitement we were apt to have in an entire week was visiting a nearby park to feed the pigeons, at least until one of us felt the need to go home and take a nap.

When it finally dawned on us that our rear ends were beginning to take root in the plaid fabric cushions of our couch, we decided enough was enough. After all, we were retired, not dead.

Within a month, we had sold our home, given away most of our belongings, purchased a travel trailer, and hit the road. We made no plans, followed no schedule, just let each day take us wherever it might take us, which on a couple of occasions was less than fifteen miles down the road.

Sometimes we moved daily from one RV Park to another, from one state to another, when we got a wild hair up our you-know-whats. At other times we would rest a spell and recharge our batteries—and I mean *ours*, not that of our trailer, or the truck we used to pull it with—and we'd stay in one park for several months at a time.

We would often work as what is commonly referred to as "workampers" to keep busy and receive free site rent in exchange for helping in the RV Park office, cleaning shower houses, doing lawn work or whatever needed to be done. As you'll no doubt come to realize, "free" is my favorite word. Occasionally we're even paid a small chunk of change on top of our free rent, which comes in handy with the outlandish price of gas these days.

But right now we actually had a schedule to keep. In the Cozy Camping RV Park in Cheyenne, Wyoming, just a couple of weeks prior, we'd met Lexie Starr, her husband, Stone Van Patten, and her daughter, Wendy. Lexie and Stone had been celebrating their one-year anniversary during Cheyenne Frontier Days. When another camper was found murdered, Lexie and Wendy had become involved in the case, and I'd ended up involved as well, to the extent we gals nearly *bit the big one* in the process of discovering the identity of the killer.

Two days after our new friends headed home to the Alexandria Inn, a bed and breakfast establishment they own in Rockdale, Missouri, I'd received a phone call from Lexie. The call resulted in Rip and I preparing to head east in order to attend a thirtieth birthday surprise party for Wendy at their inn.

There was an RV repairman in Rockdale who we'd arranged to have do some repairs on our trailer while we were there. Lexie had insisted we stay at the inn as their guests while our trailer was in the shop. Along with the word "free," I was also quite fond of its cousin, "guest." My favorite thing about being sixty-eight was the senior citizen discount that came with it.

Less than an hour later, we had Wyoming in our rear view mirror as we crossed over the Nebraska border. I had a feeling this trip would turn out to be one we wouldn't soon forget. Call it a premonition, or just a fit of fancy, but it was a feeling I couldn't shake. I was anxiously looking forward to finding out if there was anything to it, because boredom was nipping at our heels once again and I was more than ready for a little excitement.

A RIP ROARING GOOD TIME

available in print and ebook

Jeanne Glidewell, a 2006 pancreas and kidney transplant recipient, and her husband, Robert, reside in the small Kansas town of Bonner Springs. She is a mentor for the Gift of Life Program in Kansas City, mentoring future transplant recipients. Promoting organ donation is an important endeavor of hers.

Prior to moving back home to Kansas, Jeanne and Bob owned a large RV Park in Cheyenne, Wyoming.

Besides writing, she enjoys fishing, traveling, and wildlife photography.

Jeanne also enjoys hearing from her readers. You can contact her through her website: www.jeanneglidewell.com